AN ELLEN THOMPSON THRILLER

Faith
of the
Curé

VICKI B. WILLIAMSON

This is a work of fiction. All characters and events portrayed in this novel are either products of the author's imagination or are used fictitiously.

Faith of the Curé

Cover by Driven Digital Services
Editing and typesetting by Kingsman Editing Services

First Edition May 2022
ISBN: 978-0-9990605-4-4

vickibwilliamson.author@gmail.com

To my readers—old and new.

old. It all began with the cold.

Fog was everywhere. Wallowed in the gray, all the woman felt, all she knew, was the pain of the bone-deep cold.

When she cracked her eyes open, the heavy mist made her blink, but this hardly cleared her vision. She raised an arm to wipe the moisture from her face, but her limb was leaden, numb. Before she'd lifted it an inch, her arm fell limply back.

She tried again. This time to reach for her face. In the dim light, her trembling hand was white like a specter and floated toward her. If she hadn't watched, hadn't been so intent on success, she wouldn't have known when her hand touched her face, her eyes. Everything was deadened.

She squinted when a burst of light filled her vision. On its heels, a clap of sound so loud, her ears rang. In the illumination, she saw stone walls that made up a small room.

Another flash and crack made her jump. It was too bright, too loud. When the flash hit again, she was already turning. The ground was as wet as she was. There was a slippery, slimy feel to it under her palms, and when she tried to stand, her feet almost slid out from under her. She barely felt her legs, they were so weak. When she looked down to watch the ground in front of her, she was startled to see she was naked.

When she tried to take a step, she stumbled and fell against one of the stone walls. It was cold, wet, and had sharp edges that scraped her hand when she tried to brace herself. In the next flash, she looked down to see blood ooze from the wound. At last, there was a sensation that didn't have to do with the cold.

Keeping her hand to the wall to steady herself, she didn't care that she left a smear of blood on the rock. Ahead of her were a set of steps. Stone, uneven, glossy with the rain, they led up. Wind whistled down from a small opening at the top of the stairs and brought a burst of rainwater. The cold bit into her skin with the torrent. Dark hair hung in a sopping tangle to partially obscure her face, rest on the curve of her breasts, and trail down her back. It was her only covering from the elements.

Focused on the steps, she moved closer. Slowly, she approached the stairs and glanced up. Wind and rain blew down and elicited a full-body shiver. Clouds swirled overhead in the gray sky as if stirred by an angry god.

In the next flash, she saw walls surrounding the area above. Walls that ended in spikes of wood where a roof once sat. For a moment, she stood, spellbound by the drama.

Beautiful.

Magnificent.

Deadly.

After a moment she shook her head and continued. Reaching the stairs, she was too weak to step up them, so she climbed on hands and feet.

When she reached the top, she pulled herself onto what was once the floor of this ancient building. A dirt floor to be sure, but with the storm, it, too, had become a sodden mess.

When she was able to stand, she slowly made her way to the

exit—a doorless portal cut into the stone. Beyond the building, a grassy expanse spread before her. The long grasses whipped in the wind, and beyond them, a cliff dropped off to reveal the fury of a rolling sea.

She stepped from the building, relinquishing the meager shelter it afforded her. Almost knocked from her feet by the raging wind, roving lights on the near shore caught her eye. They shifted and reflected within the rain, seeming to come nearer.

Another step from the building and her strength gave out; she dropped to her knees. Curiosity pulled her to look back the way she had come, where she saw the ancient cross affixed to the front of the building.

CHAPTER 1

Not fully waking, in a kind of twilight dream world, the woman tried to concentrate on where she was. Her eyes were heavy, as if they were weighted down with bags of sand. She couldn't move her body—couldn't even turn her head. When sound came to her—voices—she listened. She tried to understand them. To make some sense of where she was.

"Bravo, Michael. You should be proud of yourself."

"Thank you, Mr. Whitman."

"Oh, Michael. You may call me Malcolm."

The second man cleared his throat, started to speak, and then with an audible swallow, he began again. "Thank you, Mr.—I mean, Malcolm. Thank you, Malcolm. We are all very proud. She's quite a prize."

"Yes, yes," the first man said. "When do you expect her to wake?"

"Well, Mr. . . . . Malcolm. We're unsure. You see, there is a lot of gray area here. This situation is unprecedented."

"Yes, of course. And, after all, you're the doctor."

The woman felt the presence of the man leaning over her. The surface she lay on shifted. She felt confined. Captured. Would he harm her? Try to kill her? Now, when she was defenseless?

The rate of the woman's breathing increased in speed, her chest rising and falling, and the man's presence disappeared.

"What's happening? Is she waking?"

"Um. Well, I don't believe so . . ."

The woman heard shifting, the squeak of a shoe.

"Why don't we adjourn to my office, Malcolm? The nurse will contact us if she begins to wake. It could be days, really."

"Of course, Michael. I would like to view the rest of your facility."

"Of course. Of course. A tour is in order."

"Oh, and Michael . . ."

"Yes, Malcolm?"

"Call me Mr. Whitman."

Once again, the man cleared his throat before answering. "Of course, Mr. Whitman. Of course."

Steps and the shuffling of papers preceded the soft closing of a door. Without warning, the woman was pulled back into sleep.

CHAPTER 2

Sounds came before she was fully awake. The murmur of voices, the squeak of rubber-soled shoes, and then the sharp odor of antiseptics.

The sun was warm on her face and body. Amid this input and thoughts was a pervasive fear, a blank spot.

Who am I?

By the sounds—the beeps and squeaks, the smells—she knew she was in a hospital.

Knowledge of mundane things filled her mind.

The warm sun was a ball of fire. When she opened her eyes, the sunlight would lend a golden aura to the room. She was prone on her back. As she breathed, air filled her lungs, her heart a steady beat in her chest.

But who was she? Her mind was blank of all personal information. Blank like a wall had been erected before her. And how did she get here?

Cold. All she remembered was the cold.

The squeaking footsteps came closer. Someone was in the room. They approached the bed but didn't speak.

At the sound of scratching, she cracked open steel-gray eyes.

Before her was an attractive woman dressed in a matching blue shirt and pants—a nurse. She stood at a desk and scribbled words in a notebook.

When the nurse glanced up to see the woman's gaze, she froze. After a beat, she spoke.

"Well, good morning. Good to see you're awake."

The woman understood the nurse. Knew the language she spoke. She knew what she meant, even understood the timbre of her voice and body language. Though the nurse hid it well, the woman saw the flush of surprise, the half step toward the door. The dilation of her eyes.

Fear.

Why would she fear me?

A garbled sound came from the woman's throat as she attempted to answer. Only then did she realize she couldn't speak. The words she wished to say formed in her mind but got no further.

Another sound, suspiciously like a growl, issued from her, and when she raised her hand to touch her throat, it was stopped short by a metal cuff that locked her arm to the bed. She spun her head and saw her other arm likewise chained.

The nurse backed toward the door, eyes wide, as the growls and clang of cuffs increased in frequency and volume.

The chained woman screamed. In her head she yelled for help.

Free me.

But it came out as a bellow of fury.

The nurse fled the room. A heartbeat later, she was back, accompanied by three muscular men dressed in white.

When the men reached for her, their skin meeting hers, she

thought her brain would explode. Sensations, images, a vast input of information she couldn't follow or control. Her body arched, her head flew back, and her legs drummed on the thin mattress.

The men grabbed her flailing limbs and ankles, and they soon had her completely strapped down. Hands on her shoulders, she was unable to fight—to even move. Once strapped, the men released her, and the images cut off.

Exhausted, confused, sweat beaded on her forehead, and the woman panted and looked into a room devoid of familiarity.

The nurse was back. She had a syringe in her hand and a gleam in her eyes.

Crazy bitch. I didn't mean to scare you.

The needle jammed into her upper arm, and the nurse whispered something in the woman's ear. The sharp stab of pain blocked out her words, and the confusion faded along with her image.

* * * * *

This time, when she opened her eyes, she told herself to remain calm.

She needed to learn what happened. Getting sedated again wasn't going to get her anywhere.

The squeak of rubber warned her she was not alone. When she glanced up, she saw that this time the nurse seemed confident. Superior.

"There you are." She neared the bed, a large smile on her face. "Dr. Daniels wants to see you. And aren't you the special one to have the top man want some of your time." On the tail of her words, three male attendants entered the room. These men were different from the ones before. She couldn't control it as a rush of adrenaline filled her system, causing a flush of heat.

Don't worry, Nurse Ratchett. I won't give you any trouble.

The final man pushed a wheelchair toward the bed.

The woman stayed docile as they unchained her. She watched them, and for the first time, she noticed she was also wearing matching pants and a shirt. Different from theirs, hers were covered in faded pink pastel stripes.

When they sat her up, a rush of dizziness flowed through her, and once again at their touch, her mind filled. This time, she was able to track some of the images. Closing her eyes, she concentrated, trying to bring order to the chaos.

Too soon, they pulled her to her feet and into a chair. As they chained her, the skin-to-skin contact was lost. She was so thankful for the chair, she didn't even care when they chained her to it. The nurse came around the rear of the chair as the attendants scattered.

The nurse didn't say anything. Just a presence, heavy in the air.

The woman couldn't stop a start of surprise when the nurse smoothed a hand down her hair, and her palm came to rest on her shoulder.

"We're going to be a good girl, now, aren't we?"

The woman sat motionless. Unable to answer.

The nurse grabbed a handful of dark hair and wrenched her head back. The woman started forward as if she could rise from the chair, but the chains kept her restrained. And this time, the images were clear.

From the nurse, the woman's mind screamed. How could they be from the nurse?

But they were. They flowed through the woman's mind, sharp and bitter. She clenched her eyes shut, attempting to stop the horrific thoughts, a quake running through her body.

Hatred.

Cruelty.

Violence.

Pulling forward, the woman tried to dislodge the nurse to get the images to stop.

Oblivious to the woman's distress, or just not caring, the nurse glared at her from over her shoulder, spittle flying. She repeated, "Aren't we?"

The touch of crazy in her last syllable had the woman's eyes flying open. Chained as she was, there was no way for her to defend herself if the nurse became more violent. If she began to act on the things that swam in her head.

Stomping down her panic, the woman took a deep, shaky breath and looked past the images in her brain. She needed to find out where she was—what had happened. She needed to see this Dr. Daniels. Moving her head stiffly due to the grip on her hair, she nodded.

"Good girl," the nurse said. She released her hair and patted the woman on the head. And just like that, the images stopped.

Then they were in motion. Out the door and down the hall. Closed doors and copies of the room they came from lined the hall at even intervals. Occasionally, a face peered through the small window in the doors. Each face crazed with a touch of fear.

How long before I have that look?

In between the door, flames flickered in wall sconces that illuminated part of the hallway. What was going on here? Why the candlelight?

At the end of the hall, a man waited. The nurse stopped the wheelchair within inches of a large double door. The man leaned over and, with a shove at the middle, rolled the doors back on runners. Beyond the door the woman saw the beginning of a ramp. They went down one floor—two? The woman couldn't tell for certain.

When they again came to a landing, the woman stared down another hallway. This one was less industrial. Dark wainscoting traveled down the length of the walls, broken by an occasional door. These doors, unlike the ones on the other floor, were dark-paneled and etched. Each, but one, had a brass placard. The one without a placard had a subtle sign stating it was a staircase. Spinning her head as she was pushed past, the woman tried to read the placards, but they were moving too quickly. All she caught was an occasional title . . . PhD, MD. All doctors' offices? And how did she know that was what the letters meant?

The woman pushed her lips together to contain a growl as a burst of frustration shot through her. A spike of temperature and a bead of sweat ran down her brow at her efforts.

How was she to know what to do or where to go if she couldn't even find herself?

The chair stopped, and when the nurse knocked on a door, the woman looked up to read the placard:

Michael Daniels, MD, PhD

"Come in," a deeply masculine voice called from within.

As the door swung open, the woman's breath caught. The heavy air inside caused a tingle to run down her spine. When she was pushed forward, a man rose from behind a large mahogany desk. Walking to the side of the furniture, he stopped and looked down at the woman.

"Hello, at last, Ellen."

CHAPTER 3

My name is Ellen Thompson, and I . . . remember . . . *everything.*

In the vacuum of a room, Ellen watched the doctor's mouth move, but she couldn't hear the words. All she knew was the high whine that pierced her ears. Dizzy, she was once again glad for the chair.

Images surged through her mind. This time, however, they were memories from her own life. A painting—small, but compelling—a train ride . . . blood on her hands. A medallion, riddles, and then the intense light. For a moment, it was as if her brain would explode with the force of all the memories. She wanted to put her head between her knees, but she was certain the action would reveal weakness.

Then, deciding it would be weaker to faint, she bent at the waist and dropped her head.

Clarity came quickly. The spinning and pressure stopped, and there was blessed silence. For a moment, she thought she'd gone deaf, but sitting up straight, she realized the doctor had gone silent at her actions.

"Thank you, Marissa. You may leave us now."

"Yes, Doctor."

When the door closed quietly, Dr. Daniels moved to the front of the desk. He looked down at her for a moment, then lowered himself to sit on its edge.

"I'm very interested in everything you have to tell me, Ellen. Why did this happen? Where have you been? How did you return? What do you remember?"

It was evident she was playing catch up in this game, but one thing she knew for certain—she wouldn't be telling this man anything.

"They tell me you haven't spoken since you woke, but I know you can, and you will."

Ellen watched the doctor, mesmerized by the sheen in his eyes. *Who is he, and how does he know me?*

"I'm sure you're in a bit of shock. After all, you were gone quite a while since you first disappeared." Pausing, he added, "And again this time."

She couldn't help the scowl his words caused, and a smile crossed his face.

"Now you see why I'm so anxious to hear of your adventures. The time you spent with my father and now with me. What you might have remembered. How you returned." He chuckled to himself. Leaning forward, he stared at her for a moment before saying, "Were you in another time, Ellen? Another space in time, perhaps?

"You'd be surprised, I'm sure, of all the stories I've heard about you. You and your hunt for the Guardian. You were smart. Able to get what everyone wanted. I've always been amazed that you were able to avoid and evade agents of The Guild."

The doctor stepped from between her and the desk to move

behind her. Cocking her head, Ellen listened and kept aware of his location.

"They were good, those agents of long ago." She heard subdued awe in his tone. "Well-trained. Deadly."

Walking back to the desk, the doctor regarded her.

"You must have been something back in your day. But"—he again mounted the edge of the desk—"now you and I will find your secrets, won't we?"

Breaking eye contact, Ellen looked down and raised her arms. The clank of the cuffs was harsh in the room. Lifting her gaze, she again caught his eye and raised her brows. Leaning back, he regarded her, a smile coming to his face. Pride. She saw his pride in her like she were a trained dog.

"If I release you, will you be good?"

Giving nothing, she held his gaze.

"Ha!" He laughed and slapped his thigh. "Nothing ventured, nothing gained. Right?"

Moving around his desk, he took a set of small keys from a drawer. Squatting in front of Ellen, he unlocked first her ankles and then her wrists. He was in a partial stand when she leaned in and pressed her lips to his ear.

"Thank you."

With a jolt, he pulled away just as she pushed the chair back with one foot and came to her feet. Trapped between her and the desk, the doctor could only stare up at her, his eyes wide and face growing pale. Her hands clasped, she drove up, catching him under his chin. The force of her hit threw him back onto his desk. Stunned, he moaned and slid from the workspace to land on his knees in front of her.

Like perfection served on a platter, she thought, then drove a knee into his face.

When the doctor dropped to the side, Ellen stooped to grab the chain with the small keys on it. Quickly, she unlocked the cuffs from her ankles and wrists. She dropped them and the keys and stepped over the doctor to the back of his desk. Rummaging through his drawers, she found little of interest until she opened the middle one. There she found another set of keys.

She scanned the room to stare a moment at another door at the back of the office. Moving to it, she listened and then cautiously opened the door to see a small bathroom. The main room had one door in and out. There were no windows to confirm her thoughts that they were underground. Entering the bathroom, she spun around, looking for anything she could use. Quickly opening the doors to the vanity, she saw precisely stacked towels and a small container of soap. She shut the doors and pushed aside a divider. A thin sheet-like cloth hung in the rear of the space. With a shake of her head, she exited the bathroom and went to the office.

Hallway first. Then the staircase. Then she would see.

At the door, ear to the wood, she paused. Leaving now with no information—how would she find anything out? Why was she here? What had brought her back? How long had she been here? Looking over her shoulder at the man prone on the floor, she wondered who this doctor was too.

She glanced around the room, her eyes again drawn to the man on the floor. Maybe she'd been hasty in dealing with him so harshly. She could have gotten some information.

With an inner shrug, she turned from him. He was going to be out for a while. The only thing moving on him was the small rise of his chest and the blood flowing from a busted nose.

She scanned rows of filing cabinets, focusing on the one

marked with a *T*. When she tried it, it was only to find it locked. Shifting through the keys in her hand, she tried two small ones before getting the right one. Opening the drawer, she quickly located *Thompson, Ellen*. She pulled the file free, then leafed through, pausing when she recognized an image. Distant, slightly murky shots of her in Paris and in Rome. Vatican City. She saw enough to know she would need to study the records further. She closed the file and spun toward the bathroom. She grabbed the sheet inside and returned to the main room. Ellen laid the sheet out, put the file in it, and strapped it all to her frame.

With a push of her hip, the drawer closed, and she turned toward the exit.

She paused in stepping over the doctor. Dropping down beside him, she felt through his pockets, but no treasures presented themselves. Ellen sat back on her haunches and studied him.

What had happened when the attendants and then the nurse had touched her? Could she make it happen again? Hesitantly, Ellen reached out with one hand. Just before meeting the flesh on the doctor's face, she stopped, the memory of the nurse's violent nature still crisp in her mind. What would she encounter in this man's psyche?

She screwed up her courage, took a deep breath, and, biting her lower lip, placed her fingertips lightly on his cheek.

The images came fast, though a bit out of focus. Staring ahead, her eyes glassy, Ellen watched the images from the mind of the doctor. A building. Large white stones. He stood with a cluster of men, all listening to each other. The leader was middle-aged but fit and good-looking. His salt-and-pepper hair was brushed back, and he wore some type of business suit. The man clasped Dr.

Daniels on his shoulder and threw back his head in a hearty laugh. Straight, white teeth gleamed. The man was the poster boy for affluence, wealth, and confidence.

Then the image shifted. Still murky, but becoming clearer, like old disused items rising from the bottom of a lake.

People were running, crying.

Buildings. Old and dilapidated.

A glass wall with something moving behind it.

A dark night, a transaction made.

Ellen's brow wrinkled as she tried to make something out of the images.

When a headache spiked through her temple, she squeezed her eyes shut, sighed, and released the man. She knew she was overstaying her welcome, and with a final glance around, she stood and approached the door.

Cracking it open, she peered out. The hall was empty, and at the end was the door marked *Stairway*. Ears and eyes alert for others, Ellen hustled to the door without incident. She cracked it open. Nothing but silence.

She slid through the door, allowing it to close behind her. Other than a small lamp a flight up and one far down, she was in darkness. It felt good—safe. She took a moment to calm down and took a deep breath. Knowing she couldn't wait here all day, she pushed herself to move.

She'd made it up two flights of stairs when a door opened above. On the tail of its closing, voices reverberated down the stairwell. They belonged to a man and a woman. They were chatting and laughing and coming her way.

Ellen fled back down a flight, silent and swift on bare feet. Pulling open the door, she peered out. The hallway beyond was empty, and she saw a closed door across from the stairs.

She angled her head to listen to the two above her. Unaware of her presence, they continued to near. She decided she didn't have another choice and slid out of the stairwell and to the other door. Cracking it open, she was relieved to see it was a small closet. When she pulled the door shut behind her, she left it open slightly and laid her ear to the gap with her hand on the doorknob.

As luck would have it, the duo entered the hall from the door to the stairs. Still deep in conversation, they made a turn and continued down the hallway, never aware they weren't alone.

When her world was once again silent, Ellen opened the door and stuck her head out. She looked left and then right. A large interior window down the hall caught her attention, and she moved toward it.

Staying back from the glass and to the side, able to peer within, Ellen saw a room of white-coated individuals. Doctors? Laboratory technicians? She couldn't tell. They were all busy, sitting at desks, or what looked like ancient laboratory equipment. She watched them for a moment more, her brows furrowing. She had no clue what they were up to, and with no way to find out, she dismissed them and headed back up the stairwell toward freedom.

CHAPTER 4

Ellen stared at the door. Visible in the light of a flickering flame, she was certain it was mocking her. The entire thing seemed to slide, but no matter how she pushed or pulled, the damn door wouldn't open. She scanned the immediate area looking for a key or swipe pad. Nothing adorned the walls around the door.

She was just thinking she would have to return down the stairs to seek another exit when the wall shuddered. She jumped back to lie flat against the wall in a dark corner, her heart beating loudly. When the door slid open, a man walked through, his gaze locked on the papers he carried. He didn't look up and didn't check to ensure the door shut before hustling down the stairs.

Before it slid closed, Ellen stuck her fingers in the door. She listened to make sure the man didn't return before she shifted and peeked out of the portal.

Another hallway, it seemed. This one showed a sprinkling of natural light, so she was above ground now. That alone made her feel more confident. No sounds came from the hall, and she shifted out, sliding the door shut behind her. Down a couple of halls, and through a large archway, she saw what seemed to be

FAITH OF THE CURÉ

an exterior door.

The door opened easily, no locks or traps. For a moment, she stood with it cracked open. Heat and the smell of dust wafted through. From what little she saw, what lay outside the door looked like a field. Dried grasses, dirt, and sunlight.

Pressing her ear to the crack, Ellen heard nothing but the wind and its rustle through the grass. Screwing up her courage, she took a deep breath to calm her pounding heart and stepped outside the compound. She pulled the door partially closed behind her as a large gust whipped by her, slamming the panel before she could stop it. She spun to lay her body on the door, twisting the knob. It was locked.

Stopping herself from panicking, Ellen reminded herself she'd been trying to get out. She turned from the exit to look first left and then right.

Well, Ellen, she thought, *you're standing here in pajamas, bare feet, and with no money. Hell of a time to realize you could have planned better.*

Around the building lay a large space that was once a manicured lawn with trees and bushes. Now, everything was dried up and dead. The trees were just bare twigs. The surrounding area was empty except for a couple of partial buildings, long since fallen.

In the distance, where a small hill marred the flat landscape, a larger cluster of dead trees stuck out from the earth. Like broken fingers they reached to the sky, which was washed out by the heat of a noonday sun. Already she was breaking out in a sweat.

Taking stock of her surroundings, Ellen saw she was alone. Really alone. Not a bird or even a rabbit fled across the prairie.

It was hot, and it was dry. She would need to locate some

water quickly, and it seemed as though she'd be doing a lot of searching. For a moment, she even thought to bang on the door. Bang and yell and let them take her back and chain her up.

"Don't be crazy, Ellen. You're better off out here, no matter what."

She took one last look around, then headed toward the trees on the hill. Perhaps, with a little height, she could see more of what was around her.

CHAPTER 5

Marissa was whistling softly under her breath by the time she returned to Dr. Daniels' office. She was having a *good* day.

Dr. Daniels had come to her personally to assist with the woman's keep and interrogation. He would see—everyone would see—that she was an asset to the organization. All her hard work and planning were coming to fruition.

When the nurse knocked gently on the doctor's door and received no answer, her brows furrowed, and with a half step back, she read the placard on the door, almost expecting it to be the wrong room. Assuring herself she was at the right office, she rapped again, harder. Hearing a slight moan from within, she wrenched open the door. Between the desk and an empty wheelchair lay the object of all her aspirations. When she saw the blood, she rushed forward and dropped down beside him.

"Dr. Daniels," she cried, reaching out a hand but pulling back before she touched him. Beginning to rise, she said, "Let me get some help," only to be stopped by his grip on her forearm.

"No," he told her, his voice garbled and weak.

Marissa dropped back down beside him, a questioning look

on her face.

"But sir. You're bleeding." This time she did touch him, flitting around his head and shoulders with her fingertips.

Slapping her hands away, the doctor made it to his hands and knees. The movement made his nose bleed again, and it dripped on the expensive rug he'd lain on. Growling under his breath, he ordered, "Get me a cloth," and with his palm cupped under his face, he used the edge of the desk to gain his feet.

Marissa jumped up and ran into the adjoining bathroom. She pulled a white towel from under the vanity. Racing back to the doctor, she flipped the cloth open, waving it in front of him like a flag.

Dr. Daniels snatched the cloth from her, guiding himself behind the desk where he dropped into his chair. With a sigh, he laid his head back, a towel to his nose.

Blood began to seep through the material, bright even in the subdued lighting.

"Dr. Daniels," she began again, tentatively approaching the man. "You're still bleeding. Please let me call an attendant with some ice and packing."

"No," he said. "Is Ellen back in her room?"

"Ellen?" the nurse said, now looking about the room.

"Ellen. Ellen, you twit." Rocking back in his chair, the doctor put his other hand to his head, his raised voice and the situation exacerbating his headache.

"Um."

Opening his eyes, the doctor stared at Marissa. "What do you mean, um?"

"Well, sir." Marissa scanned the room, her eyes resting on

anything but the doctor. "She was here with you. I didn't want to interrupt."

"Didn't want to interrupt . . ."

When she looked into his eyes, the glare held her.

"Didn't want to interrupt," he said again louder, this time rising to his feet.

Marissa scuttled back, tripping on her feet. Afraid to turn from him, she backed toward the door, watching him as if he were a growling dog.

"I was in here. Alone with what might very well be a lunatic from the past . . . future . . ." He shook his head. "Whatever! I'm in here, alone, and you never once think to stop in."

Marissa tried to get some words out. Tried to defend herself. In her mind, she saw the situation where she knocked on the door to check on him. The situation where she interrupted the doctor and his interrogation of Ellen Thompson. Neither situation showed her in a good light. She knew there was nothing she could have done not to be where she was now.

Marissa quaked as the doctor took another step toward her, and she pressed against the inside of the door.

Giving a small gasp, Dr. Daniels placed a finger to his injured nose. In that moment, Marissa swiveled, cracked the door, and was through and moving down the hall in a second.

She looked over her shoulder twice, but the doctor didn't follow her. Opening the door to the stairs, she turned back and muttered, "And it had been such a good day."

CHAPTER 6

Ellen stood on her toes, hoping to give her view more distance. She'd thought to climb a tree, but they looked as if a good wind would blow them down, and the last thing she needed was an injury.

Even from this height, there was very little to see. Mountains rose to the north—if the sun were any indication—but they were miles away. Their image was distorted and out of focus. Spinning, she looked again to the south. What appeared to be an ill-repaired highway stretched across the surface of the land. Weeds grew from its cracks and, in places, the pavement was completely gone.

Following instinct, she made a hurried exit down the slope and headed toward the highway. When she made it to the road, she scanned the distance. Hearing and seeing nothing, she walked out into the middle of the paved road. She felt a pull in one direction and made her way on that path without questioning her instinct.

The pavement, broken and worn, was super-heated from the sun, and soon, her feet were burning. She moved just off the pavement. Though the dirt was hot, and the dried grasses and weeds poked into the soles of her feet, they were a blessed relief from the burn of the asphalt. The fabric of her scrub shirt and pants was light and airy, but it clung to her, plastered to her skin with sweat, heavier where the sheet hugged her.

Her lungs stung with the heat of the midday air, and if given the chance, she'd have traded her soul for a drink of water.

Ellen thought soon she had to come across some evidence of civilization, but as the sun dropped behind her in the sky, she looked around for a place to spend the night. There were no trees to speak of, just scrub bushes and no real cover. She didn't want to wander too far from the road as it was her directional center. Afraid to wait much longer, she moved from the road into the wilderness.

Within a few hundred feet, the land dipped down into a crevasse, a mass of dead plants and grasses shooting up from its base. This seemed like the safest place she'd seen, and so moving gingerly, stepping from large rock to large rock, she made her way to the base of the chasm. She cleared a small spot and lay down to sleep. She thought it might be cooler here, maybe even a little damp, but everywhere she touched was dust, heat, and broken plant life.

Exhausted as she was, sleep did not come easily. Her mind, always agile, wouldn't calm and give her peace.

Why was she here? Where was here? How long before they came to find her?

She remembered her past, both as Ellen Thompson and as the Guardian. Who was she now? What was she to do?

Ellen had just begun to drift off, entering that twilight of sleep where you couldn't tell if you were in the real world or a dream world, and she was startled awake by the sounds of a motor. Groggy, and weak with dehydration, she tried to pull herself into a sitting position but fell into a deep sleep with a heavy sigh.

* * * * *

A rush of lights and wind whipped by her as she was pulled down a tunnel. There was no fear, just an exhilaration unlike anything she'd known before. At the end of the tunnel, she was propelled out, but she floated, weightless in the air. The atmosphere around her swirled, her hair floating out to crown her head. She peered down to see multiple beings, all varied and unique. They paced in a circle. Constant and timeless.

With a gasp, she was pulled forward to float in front of one figure. It was garbed in black and covered in a mask. Within the mask she saw eyes, her own eyes, gray and determined, staring back at her—through her.

Time sped up and the figures jumped places, streaks of color flowing from them as they sped forward. As varied and unique as the figures, planets moved quickly through the heavens above, their orbits eternal.

How much time passed?

Once again, the heavens opened, and a portal awaited her. In absolute silence, a blinding light filled the space. She was sucked back in, but this time she was not alone. Spinning through the lights was the black-clad figure with her eyes. The figure morphed. The battle armor fell away, dark hair grew before her eyes, and soon she was staring at herself. Like a mirror image, they stared at each other. Closer yet, they moved, 'round and 'round, circling one another. When the figure touched her, she welcomed it—the sense of completion, comfort.

Then, she was alone.

CHAPTER 7

D r. Michael Daniels stared at the note in his hand, a note he had to send. Fear filled him, but it was dissipating with the knowledge that he'd had time to dodge the proverbial bullet. By the time the runner got the message to Malcolm Whitman, he was sure to have Ellen back.

Sealing the missive, he spun his chair to again face the woman in front of him. Marissa, Ellen Thompson's nurse, stood with a cool rag in her hand. She stooped, applying it to the growing bruise on his face.

The skin around his eyes was already black and blue. His broken nose was disinfected and wore a bandage. The nose really pissed him off—he'd always been proud of its clean Roman lines. If it didn't heal correctly, he'd have to have it rebroken and set.

The woman had only been awake for a few days, and she was already causing him pain.

When he got her back, he thought with narrowed eyes, he'd take all these aches and pains out of her skin.

He dreamed of the things he would do until a sharp stab of pain had him wrenching back, slapping at the nurse's hand.

"Christ, Marissa!"

She backed off quickly. Storing her implements and medications back on their tray, Marissa snapped off her gloves and, without saying anything, headed for the exit.

"Marissa."

Turning back to him, her expression closed, she raised an eyebrow.

"We need to get the staff together. See if anyone saw Ellen leave."

"Yes, Doctor," she said, opening the door.

"And get someone in here to take this message to Chicago."

With a curt nod, Marissa was gone.

When the door closed softly behind the woman, Michael rose from his seat and went into the bathroom attached to his office. He was shocked to see how much darker the bruising had become in just the span of a day. Gingerly touching his skin, he issued a hiss.

"Crazy bitch," he whispered to his reflection. He would turn over the world and shake it to find her. She'd see bruised when he was finished with her.

CHAPTER 8

A gasp woke Ellen, causing her to sit upright. She still lay partially under the brush at the bottom of the coulee. Her mind spun, so she lay back to gather her thoughts. She knew where she was—relatively—and she knew she had to keep moving or the psycho doctor and his men would have her again. She didn't know what was going on, but she knew she needed to stay out of their hands.

After a moment more, she rolled to her feet to slowly make her way up the side of the ravine back to the paved road. Instinct pulled her in the same direction as yesterday, and she didn't question it. If she didn't find something or someone soon, she'd need to stop during the heat of the day. She could not go too much longer without water.

She didn't know how long it had been or how far she had come. Putting one foot in front of the other was the only thought in her mind.

The air in the distance, where the line of the highway disappeared, was distorted with heat waves, and she imaged it might be the ocean. The back of her mind knew this was unlikely, and she knew what a mirage was, but just the idea of water was so appealing, she was willing to entertain the fantasy. Dreaming of diving into cool, blue water kept her moving.

By the time she saw the little white church in the distance, she was so dehydrated she was not sure if it was part of her illusion or not. For a while, no matter how hard she tried, she couldn't seem to get closer to the chapel, and this seemed to confirm the deception.

Dropping her gaze from the church, she stared at the ground in front of her, willing herself to keep moving. She kept putting one foot in front of the other until she stumbled up the stairs to the church and collapsed.

CHAPTER 9

Father Thomas Johansen moved slowly down the aisle of his church. When he reached the end, he laid his forehead against the door of the sanctuary. Another day without worshippers. Another day for him to question his faith.

So many had moved on, shifting their lives into the city where there was more abundance. More ability to forage. Food and water had disappeared from the outlying communities almost entirely. Unless you had a well and were able to grow a garden, you would starve. And usually, roving bands of looters would get to you first. People preying on people. This world was harsh and would kill you if you weren't careful. He knew only dumb luck had kept him safe for this long.

When he heard a bang and reverberation from the other side of the door, Father Thomas thought perhaps he'd been wrong. Perhaps they were coming for him after all. Lifting his head, he stared without seeing for a moment and then, with a sigh, resigned to his fate and pulled the door open.

At first, he thought he'd been mistaken and that he was still alone. But then, he saw the body prone on the porch that surrounded the church. It was dressed in striped pajamas and seemed to have something tied around it.

He glanced back the way he'd come. Exhaustion draped over him like a heavy shroud. Maybe he should just go back inside. Lock the door. Worry about dealing with the body later.

When it moved and gave out a moan, he knew he couldn't do that—no matter how tempting the thought was. He kneeled beside the form and turned it over.

A woman.

Other than the old and the very young, it was a rare thing these days to see a woman. Especially one unaccompanied by men.

When the woman moaned again, her eyes opened, and she looked right at him. A shiver passed down his spine. His brows drew together, and he whispered, "It can't be."

When the woman shut her eyes and went limp, Father Thomas stood to walk away from her. Keeping her at his back, he stared off to the horizon, thinking. He rubbed his chin. When he made his decision, he spun back to the woman and kneeled. With a small groan, he picked her up and carried her into the church, through the sanctuary, and into the rectory. Laying her upon his mattress, he again stepped back to study her. She didn't wake. He went to the bathroom and retrieved a wash bin, towel, and jar of well water.

Dampening the towel, he wiped the dirt from her face and hands. When she opened her eyes to stare at him, he put some water in a cup and placed a hand behind her head to lift her, urging her to drink. She drank all the water, and he laid her back. He thought she'd again lost consciousness when her hand flew up and grabbed him by the forearm. He recoiled, but the force of her grip kept him close.

Her form gave a full-body shiver. "Eric," she whispered, and he knew the change he'd prayed for had come to his door.

When she didn't say any more, when she seemed to drop back into unconsciousness, the priest moved away from her. Time ticked as he studied her, waiting for something to happen. When nothing did, and she didn't awaken, he left her alone in his room. Passing again through the sanctuary, Father Thomas climbed a flight of narrow stairs just off the entry. These stairs led him to a small attic. He knew where he was going, and for what he was looking.

At the rear of the room, he located a small packet. Leather and worn, it was practically bursting with papers. He pulled the packet to his face and inhaled. A blend of the earthiness of leather, old pipe smoke, and dust brought an image of his grandfather to his mind. With a sigh, he reversed his steps across the room and down the stairs. Through the sanctuary, he again stood before the woman. She hadn't moved.

Could she really be the same one?

Without the patience to wait until she woke, Father Thomas opened the packet and spread the papers on the desk near his bed. Out of the packet tumbled sketches of the woman.

It had to be her.

There were studies of her. Profiles and frontal. Smiling and somber. All in pencil on paper. They were true likenesses. His grandfather—Eric—had a rare talent for capturing images. And this image, this woman, had filled his mind.

Thomas remembered his grandfather's obsession.

Ellen Thompson.

The woman who disappeared into the light.

CHAPTER 10

Ellen awoke with a violent start, her mind full of the memories of a tunnel. It was difficult to breathe in the dry, dusty space. Fear was a constant companion—fear of being buried underground. Fear of her light going out. The absolute dark. And there, in the underground, was a giant spider. A spider with a man's face.

She knew where the memory had come from. She knew who she'd been with.

Back in the present, she recalled waking off and on. The man—the priest—was always there. Always ready with a cup of water. Stale, tepid water, but delicious all the same. Even without the touch, her newfound insight, she saw Eric in the lines of his face. She heard him in the priest's accent. She remembered thinking of windswept fjords and Vikings when Eric had finally spoken. Though fainter, the same images went through her brain with this priest.

Ellen scanned the room, surprised to see she was alone. On a small bedside table lay the folder she'd been carrying. The sheet was folded and laid beside it.

She swung her legs over the bed and sat up just as the door

opened. There he stood, his sleeves rolled up. A Roman collar at his throat. A stranger, but someone who had taken care of her when she'd needed it.

"Ah, so you're awake. And looking better than you have." When he saw her glance toward the exit, he added, "You're safe here."

When she made to stand, he rushed to her and put his hand on her shoulder.

"Now, don't be too hasty."

She relaxed back into a sit, not sure if she had the energy to fight him. "Where am I? Who are you?"

The priest pulled a chair closer to her and sat. "I'm Father Thomas. Thomas Johansen. I'm the priest of this church."

"And where is this church?"

The priest didn't answer right away. He stared off, seeming to study the skyline outside the window across the room, as if he didn't have a ready answer for her question. When he looked at her, he shrugged.

"This town has been called many names over the years. Currently, it's referred to as Hopewell. Hopewell, Illinois. We're about seventy-five miles outside of Chicago. Or what used to be Chicago."

"Father, this might seem like an odd question . . ."

"Ask, my child. These days, there are no odd questions."

Now it was Ellen's turn to stare out the window. The sky was blue and cloudless. Robin's egg blue, her mother would have said. Beautiful until you stood and saw the land. Dry and burned out. Bereft of life.

The priest seemed to be giving her time to think, but when she looked at him, it was to see him staring at her intently. She returned his stare until he dropped his gaze. Only then did she ask her question.

"What year is it?"

At her question, Father Thomas regarded her with a narrowing of his eyes and cock of his head. "Thirty-one seventeen."

"Thirty-one seventeen? So the doctor was telling the truth," she muttered.

"Doctor?"

"At that place. He said I'd been gone."

"What place?" the priest asked.

"I don't know," she said and shook her head. "I don't seem to know anything."

Father Thomas poured water into a glass and handed it to her. She accepted it and took a sip.

"Let's back up a bit, shall we?" He waited until she gave a small nod before continuing. "As I said, my name is Thomas Johansen. Father Thomas Andrew Johansen." When she simply watched him, he added, "And your name is?"

"I'm sorry, Father. My name is Ellen Thompson."

He was already nodding before she got her name out. Ellen's gaze sharpened. "And what is it you want, Ellen?"

"Well," she said and looked around the room, "that is the million-dollar question, isn't it?"

"What do you mean?"

"I know I'm here. But I don't know *why* I'm here."

"I might be able to help you with that," he said and turned away. He reached behind him for the leather packet. "You see, Ellen, I knew who you were before we officially met."

"How . . ." she began, but he cut her off.

"Let me show you."

Father Thomas shifted to sit beside her on the bed, opened the packet, and pulled out the first of many images. Ellen didn't say anything. She took the paper and studied the drawing. When he pulled out another, and then another, she took each of them silently.

By the time her hands were full of images of herself, she'd turned to him with a question in her eyes.

"My grandfather . . ."

"Eric," she said.

"Yes. So, you do know some of what's happening."

Ellen shook her head and looked again at the drawings covering her lap. "No. No, I don't know what's going on at all. I do remember Eric and know of your relationship to him, though."

"My grandfather told me a bit about you. About how you disappeared into the light."

Ignoring the implied question in his words, Ellen set the pictures aside and leaned to take the folder from the table. She opened it on her lap, causing Father Thomas to lean in. Starting at the beginning, it held a history of her life. Images of her and her parents. Christmases. Even her first day of school and graduation from high school. Then the pictures changed. They became more covert, with fewer people from her family. Images of her in Paris. In Rome.

The last dozen pages of the folder contained a synopsis written by a P. Oliver, whoever the hell that was. Why had they been watching her since childhood?

"Where did you get this?" the priest asked, reading the brief over her shoulder.

"In that place."

"The place you were? The place you don't know where it is?"

"Yes. The place I escaped from."

"I'm sorry, Ellen, but I really don't understand. Why would someone hold you captive? How did you escape?"

"Okay," she said with a sigh and twisted toward him. "I'll explain what I can, but I really don't know much."

Father Thomas also turned to her, leaning in, his face intent on hers.

"It's kind of starting from the ending, but you know about that day. The day your grandfather told you about."

Thomas placed his hand on the file to keep it closed. "You tell me about that day."

Her brow crinkled. "Me?"

"Yes. I'd like your point of view."

"But you already know your grandfather's."

Thomas nodded slowly. "Yes, you're correct. But his tale was full of emotion—fear, longing, awe. I want to know yours."

Ellen tried to take herself back to that day. The adrenaline and anticipation. The home guard crashing through the door and taking Eric to the ground. The all-consuming bright light.

And then the sense of speed.

"There was nothing. Light. Motion."

He leaned forward. "And after? Do you have memories of where you went?"

The circle. The beings. The sense of oneness. She couldn't truly explain it to him. Not to anyone.

"There was a place. Beings. Other planets."

"Another dimension?" His voice, attentive before, grew excited.

"Maybe . . . I don't really know."

"You've been gone a long time, Ellen. What happened in that time?"

Hedging, she shifted back. "I don't really remember." With a nod toward the file, she added, "If you want to look at it, do. I need to figure out my next move. I can't stay in one place for long. They'll be coming."

Thomas nodded his agreement, if not his understanding, and took the file from her lap. He read the brief, turning the pages almost silently. After a few moments of watching him, Ellen got up to pace. She'd never been good at inactivity. This waiting—not having a plan.

"Ellen." The priest's call broke through her thoughts. "Have you seen this?"

Moving behind him, she peered over his shoulder. "What? I don't see anything."

"Here." He pointed out a sentence. "It's talking about my grandfather."

Ellen grabbed the page, reading avidly.

When Thomas stood, it was his turn to peer over her shoulder.

"They questioned him. Tortured him." Continuing to read, she added, "They thought he knew something. That I'd given him something they wanted."

Her mind jumped back, clearly seeing the amulet as she laid it in the circle. It was the only thing she'd had. It had made her journey possible. As soon as she thought that, her mind flipped to her return trip. Losing the strappings of the Guardian. Once again being Ellen. No talisman acted as a catalyst. Just a call—a pull.

Thomas turned the next sheet. "It looks like there was a whole investigation into your disappearance. References to an

Adrian." He stared at her.

"A friend," she muttered.

He watched her for a moment and then returned his gaze to the papers. Ellen paced from him again, her mind in turmoil.

"There must be a reason for my being here. A reason I was brought back. Something to be done."

Not raising his gaze from the papers, Father Thomas muttered, "My grandfather had a place in the city."

Spinning, Ellen rushed back to him. "The city?"

"Yes. In Chicago."

"What kind of place?"

"A home," he said and shrugged. "An apartment in one of the high-rises."

"Do you think there would be information there? Something about what happened to him. What he might have known?"

"I know he had a safe."

Ellen about jumped on him, excitement plain in her every motion.

"He showed it to me once."

Her smile was so bright, Father Thomas had to smile back.

CHAPTER 11

Ellen laced up the boots Father Thomas found for her. In a small side room, along the back entrance just off the kitchen, the church kept items donated for helping the poor and downtrodden.

Now, those items were to help Ellen.

Along with the boots, they'd located other pertinent items a woman might need. Three different T-shirts—one white, one black, and one with a bright, smiling Tweety Bird on it. A pair of cargo pants in a dirty, worn khaki color, two pair of socks, a heavy-duty black belt, and a lightweight windbreaker. After looking awhile, Father Thomas found a navy-blue baseball cap with a large red *A* front and center. When he'd brought her a couple of pair of panties and an exercise bra, she had to laugh at the blush that had covered his face. He'd even found a backpack covered with images of a flying hero with a hammer.

Ellen braided her long, dark hair and pulled the tresses through the hole in the back of the cap. She stuffed the jacket in the backpack along with the extra socks and underwear.

When she stepped from the room, Father Thomas was filling bottles with water and placing them in another bag. He straightened when he saw her. "I thought at first we could bring a wagon full of supplies, but we'll be going overland and that really won't work."

"That's okay," she said. "I'm strong. We'll make do."

"We'll be walking for a couple of days over rough terrain, maybe a week. It might take longer than I'm thinking, and that's if we're lucky enough not to meet up with anyone."

She nodded to let him know she understood, but he moved toward her, his gaze intent.

"I don't think you are understanding me, Ellen. We do *not* want to meet anyone. Nothing good will come of it. Not around here, at least. It would be easier to take the roads, but packs of gangs run them. They've got vehicles. They make or steal their fuel."

When she didn't comment, he stared off into the distance and again nodded.

As if the words were pulled from him, he admitted, "Okay. Yes. There are some good people. And even some people who may need help. The problem is most people you will meet are only out for their own benefit. If we're to get where we need to be going, we're going to have to be smart."

"You don't sound much like any priest I've ever met."

"I was idealistic once. But lately . . . I think God has left this place." Turning away from her, he continued to pack a couple of bags. Letting the discussion lie, Ellen walked to him to gather half of the food and water in her pack. She glanced at the priest to see him holding a book.

"What do you have there?" she asked.

He hefted it for a moment, and then handed the Bible to her. "It was my grandmother's. She was a devote woman. Her faith gave her strength." Under his breath, he muttered, "I could use a little of that now."

Opening the book, Ellen flipped through it and then went back to the first few pages. There she found an inscription written in an aged hand. The words were foreign, and when she flipped the book and showed Father Thomas, he confirmed it was French.

Le curé était un parent
Uncousin bien-aimé

Attempting to read the inscription, Ellen stumbled over it.

With a chuckle, Father Thomas took the Bible back, read the inscription in fluent French, and said, "Roughly translated, 'Your cousin is the parish priest.' He is the one who gave her the Bible. They were very close."

Watching him, Ellen thought he might leave the Bible behind, but then at the last moment, he slid it into his pack.

When they were ready, Father Thomas led her out of the sanctuary and into the darkening day.

CHAPTER 12

They had walked for about a mile in silence when Ellen asked, "So what happened here?"

"Here?"

"This time. This place. It's like I'm in a *Mad Max* movie or something." When he looked at her, his brows drawn, she stumbled for something to say and ended up with, "Never mind."

After another moment of silent travel, she tried again.

"The last time I was in America—granted it was near a century ago—it wasn't like this. Not so dry. Not so wild—the people, I mean. And really . . ." She stopped walking to scan the area and shielded her eyes with a hand to peer at the setting sun. ". . . not so intense. The sun seems brighter."

"The Rush," he said, turning to consider her.

"The Rush?"

"It happened before I was born. A solar flare, people said. Electrical devices got fried. Electricity in general was shut down. People didn't know what to do. Everything we used was electronic. Cars, communication, even money in the bank. People were barely coping with that, then panic set in, and then the weather changed almost overnight. Things were bad. Large groups fled the cities. But they brought more of the same to the outlying communities. I suppose we would have been all right, been able to recover, if it weren't for the riots. Control became lost completely. Whole cities burned."

They began to walk again, slowly.

"People panicked as people will. As I said, it was bad in the cities. Across the world—you'll see when we get to Chicago." Stopping, he faced her, his eyebrow raised. "Have you ever been to Chicago?"

"Once," she answered. "Years ago. For a conference on impressionist painters."

"You'll notice right away. I've been told the entire skyline is changed from what it once was. Back before The Rush."

"You grew up afterward. And became a priest. It couldn't have been all bad."

"Oh no." He shook his head. "It was decent. And, you know, I didn't know any different. In the small towns, it probably wasn't too changed. Fewer amenities. All the electronics were gone so it was hard on the older folks. Those who'd lived with the convenience of machines. With the weather—they said large chunks of the ozone fried away—it was hard to raise crops. No plants, no herds, both domestic and wild, so we grew up on different fare than you would remember from your childhood. And with the weather, we didn't play outside much. Evenings and nights mostly.

"You were wrong to walk during the day, but I get you didn't know that. It's just too hot. Too dry. Almost everything lays low while the sun is out. Except for the occasional raiders, you won't see anyone in daylight."

"I always liked the nights." When he glanced at her, she

added, "As a kid. I loved to play in the evenings. Hide-and-seek as the sun was sinking. The smell of the night. Dew just forming on the grass. The sounds of kids echoing through the neighborhoods."

"It sounds lovely."

"Yes, it was. I don't think I appreciated it enough while I had it."

Ten miles later, Ellen followed Father Thomas over a hillside to look down on an abandoned farmhouse. A partially broken barbwire fence still encircled the home, and a pile of tumbleweeds had accumulated in one corner of fencing. Wind blew through and swirled for a moment, turning into a mini tornado in the yard.

"What's this?" she asked.

"Somewhere to spend the day."

"You want to stop already? I think we can push on."

"We need to take the rest while we can. Your health is still fragile—"

"Fragile?" she interrupted him with a scowl.

"I'm sorry. I don't mean to offend you. You've just come out of an experience neither of us understands. You were unconscious just yesterday. I see no reason to possibly push you too hard. Not now. You may well need your strength soon enough."

Prideful, yes, but not stupid, Ellen saw the reason in what he said. "Fine." Again, studying the farm, she asked, "Do you think it's empty?"

"I do, but we'll be careful. There used to be an artesian well on-site. If it's still functioning, we'll be able to refill our water."

Following the priest down the hill, Ellen moved toward the farm.

CHAPTER 13

With a start, Ellen awoke to the fading light of a late-afternoon sun. Across the room, on the other sofa, Father Thomas slept, a soft snore issuing from him with each exhale. Ellen was surprised by how comforting the priest's small sounds were.

In the next room, beyond the open doorway, soft light streaked into the room through the dirty pane of a large picture window. That same light spilled into the area where she and the priest had slept out the day. Turning her head, she could make out the figure of Father Thomas, his chest rising rhythmically with each breath.

Finding sleep in the heat of the day hadn't been easy, but luckily, they were both exhausted. Now, she felt rested, stronger than the day before, and ready to continue their journey. If he didn't wake up soon on his own, she'd rouse the priest so they could eat something and be on their way in the dying light of dusk.

Sitting, she wiped a hand over her face and combed her fingers through her hair, then rebraided the tresses. She moved out of the room, neither silent nor noisy, and after crossing the outer space, she moved into what was once the kitchen for some family.

Curious if there might be hidden treasures, Ellen went from cupboard to cupboard searching for something useful. Anything located, she placed on the small table in the eating nook for further consideration.

Opening a door, thinking it might lead into another room, she was pleasantly surprised to locate the pantry. Mostly bare, she found two jars of canned peaches and a dusty box of crackers on the top shelf. She opened the box and took one out to study. Popping it in her mouth, she chewed the stale biscuit and, with a hard swallow, got the chalky consistency down.

"Delicious," she said.

"What did you find?"

Ellen whipped around, her fists up in a fighting stance. The box hit the floor at her feet, spilling part of its contents.

Father Thomas stepped back, his hands raised in a warding gesture. "Whoa, whoa. It's just me."

Ellen dropped her hands and bent to retrieve the box of crackers. Gingerly picking up the spilled ones from the dusty floor, she dropped them back in the box. "Sorry, Father. You surprised me."

"No, it's my fault. I should have made some noise. Let you know I was here."

Ellen took the canned peaches from the shelf, stepped from the pantry, and with a shrug, she moved past the priest to the table. "I guess we'll both need to get used to each other."

Father Thomas came to the table to study her findings. "You've been busy."

"Just thought I'd look around while we had some time before we leave." She set her items down. "You did say there was a well on this property?"

"Yes. I think so. In one of the outbuildings." He gestured toward the back of the property. "Might be a well house. We need to check them out."

Without any comment, Ellen returned to the room they'd slept in and picked up her pack. Pulling on her hat, she tugged her braid through the back.

When she returned to the kitchen, Father Thomas was still examining the goods on the table.

"I'm ready. Let's do this."

Father Thomas hustled to grab his things, and together they filled their packs with the items from the table.

When they stepped outside, the sun was nearing the horizon, its glow shooting yellow and orange streaks. For a moment, Ellen stopped and tilted her head back, bathing in its dying glow. With a deep breath, she opened her eyes and turned to follow the priest.

The first building was a shed that might have been used to house small equipment for maintaining the house and yard. It still smelled of oil and gasoline. It was empty, long since scoured of anything useful. As they turned to step out, Ellen saw a gleam against a back wall and located a screwdriver encrusted with dried dirt and rust. She rubbed it between her hands for a moment to free most of the debris and then shucked off her pack to place it inside.

They got lucky on the next building. Small and dark, the interior contained a hand crank water pump. Father Thomas wrenched the rusty handle up and shoved it down again. Within two more pumps, a groan sounded, and a small trickle of water flowed.

Ellen dropped her pack and pulled bottles from it as Father Thomas gave another pump of the mechanism. More water hit the dirt floor and flowed to the back of the shed. Ellen uncapped the first bottle, shoved it under the flow, and smiled.

When her bottles were full, she and the priest switched places. She pumped, and he filled the bottles he carried.

The two stepped back outside the shed with their bottles stowed away. By now, the sun had sunk below the hills, and stars had begun to appear in the early night sky. Using what remained of the sun as their guide, the duo set out on their second night of travel.

They'd barely reached the top of the next rise when the sound of engines cut the night.

"Get down!" Father Thomas grabbed Ellen's arm and fell to the earth, pulling her down with him. They positioned themselves behind a scrub bush and peered down the hill at the farmhouse. Two vehicles, which looked like they were piecemealed from a dozen random machines, roared up to the home. Doors flew open and men spilled out.

"Damn," the priest muttered, causing Ellen to look at him, a question in her eyes.

Making no effort at secrecy, the men spread out, three of them entering the building. Even from where they lay, Ellen and Father Thomas could hear the crashing and breakage of items in the house. When a chair crashed through the large living room window, Ellen instinctively ducked her head. Moments later, a small flicker of light lit the window before bursting into flame.

The men hurriedly exited the building only to turn at the vehicles and watch the fire grow quickly to encompass the structure.

"What's going on?" Ellen whispered. Leaning against the priest, she grabbed his forearm. "Do you know who they are?"

"The Main," Father Thomas said without taking his eyes from the fire below.

"The Main?" She faced the house again. "Do you know them?"

"They're run by a big wannabe thug named Little T," he answered. Pushing backward until he was behind the hill, he stood and urged her to follow his lead. "We can discuss them later. Let's get some distance between us and them."

CHAPTER 14

Little T always told people his name was ironic.

By the time he was twelve years old, he'd reached a height of six feet tall and didn't seem to be stopping any time soon. And he had the girth to go with it. He didn't know if he came from big people or was an anomaly since he'd never met his parents. For as long as he could remember, he'd been on the streets. The city of Chicago had raised him. He'd suckled at her breasts and had been comforted by her lessons. Sometimes she mothered with grace and love, and sometimes with an iron fist. He was the man he was because of his true parent, and he loved her.

Little T ran one of the largest organizations within a few hundred miles of Chicago, Illinois. His baby, The Main, was large and complex. Even he didn't know the exact numbers, but he had thousands of men and women working under him. Some were collectors, some negotiators, and some were just good at killing. He, in turn, answered to a bigger boss.

Little T had plans for the future—his future—but for now, he answered to Malcolm Whitman. If there was one thing he'd learned on his mama's knee, it was to obey the boss. So he went about his business, accumulating assets of goods and people, giving the cut to the boss—after skimming his own piece of that pie—and keeping his eyes open for the day he could take all the pie.

Staring at his reflection in the large ornate mirror in his office, Little T smiled.

"Boyo, it looks like your day has come."

CHAPTER 15

D r. Michael Daniels relaxed into aged upholstery and enjoyed the experience of riding in a vehicle. It didn't happen very often, and he didn't know when, or if, it would happen again.

He had a meeting with Malcolm Whitman, and though he was worried about what would happen when he got there, he planned on reveling in the trip. He'd be in the car all day, with a couple of small stops for breaks and eating. Mr. Whitman kept himself in his place in Chicago—mostly. For this meeting, Dr. Daniels would be going to him.

Even though the doctor was important in his field, he rarely got treated with the deference he enjoyed when at the beck and call of Mr. Whitman. He peered out the side window, watching the passing of the scenery, when the man in the front passenger seat spun to face him.

"You all right back there, Dr. Daniels?"

"Yes. Thank you. Everything is perfect," he answered and took another sip from his glass of water. The fact that it had little taste, if any at all, let him know how special he was. It was devoid of the lasting residue of metals and impurities.

When the man in front gave a little nod and faced forward, Dr. Michael Daniels leaned back and allowed himself the indulgence of a daydream.

CHAPTER 16

Nearing the end of another night of travel, Ellen and Father Thomas saw the flicker of a campfire in the distance. As they neared, a small group of people came into view.

"Stop right there," came a voice from behind them. Ellen and Father Thomas stopped in their tracks, hands held high.

"We're no harm," Ellen said, angling toward the stranger. A young man stood next to a tree trunk—not older than fifteen. He aimed a hunting rifle at her. "We're just looking for somewhere safe to spend the day."

"Let them be, Jeremiah." Ellen spun to see a woman in bib overalls standing in front of them. "Can't you see this one here is a pastor?

"Sorry about that, Father. He's not used to seeing a man of the cloth. You and your lady friend can share what we have." The woman turned and moved back toward the fire where three other people rested. Ellen and Father Thomas followed her, and the boy followed them.

Seating them, fussing over Thomas, the woman soon had their hands full of food and a weak, lukewarm tea.

Ellen sat back to eat. She didn't care what the food was or what might be in the tea — she was just happy to have something warm to fill her belly. She smiled as she watched the family. For a family was what it was. A mother, father, four children, and what might have been an uncle. After they'd gathered around the fire, two younger boys had come out of their hiding place in the brush. Now they ran around the people, calling out, playing a game of tag.

When Ellen saw Thomas shake his head at the woman, her attention turned from watching the children play. It was obvious the woman was attempting to convince him of something. Something the priest was having no part of. Ellen set her dishes aside and moved to listen.

"I'm sorry, Martha. I don't think I'll be able to do that."

"But Father, the family, the children, would learn so much. I want them to believe, but life here is hard. Don't you have some words for them?"

When Father Thomas caught sight of Ellen, she saw the desolation in his eyes. But she also saw resolution. He was a priest. He hadn't given that up. He no longer felt the stories in his heart, and he hadn't in some time. But he couldn't walk away from it. He projected his faith for anyone who saw him with his choice of clothing. Now, when asked to stand behind it, he had very little choice.

Nodding and bowing his head, he whispered to Martha, "All right. I'll try. I'll try and give you and your family what comfort I can." With those words he sat on a stone a little distance from the fire and gathered the children to him.

He began telling the children stories. Stories of choices and good deeds. The children sat before him, legs crossed, heads tilted back. They listened, enraptured by his tales.

Not so much a sermon, Ellen thought, but more a teaching of life.

Father Thomas's tone was friendly, but she noticed it never warmed. Ellen doubted the others noticed, but she could sense his distance from his subject.

When Father Thomas seemed to be drawing to a close, he paused, took a deep breath, and said, "Jesus said unto him, thou shalt love the Lord thy God with all thy heart, and with all thy soul, and with all thy mind. This is the first and great commandment."

Martha herded the children to tents in a copse of dry woods when he finished. As she passed them, she placed a hand on Father Thomas's arm and whispered a quick thank you.

The sun would be up soon, and they would all need to take shelter and get some rest. While they'd eaten, Martha had told them that the men—her husband and his brother—would take turns at watch for the daylight hours. She said she and Father Thomas could rest in one of the tents. That they would be safe.

Father Thomas sat alone after his talk with the children. Ellen was just about to approach him when he stood and wandered away from the campsite. She was asleep before he returned.

The next two nights passed without incident. They made good time and found safe locales to spend the daylight hours. Every time Ellen brought up the subject of The Main, Father Thomas put her off and promised her he'd tell her soon. After two nights of this, she knew that when they again rested, he would tell her everything.

It took until the sun was rising to find safe lodging for their rest. They were nearing the city, and buildings had become common. Mostly industrial, she was certain they could find useful items if they had the time to stop and search each one—to risk possible inhabitants. Their primary concern, however, was to get to Eric's place in Chicago and see what, if anything, he had pertaining to her in his safe.

When Father Thomas turned in to an old gas station, Ellen fell in step behind him. This was as good a place as any, and she was feeling fatigued after another all-night trek. Entering the building, the priest and Ellen fell into the pattern of clearing each room before shutting them off. They cleared the rear exit and then locked it. After the burning of the farmhouse, unless they felt particularly secure, they would take turns standing watch while the other slept. Though he had yet to tell her about The Main, she was aware that they were a threat to each of them.

Spreading a bedroll she had acquired a couple of nights ago, Ellen sat cross-legged and faced the priest.

"Okay. Tell me about The Main."

Father Thomas sighed loudly and turned from her. "Not now, Ellen. I'm tired. Tomorrow we'll discuss—"

"No, Thomas. I need you to fill me in on this threat. What if we get separated or something? I need to understand more of what to expect in this world."

"You don't have to worry about it. They were just burning."

"I don't agree," she insisted. "I think they were looking for us." When he turned to her, she added, "Or at least looking for you."

He seemed to want to tell her. It was as if the story were fighting to clear his lips, but something continued to stop him.

"What is it, Thomas. Why do you hesitate to tell me what your history is with this group?"

Father Thomas took a last resigned look around the back room, and with a heavy sigh, he sat across from her. A small lantern's flickering light threw a shadow across his face as he bent forward to study his hands on his lap.

* * * * *

Father Thomas kept his head lowered as Father Patrick said the benediction. The baritone made the words resonate. Oh, how he loved the mighty words of the Bible. Sometimes, he would sit and read passages just to have the words in his mind.

He loved learning from Father Patrick. He was what some would call an "old-school pastor." His teachings brooked no argument—there were no gray areas in the Bible as far as he was concerned. Father Patrick's faith was comforting in a world that was anything but.

The engine noise came, softly at first, in the distance. As it got closer, it increased in power and volume. Behind him, where the congregation gathered, a low murmur began. It, too, rose in volume, and soon a word or two became plain.

"What will we do?"

"Why won't they leave us alone?"

"No. It's too late. They'll see us."

Father Thomas looked up from his position, his gaze automatically going to Father Patrick. The older minister was already moving down from the pulpit. He raised his hands, the sleeves of his robe sliding down his arms, and called to the people.

"Listen. All of you. Please, everyone. Be calm."

From where Father Thomas stood at the top of the pulpit, he saw over the heads of the anxious congregation. They clustered around Father Patrick, all talking at once, grasping at the sleeves of his robe.

When the engines entered the grounds around the church and then cut off, communication stopped. As one, they spun to face the main entry. A baby wailed but was instantly hushed.

The sound of boots stomping up the wooden stairs and across the porch had the babble of voices starting up again. Father Patrick reached out to them, opening his mouth to speak.

"Pl—"

And the double doors flew open. There, on the vestibule, a large group of men and women stood. They were young, probably none older than thirty. Men had arms around women who giggled and scoffed at the churchgoers. When the gang took a step within the church, the mass of Father Patrick's flock fell back equal distance.

Father Thomas had a clear view of the standoff. When Father Patrick made his way through his people, in an attempt to placate any possible altercation, Thomas put up a hand to stop him.

The cleric had barely gotten through the throng surrounding him when Thomas heard the twang of a bowstring, and it appeared as if an arrow had sprung from Father Patrick's stomach. The priest clenched the shaft of the arrow, bending slightly. Chaos erupted around him—people screaming and running. Tripping over each other, some went down behind pews. The raucous laughter of the horde by the doors cut through the screams as Father Patrick fell on his side. Some of the congregation had stayed with him, holding his bloody hands.

Father Thomas stood above it all, frozen.

* * * * *

Ellen listened silently, letting Father Thomas spin out his tale in his own time. He didn't look up, didn't shift his body, but occasionally he would wring his hands as if the anxiety of his telling had to be expressed in some way.

He didn't know what to do. Frozen, sounds muted, all he could do was watch as the drama unfolded.

When another arrow launched, finding its target in the throat of one of the parishioners, Thomas's fear finally broke through his paralysis and had him ducking behind the first pew, Noise overwhelmed him. His senses went into overdrive, and he could even smell the blood.

Then people stampeded past him to the only other exit in the church. Father Thomas peeked up, his blanched face a specter against his black suit. From his position, Father Patrick's legs and feet were visible. He wasn't moving, and Thomas feared he was dead.

When the black-clad legs stopped between him and the other pastor's prone legs, Father Thomas looked up. A man smiled down at him, the area around them quickly filling with others from his group.

"Lookee, lookee," he chimed. "Seems we got us a spare." The crowd around him broke into peals of laughter. The leader stepped around Thomas and headed for the back door. Over his shoulder he said, "Bring 'im."

Father Thomas stopped in his recitation, giving a hard swallow.

"Thomas," Ellen said gently.

The priest looked at her from under his brows.

"You don't need to tell me anymore. I get it." He nodded, dropping his gaze to his lap. After a moment, she asked, "Are you sure they were part of The Main? I guess it doesn't matter—raiders are raiders—but perhaps they were another group."

"No," he insisted. "Little T, smug as he is, is a powerful man. I can't imagine another group working in his territory."

"Thank you for telling me. I agree. We need to do anything we can to avoid them."

Nodding, and relieved, the priest stood. "Get some rest. I'll take first watch."

Ellen watched for a moment while the priest walked out of the room. Knowing there was nothing else she could say, she lay back and closed her eyes.

CHAPTER 17

Dr. Michael Daniels leaned back in the comfortable chair, crossed his legs, and enjoyed the smell of his coffee.

When they'd arrived in the city, the men had delivered him to the entrance of one of the mighty towers that still populated this area. He'd never been here before, and before he'd even gotten out of the car, his first thought was that he hoped to be invited back again.

Just as the car to his back pulled away, one of the double glass doors at the front of the building opened. A young man in a black suit stepped out, the door held ajar.

"Dr. Daniels?"

"Yes." Michael Daniels cleared his throat and stepped forward.

"If you'd step inside, Mr. Whitman has asked me to bring you to him just as soon as you arrive."

Giving a gracious bow of his head, Michael Daniels stepped into the building. Once in, the intensity and heat of the sun cut off. The atrium, towering many feet above their heads, allowed some light to enter where the shadows played with the rays, weaving in and out with the patterns of the clouds outside.

Michael Daniels' footfalls wavered once upon entering the building, the grandeur of the entrance causing a pause he quickly covered. Following the man across the polished floor, their shoes clicking, he couldn't contain his surprise at being led into an elevator. When his guide noticed his hesitation, he gave a small chuckle.

"Mr. Whitman says for every desire, there is a way." And with that, the heavy double doors slid closed, and with a slight jerk, the elevator began to rise, causing Michael Daniels to widen his stance and grip one of the silver bars that ran around the interior of the car.

When the car gave a small jerk and came to a halt, Michael straightened and released what he realized had become a death grip on the bar. Flexing his hand, he turned toward the opening doors. His escort extended an arm, indicating he was to exit the elevator. When Michael raised an eyebrow, the man only said, "Mr. Whitman will be right with you."

What followed was a relaxed, and welcome, dinner with the only guest being himself. Malcolm Whitman had been a gracious host, charming and attentive. Once, Dr. Daniels had brought up work, his explanation of Ellen Thompson's escape at the forefront of his mind, but Malcolm Whitman had halted him mid-sentence.

"Let's keep the work talk for after dinner, shall we?"

To which, Michael Daniels had readily agreed.

Now, Michael was in a post-dining stupor. He wasn't completely sure what they'd eaten, but it was real meat and fresh vegetables—some things that were in short supply. And coffee! He almost didn't want to drink it and waste the sweet smell.

"So, Michael," Malcolm Whitman said as he entered the room from behind the doctor. His words caused the physician to sit up and give a mental shake of his head. Malcolm Whitman sat across from him, his own hands free of any incumbents such as a cup. "Tell me what you're doing to retrieve Ellen Thompson."

His voice low and hesitant at first, but growing stronger as he gained confidence, Dr. Daniels explained that he had groups of security agents out as they spoke. They would find her; he was confident of that.

When Malcolm Whitman put up a hand to stop his recitation, the doctor's voice stuttered to a halt. "What I want you to do is locate her. Don't stop her."

"But sir . . ." The doctor stopped, not quite sure what to say.

"I think she has information or can locate the information— the knowledge of something I want. Once she has it, then, and only then, is she to be reacquired."

Nodding as if he completely understood, Dr. Daniels said, "Yes. Yes, of course."

CHAPTER 18

Little T had worked for Malcolm Whitman for years. He'd been a good and loyal soldier in the Army of Whitman. But he'd never been invited to where Malcolm Whitman worked and lived.

Stepping through the doorway of the downtown high-rise, the leader of The Main stopped, spun, and gave a low whistle.

"Swanky," he muttered under his breath.

Giving a cocky smile to the two men who approached, obviously security, Little T said, "I'm here to see the big man." When they looked him over from his size fifteen boots to the top of his impressive height, his smile extended. "I got an appointment."

One of the men unclipped a small notepad from his waistband, sure to let Little T see the sidearm strapped in a shoulder holster under his suit jacket. Scanning it, he confirmed what Little T said.

"You can go straight up." The man gestured to the bank of elevators.

Surprised, but not daunted, Little T made his way to the conveyance, and a moment after he'd arrived, the doors opened.

Within, stood a man—white, middle-aged, arrogant—and he stared back at Little T.

Neither man moved to allow the other to enter. It seemed as if they had a standoff.

*****

When the doors opened and Dr. Daniels saw the man on the other side, his pulse gave a little jump. The size of him. It was just the size of him. Never mind his foreboding presence.

Ever believing himself above most men, Michael Daniels waited for the other man to move out of the way and allow him to exit the conveyance. When this didn't happen, Dr. Daniels couldn't bring himself to be the one to step out of the way.

It looked as if the two of them might stand where they were forever. One inside the elevator and one out. When a clearing throat broke the silence, they both looked at the guard.

"Mr. Whitman isn't going to wait all day."

Finally, they moved at the same time, sliding by each other. After he entered, Little T turned to watch the door slide closed with a barely audible *snick*. When the car gave a small jolt and moved up, the leader of The Main grabbed the bar and gave a small chuckle.

"Must be the only building with a working elevator in the whole damn city."

Little T watched the floors pass by—light peeking through the crack between the doors—and waited for the elevator to stop, not certain how high it would go. He thought about the building from the outside—he'd always liked its look. The big letter *T* was the only evidence of a name that was once on the skyscraper, and he told himself one day the building would be his—it already had his name on it. But he didn't know how many floors the structure had.

Would Whitman position himself on the top floor? Little T knew *he* wouldn't—it would not only be too hard to defend, but the avenues to escape would be limited.

But Little T knew Malcolm Whitman was cut from a different cloth than most men. He wouldn't even know how to look at the world like Little T did. It was obvious nothing in the man's history, nothing in his memories, had lent him to the supposition that he was vulnerable.

When the elevator stopped, and the doors opened, Little T thought he was somewhere around the ninety-fifth floor. He was only surprised by the fact that it hadn't reached triple digits.

Little T wasn't used to facing any aspect of his life with trepidation, but as he stepped hesitantly from the elevator, he looked both left and right. Two men, like twin statues, stood on either side of a two-paneled wooden door. They didn't look at him as he approached, and just as he was going to speak, one pushed the door open.

Little T again hesitated, quickly becoming irritated by his reactions. Due to his wariness, and his own annoyance for it, he almost rushed through the door. He screeched to a halt when the view on the other side captivated his attention and left him without words.

"Little T," a voice greeted him.

Unable to tear his sight away from the grandeur out the window, Little T didn't immediately answer but moved the distance to the window to truly study the awe-inspiring vista. Below and beyond him, the riverbed splayed. In his mind, he could almost see what it must have looked like full of water. He'd never been so high that the grittiness of the streets wasn't evident. From here, the city looked like a land of enchantment.

After a moment, he heard his name again from behind him — he wasn't sure how many times it had been called.

"Little T."

When he turned, putting the view behind him, he faced Malcolm Whitman. "Mr. Whitman," Little T greeted his boss with a nod.

"Welcome." The leader gestured to a comfortable seating area.

Little T, never one to willingly put someone at his back, showed not his trust but his usefulness to his boss by preceding him into the lounge. When Malcolm Whitman offered a brown liquid in a crystal decanter, Little T only nodded.

Malcolm Whitman joined his guest and handed him a glass with two inches of liquid in the bottom.

"Cognac," he said.

Little T nodded as if he'd known this all along, and with a swift motion, he shot the liquid down his throat.

"Ugh," was all he could say before leaning forward and giving in to a vicious coughing attack.

Malcolm Whitman leaned back with his own snifter, gave a small smile, and sipped at his drink. "Cognac is made to be sipped."

"Wha—" Little T began and then had another, though abbreviated, coughing fit. "What is that?" he asked when he got his breath back.

"Cognac," Malcolm said again, not choosing to embellish his description.

Little T sat up straight and peered with interest at the flask on the side table across the room. "Can I have some more?" he asked, already beginning to rise.

"I think not," was the reply.

Catching his upward motion, Little T again relaxed into the chair, but for a moment, his gaze remained on the tempting copper-colored elixir just out of his reach.

"T," Malcolm Whitman spoke. "Tell me about your surveillance of Ellen Thompson."

"Well," Little T began, turning his body and attention to his boss, "she's a slippery one. I'll give her that. But I have eyes and ears in every town and city for hundreds of miles." Seeing his interest, Little T got comfortable, ready to ensure his employer of his worth. "Her and the priest left his church. They headed into Chicago proper."

"Do you have any indication of where they are going?"

"None right now, boss. But we'll watch them. They won't get away from us, and we'll have that info for you, right quick."

Malcolm Whitman gave him a small nod and took another sip of his drink, causing Little T's gaze to jump back to the decanter on the table.

"I cannot stress enough"—the big man's attention returned to Malcolm Whitman—"how important this woman is to me. I want her to go wherever she wants, but I always need to know where that is."

"Yes, sir." Little T nodded his understanding.

"She has information. Information I'm not even sure she is aware that she knows. Information that I will have. I *must* have." Shifting so he sat forward on the sofa, Malcolm Whitman leaned into the space between him and Little T. "Can I trust you to follow her and deliver her to me when I tell you to?"

Now Little T sat forward, gaze intent on his employer. "Yes, sir, Mr. Whitman. You can trust me. I'm your man."

Malcolm nodded and sat back in his chair. He gestured to a man who had materialized behind Little T. "Stuart will show you out," he said before again sipping his cognac.

Knowing his time with the man was over, Little T nodded, rose, and left the building, again thinking that one day, somehow, he would have this place for his own.

CHAPTER 19

When Ellen heard a car door slam, her eyes popped open. From the back wall where she'd been sleeping upright, she pushed forward to rest on her hands and knees, face toward the front of the gas station. Sparse illumination came from a small window high on the wall.

Thomas stirred on the floor against the other wall, rubbing his eyes and yawning.

"Wha—" he began, but she cut him off with a wave of her hand.

Another car door slammed, and voices sounded faintly in the distance.

Now he was awake, his eyes large. Gaining her feet, Ellen moved past the priest and approached the door at the main area of the station. She cocked her head, listening. When all remained silent, she inched forward along an interior wall and peered into the night through a slice of window.

"What do you see?" Thomas whispered.

Putting her hand up to still him, Ellen kept her sight on the parking lot. After a moment, she stepped back and returned to the priest. "Quietly. Get your things."

"What's happening?"

"They're here. We're out of time." She sat and began to pull her boots on.

Thomas flew back to his bedroll. He'd slept in his trousers and undershirt. He pulled his dress shirt from where he'd hung it, grabbed his shoes, and sat across from her on a folding chair to pull on his loafers. Closely watching her, he buttoned his shirt. When she stood, then squatted to roll up her blankets, he gathered his belongings. Next came his suit jacket. Pulling his collar from the inner pocket of his jacket, he affixed it to his shirt. He righted his jacket and reached down to grab his pack.

She nodded upon seeing that he was ready to go. Again, she leaned against the corner of the front window to peer out.

"They're getting out of their cars," she whispered.

"They know we're here."

"Then we need to leave."

Thomas moved next to her, trying to see out the window over her shoulder. "We only have one option. Will they see us when we go out the back door?"

For a moment, she didn't answer. She took a deep breath before she turned toward him. "We're going to have to risk it."

With a small nod, he led them to the back door. Gingerly, he cracked it open and listened. He opened it farther and peered out. When he didn't see anyone, he glanced at Ellen and then slid out of the door with her right behind him. Quickly, they ducked into an alley that intersected with the street behind the station. Curiosity had them halting to peer back around a building. When Thomas moved on, Ellen looked back, watching for a moment before following the priest into the dawn.

They hadn't been gone for more than a few minutes when

they were stopped by the sound of automatic gunfire echoing off the concrete of the outer city. Both stared back the way they'd come.

"What do you think is happening?" Father Thomas asked.

Ellen just shook her head. Taking the priest's arm, she got them moving again.

They'd barely walked a mile from the gas station when Ellen saw furtive movement ahead of them.

"You see that?"

"Yes." He panned his gaze left and right. "Let's just keep moving."

A block later, the movements became men, all dressed in black jogging suits with white tennis shoes. The only way to tell one from the other was by the painting of their faces. Cut directly in two, each side was a different color. From what Ellen saw of them in the steadily lightening day, no two were alike.

At first, they just seemed to be watching. Ellen and Father Thomas moved quickly through the city street, keeping an eye on those who kept an eye on them.

Ellen was just thinking they may get out of this unharmed, when one of the men following them gave a whoop and they began to close in. Not quickly, but slowly and methodically. She had a moment to wonder if they were being herded when Father Thomas took them down an alley that didn't have an opening at the other end.

Pivoting, they attempted to reverse directions, but the gang was already filling the gap.

Ellen grabbed Father Thomas's arm, and frantically, they began trying doors that opened to the alleyway. They were almost at the end of the alley, while the crew seemed to be growing in number every moment.

"Ellen!" Father Thomas yelled. She spun to see him with his hand on an open door. The whoop came again from behind them, and she ran. She and the priest slid through the interior darkness, and she heard Thomas throw a bolt.

Ellen took off her pack and pulled out a small lantern. With a quick strike of a match, and match to the wick, the hallway was sparsely illuminated. They stood at the base of a staircase, the steps rusted and only a partial handle still attached to the wall leading up. With a quick glance at the priest, Ellen shoved her arms into the straps of her pack and began climbing the stairs. They'd need to be quick. Behind them, the men outside were banging on the door, trying to get in. It wouldn't be long before they found an alternative entry.

Ellen flew up the stairs, Thomas hot on her heels. They came to another door about four stories up. They cracked it open and peered into the building. Silence greeted them. The room was partially illuminated with the diffused early-morning light.

Not sure where the gang was or what other threat might be in the building, the two exited the stairway on silent but quick steps to the open floor, locking the door behind them.

Scattered across a large room, desks were set at odd angles. Some were on their sides, giving evidence to the fact that the room had been ransacked. That had little bearing to them as they weren't looking for anything but a safe exit, and with that in mind, Ellen headed across the room. She moved down the bank of broken windows. Father Thomas stood behind her, his eyes on the door.

"Do you hear something?" she asked when she saw him intent on the exit.

"No. Not yet." But he wouldn't take his gaze from the door.

"Out of the frypan and into the fire," she muttered, returning to him. "Looks like we have to keep going up."

When they reentered the stairway, Ellen was about to relight the lamp, but she hesitated. Far below came the sounds of crashing and smashed glass. Loud voices filtered to them, echoing up the stairwell.

Ellen grabbed the priest by his arm and, with her other hand on a wall, made her way up the flight of stairs. Silent as cats, hyperaware of their pursuers, the two reached the top floor without incident. When they opened the door to the roof, it let out a loud scream that reverberated down.

"Shit," Ellen breathed. She tossed aside any idea of secrecy, and they rushed out the door and slammed it behind them. While Father Thomas held the door against possible force, she hurriedly searched the roof. Coming back to the priest empty-handed, for a moment they simply stared at each other.

Hearing a whoop coming up the stairs, Ellen shucked off her backpack. She dumped the contents and furiously searched. When she pulled the old, rusted screwdriver from among her things, she almost shouted with triumph.

At the juncture of the door, Ellen shoved the screwdriver into the gap by the knob. Grabbing the handle, she gave such a shove, she screamed with the effort. She and the priest knew it wouldn't hold them for long—if at all. They had to find a way off this roof.

Quickly, Ellen and Father Thomas separated to search around the outer walls of the roof. There was no ladder down. No emergency escape from the height of the building.

On the path around the roof, Ellen noticed piles of debris, wood, and scraps in the middle of the floor. Hoping for a ladder, she moved past, her attention on getting off the top of the building. When she again met Father Thomas and neither had seen a quick way down, she began to think.

Just as she neared the largest pile of rubble, the first sounds of banging could be heard on the door. They were running out of time.

"Help me, Thomas. Look for anything we can use."

The priest was quick to scavenge through the piles, but they found very little. Wooden planks, though frequent, were all too short a length to span between the buildings. Likewise, there was rope, but nothing to tie to and all too short to be of any benefit.

In desperation, Ellen made another trip around the roof, looking this time at the buildings on each of the four sides. "Thomas!" she yelled to get the priest's attention. When he looked up at her, she gestured. "Come here."

When he joined her at the side of the building, she pointed to the one neighboring theirs.

"Look. Balconies."

"Yes?" Father Tomas asked with a shake of his head.

"Okay," she began. "Hear me out."

Even as she talked, the priest was shaking his head and backing away.

"No, Ellen. That's impossible."

"Not impossible. I believe we can do it."

"You want us to *jump* to that lower ledge?" When she nodded, he shook his head. "That's insane."

"It's not," she insisted. "It's not, and we're out of options."

"Ellen . . ." he said and took a seat on the wall that surrounded the roof.

"And when we're in the other building, we can get down to

street level and run into the city. Look." She pointed. "There are plenty of places to go. Plenty of places to hide."

A heavy banging came again from the other side of the door. Looking down, Ellen was surprised she didn't see any of the gang members on the street. Apparently, they didn't think she and the priest could escape.

"I think we're out of time."

When the priest sighed deeply, she offered her hand. He reached to take it, and she hauled him to his feet. For a moment, she held on to him, skin-to-skin, staring into his eyes.

"What?" he asked. "What did you see?"

When she gave him a small smile, released his hand, and gave him a pat on the back, she said, "It's all going to be all right."

They studied their target building for a moment and then walked to the middle of the roof together.

"I'll go first?" she asked.

"I guess that would be all right," the priest said with a lack of conviction.

"Okay. I'll go, and you make sure you head over right behind me."

"All right," he agreed. "I'll be right behind you."

Having already blown out the lantern, Ellen put it in her pack before strapping it back on her frame. She gave the priest one last look and then concentrated on her path. With a deep breath, she took off running as fast as she could. When she reached the edge of the building, she took a final step to the knee-high wall that surrounded the roof. Pushing with that step, she aimed for a balcony about three stories down. She didn't know at what rate she would fall, but the three stories seemed good.

When she hit the open air, all sounds, except the whistle of wind in her ears, stopped. Her stomach gave a small tilt, and then she hit the bars of the balcony with a muffled clang. One foot landed on the floor of the platform while the other hung in midair. Scrambling, she grasped, slipped, and then put a death grip on the railing. She pushed with her foot and got the other one on the flooring. Turning, she saw Father Thomas on top of the far building. She swung a leg over the rail and gave the priest a wave. He waved back and then disappeared from her view.

Then he was hitting the wall of the building and flying through the air—right toward her.

Clambering back, she fell from the rail onto the floor. Scrambling on her hind end, she crab-walked away from the edge, her wide-eyed gaze on the priest.

When he hit, he missed with both of his feet, his arms quickly slipping from the top of the rail. Ellen jumped forward and grabbed him by the upper arms. His fall stopped, and he was able to get a foot on the balcony and heave himself over the side. The two of them fell against the door, pushing it open to fall inside the building.

"Oh Lord," Father Thomas whispered.

"Yeah. I'll second that one, Father," she said.

She allowed them a couple of seconds to get their minds and breath back, and then they were up and moving.

"Let's get to the bottom floor and out before they know we're gone," Ellen said.

They moved through the room. It was an apartment, so Ellen rummaged through the kitchen and confiscated a couple of large knives. She slid one through the loop of her belt at her waist and handed the other to Father Thomas. When the priest tried to refuse the knife, Ellen would have none of it.

"For your protection, Thomas. Just in case you might need it."

When he put it in his pack and returned the pack to his back, she nodded and led them out of the apartment. The hall was littered with trash and destroyed furniture. At the end of the hallway was an elevator, the door partially open.

"Stairs. Do you see a door for the stairs?" she asked, swiveling her gaze around the area.

"Here," Father Thomas said, pointing down an adjoining corridor. "Here at the end of the hall."

The two hurried through the door and moved down the stairs. Diffused light came in from small windows high on the walls. Twice the squeak of rodents came to them with the scurrying of small feet. A stench permeated the small area, telling Ellen something had died here not too long ago.

On the third flight down, Father Thomas put a hand on her arm, halting her.

"Do you hear that?" he asked.

Ellen listened. "I don't . . ." And then she did. A child crying.

CHAPTER 20

Ellen led Father Thomas from the stairwell, her attention intent on the sound. When the priest tried to talk, Ellen turned to him with a finger on her lips. She didn't know what it was about the crying, but it had an odd sound. Perhaps it was the reverberation of it through the hallway. Perhaps it was the lack of any other sounds. Perhaps it was her heightened state of awareness. She didn't know, but she didn't want to alert anyone that they were close.

The hallway, smelling of rotten meat and laundry detergent, was narrow in its clear spots, almost impassable in others. Sliding through, Thomas close on her heels, Ellen stepped lightly, twisting her body this way and that. Twice she had to duck under first a pair of upended bedsprings and then a refrigerator, which proved to be from where the scent of old meat permeated.

Ellen and the priest were almost at the end of the hallway when the crying abruptly cut off. She froze and the priest froze with her. Barely breathing, they waited to see what—if anything—would happen.

A few seconds into their vigil, her breath came deeper, and a cold sweat broke out on her upper lip. Fear, she realized. It was as if the pressure in the hallway had intensified.

When the crying began again, it was almost a relief. At least until she realized the sound now came from behind them. From a room off the hallway that they had already passed.

Perhaps they should just make their way back down the hallway to the staircase and leave. They had enough to worry about without increasing their load.

As the oppression of the hallway increased, Ellen decided she'd had enough.

"Thomas," she whispered, and the priest turned from the hallway behind them to peer at her. His eyes were large and his pallor was almost white. She was sure she looked just the same to him. "We need to get out of here. We need to get out of here *now!*"

Nodding vigorously, Thomas stepped back the way they'd come. As he was ducking under the refrigerator, his elbow hit the sagging door, and a wire shelf slid out to hit the floor with a clang.

Both Ellen and Father Thomas froze, and the crying cut off. Absolute silence filled the hallway.

When the floor shook, she had to bend her knees to stay upright. It took another percussion before Ellen identified the small shockwaves as steps.

"What in the h—?" she began as a silhouette filled the doorway and darkened the hall. With the light behind it, Ellen couldn't tell what had come to join them. Then it moved toward them.

"Mama!"

The largest man Ellen had ever seen pinned its beady eyes on her. He was dressed in what could only be described as a diaper. It sagged from his hips, pushed down by the weight of a very impressive gut that hung over the front of the garment. He was bald, no hair adorning his body at all from what she saw. Saliva dripped from his mouth and ran a path down his chest and stomach.

"Mama!" the behemoth bellowed again.

"What. In. The. Hell?" Ellen yelled as she backed away from the freakish man who'd begun to advance on them. Turning, she pushed the priest in front of her, almost tripping over him as they ran for the stairwell at the end of the hallway.

She heard the monster coming up on them from behind. "Run, Thomas!"

As they shot through the door and started to descend, the man began to cry again, his voice following them down the stairs.

CHAPTER 21

Ellen and Father Thomas exited the building at a speed not conducive to stealth. They weren't thinking of the gang or anyone who might be after them other than the large man-baby upstairs.

Outside the building, they kept at a fast clip down the street, farther into the city.

Blocks later, Ellen pulled the priest to the side of the street, under an old, torn canopy with the remnants of a bakery's name on it. She leaned against the wall, her hands on her hips, and took deep, cleansing breaths. Father Thomas slid down the wall to sit on the sidewalk in front of the shattered bakery window.

"What was that?" Ellen asked.

"I don't know," Thomas said. "People have adjusted in many ways to their world."

"Adjusted?"

With a nod, the priest added, "Well, yeah . . ."

"Okay," she said and moved to the middle of the street to look both ways. "Which way do we go from here to get to Eric's?"

Thomas pushed himself to his feet and, with slightly wobbling knees, joined her in the street. "We're a few miles from the building. It won't take too much longer, and we'll be there."

Ellen shucked her pack off and rummaged through until she found a water bottle to take a long drink. She handed the bottle to Father Thomas, and while he drank, she walked across the street to peer into the building.

Surprisingly, the front pane of glass was still intact. Reflected in the glass, she saw herself with Father Thomas behind her. She brought both hands up to cup around her eyes and peered inside.

"What is it?" Thomas said from behind her. "Do you see something?"

Ellen waited a moment more, sure she'd seen something move inside, and then, with a shrug, she stepped back. "It's nothing."

"Let's get going then," Father Thomas said. "We should be there within the hour if we don't come upon any more complications."

With a snort, Ellen said, "Complications."

"Well, you know. Anything that will keep us from our goal."

Within the hour the two were walking down a wide avenue closer to the center of Chicago. There were high-rises on either side of the street, though some of the skyscrapers had been burned out or had large chunks of their facades broken off. Along the avenue, cars were strewn as if by a strong wind. Windows were broken out of most of them, and doors hung open. Walking beside them, Ellen kept farther than arm's length away, not trusting what might be in the automobiles. She still scanned the interior of each, hoping to see something that might prove useful. Nothing presented itself as all the vehicles seemed to have been thoroughly picked over.

Her attention was on moving and looking over the interior of each car when Father Thomas called to her.

She was surprised to see he had stopped. When she walked back to him, he gestured to large double doors on one of the buildings. The doors were made of thick, darkened glass. Most of their bulk was broken out, but Ellen still saw evidence of its past grandeur.

"This is where my grandfather lived. At least for the better part of his life."

"I never did ask . . . how long did Eric live?"

"He was well into his eighties. The last five years or so, he couldn't live alone. He and I talked about him coming to live with me, but he wouldn't have it. He said that this was his home, and he wouldn't be leaving it. At least, until they had to carry him out." The memory, though painful, brought a small smile to the priest's lips. "I miss him every day," he whispered.

"You weren't able to live with him?"

"No. The city is too far from my parish. I needed to be available to the people there." Father Thomas paused and stared up at the tall building. The sun reflected off the mirrored surface, causing him to squint. "I visited him as often as possible, though."

The priest stopped studying the building and, with a glance at her, headed toward the entrance. When Ellen fell into step beside him, he continued with his story.

"I hired a lady to come in daily. I told Grandfather that she was there to clean and cook, but she was a nurse too. She made sure he took his medication correctly and on time, made sure he ate nutritious meals, didn't wander. Things like that."

"He didn't mind having her there?" Ellen asked.

"Well." Father Thomas hesitated. "The woman who stayed the longest was the third we tried. He kept chasing them away. I don't know why he accepted her."

"It's odd to hear stories of Eric as an old man. I met him in the prime of his life. He'll always be young and strong in my mind."

Stepping through the broken-out door, the two stopped just inside to listen and look about. The main atrium was wide open, the floor still covered with a rich-looking tile. Two different seating areas once adorned the sides of the space. Now the settees were overturned, their stuffing spilling out of ripped upholstery. One had a shattered china set spewed across the floor from it. In the far corner, a perfectly preserved china cup sat as if brand new. A faded painting covered the high ceiling. One wall sported a banister and what appeared to be a loft.

Along a far wall, a bank of elevators stood, all the doors closed.

Through an open wooden door, Ellen saw the remnants of a dark wood bar. The wall behind looked like it had glass shelves once full of liquor, but no more. The mirrored backsplash was shattered, and any shelves that may have been were long gone. Two barstools, red leather with plush seats and backs, faced each other at the bar. If this room could talk, what wonderful and awful tales it would tell.

Back along the other side of the room, a large winding staircase rose from the first floor. It was toward that staircase that Father Thomas led them.

"What floor did he live on?" she asked.

"The ninth. I swear, all we've done today is climb up and down stairs."

"Yeah. My kingdom for some electricity."

Father Thomas stopped his climb and turned to study her. "You have a kingdom?"

Ellen chuckled, and when his expression didn't change, she realized he was serious. "Um, no," she said. "It's just a saying. I guess it's a pretty old saying."

Nodding, but still with a confused look on his face, Father Thomas continued to the second floor. Here the floor spread, open to the first floor, just the banister providing safety. Ellen walked to it and peered down.

"Ellen."

She turned to see him stepping onto another, smaller, set of stairs. These were enclosed, though wider than most, and windows allowed light in from exterior walls.

With a sigh, she followed the priest up the next flight.

Each consecutive flight had a number where the floor branched from the stairwell. When the number nine showed, the two shared a small smile.

"It's right this way," Father Thomas offered and led them down the hallway.

Like the other buildings they had been in, this one was ransacked. Wallpaper ripped, carpet long gone, doors to rooms broken or removed entirely.

When they reached Eric's apartment, it didn't look any different from the dozen they had passed. The door was missing. Sometime in the past, it had been broken from its setting. The jam was busted, half of it projecting into the apartment as if kicked by a heavy foot. When Father Thomas moved inside, Ellen grabbed him by the arm. With a small shake of her head, she moved in front of him carefully into the room.

Nothing immediately jumped out at her, and she could feel the priest at her back, but after all they'd been through today, she was jumpy. After scanning the front room, she turned to Father

Thomas, put one finger to her lips, and made a "stay here" motion. He nodded his agreement, his eyes large in a slightly pale face.

Ellen made her way into the kitchen, noting absently the pulled and empty drawers and cabinets. When nothing happened, she continued through the apartment, scanning around every corner before moving on.

In the bedroom nothing remained of a room she was sure was once full of furniture. The empty room left no place for a foe to hide. When she'd checked all the adjoining rooms, she returned to the front of the unit where Father Thomas still stood.

"It's empty."

Still visibly shaken, the priest asked, "What was that all about?"

Ellen could only shake her head. "I don't know. I'm just edgy." She moved out of Father Thomas's way to allow him to precede her back into the unit. A bit flustered at herself, she said, "What are we looking for anyway?"

From over his shoulder, he said, "The safe. I don't know where it is, but for some reason, I've always thought it was built in or something. Must have been something my grandfather said."

"Okay. Well, let's get searching."

They decided to start in the back of the apartment and work their way forward. That way, the longer they stayed, the closer to the exit they would be, more aware of anyone coming or going.

The sun had reached its midpoint in the sky and had begun to lower when they got back to the front room. An overturned armchair lay by a front window. The underside was ripped open, and it looked as if rodents had been harvesting the stuffing for their bedding.

Built-ins were on the far wall with a gap for electronics in the middle. Most of the shelves were empty, all of them covered with a thick layer of dust and bug carcasses. Four framed photos stood on one side along with a small case open to show a gold pen. When Ellen got closer, she read *For Exceptional Service* emblazoned on the case. The photos all contained images of Eric with others. She studied his face in one and then another, trying to recall the exact emotions of their time together.

"Ellen," Father Thomas called softly from the kitchen. With another glance at the photos, Ellen went to where he squatted in front of a cabinet.

The priest had the cabinet open and the floor of it removed. Under the space where the planking had sat, Ellen saw the front of a dial safe.

"How did you find that?"

"I was opening the cabinets, and it all looked so familiar. I just followed my instincts." From where he crouched, he looked up at her, his face glowing. "It was as if my grandfather were right here guiding me."

"Well, cool. Can you open it?"

His face darkened as he considered her question. "Um. Yeah. I think so." The priest gave the dial a spin. When Ellen kneeled beside him, she had her lantern in her hand. She lit, then held the lamp toward the face of the safe. Father Thomas returned his attention to it, and the dial made a low metal-on-metal sound almost too small to hear as Father Thomas turned the dial, first one way and then the other, sitting close to see the numbers on the face.

After the third one, he grabbed the handle, but it wouldn't turn.

"Maybe you didn't get it right," she offered.

The priest gave a small sigh and muttered under his breath,

"I was sure that was the combination."

"Give it another try."

Father Thomas sat back for a moment and rubbed his hands together. Then, with barely a glance in her direction, he leaned toward the safe. Ellen sat forward, too, directing the glow from her lantern onto the face of the safe.

Again, he went through the motions.

Spin. Stop.

Spin the other direction. Stop.

Spin the other direction. Stop.

This time, when he grabbed the handle, they both held their breaths.

With almost no effort, the handle turned, and he pulled the door open.

"Ha!" Ellen said and patted him on the back.

With the light shining in, they peered inside the safe.

CHAPTER 22

Little T cruised along in the passenger seat of the sedan. He dreamed often of what it would have been like to have ridden in the automobiles that had once populated the world. Now, the only ones running were rudimentary to their decedents. Carcasses of the truly grand ones could be found, but only in books could they be seen as they were. And those gave no feeling as to what they'd been like.

Little T sighed and sat back on the padded upholstery. The meeting with Malcolm Whitman had gone about as he had thought it would. Nothing got settled, and all the work was put on him.

Now, he had a meeting with his top lieutenants to determine where the priest was and if the woman was still with him. Last he'd heard, they had slipped by his men just outside the main part of the city. There weren't many options for them though. Little T was confident they would find the two. And when they did, he'd get all the information he could out of them, and what it was Whitman thought they had. Now he was curious, and now, as always, information went a long way toward success.

Little T had multiple places he used to do business in and out of the city. He never wanted to be too predictable since that was a good way to get dead.

He remembered hearing, as a young child, that his great-grandfather had been a city councilman or something in some small backwater town. He guessed, with the way things were going, that his current status was higher than anything his predecessors had aspired to.

"Take the back way in, Simon," he told the man driving him.

"Sure thing, boss."

When they pulled up to a large overhead door, it rattled up, aided by another of Little T's employees. As the vehicle pulled in, the door was pulled down.

Little T never considered it advantageous to be caught out in the open. One thing a man of his size could guarantee was that he made for a large target.

Exiting his transport, Little T put one hand on his abundant hip and scanned the area. About a dozen men worked on a variety of jobs, including taking apart objects they'd found, packaging up different weapons, and planning a run into another territory.

When his driver approached, Little T said, "Call them together, Simon."

With a swiftness the big man appreciated, the men dropped what they were doing and hustled over. He knew it was in part from good training, but also good old fear. They knew that for any reason, real or imagined, if he was dissatisfied with their performance, they might become the next body buried.

"Okay, boys. We have a goal." And all his hirelings fell silent to listen.

CHAPTER 23

The object gleamed in the illumination thrown by the lantern.

"A key?" Ellen murmured.

Father Thomas gingerly reached inside the safe and plucked the key out. It was lying on a folded piece of paper. He laid the key in his hand, turning it this way and that.

"What do you think it goes to?" Ellen asked.

He shrugged and muttered, "I have no idea."

Father Thomas reached up to place the key on the counter above them and then returned to the safe to pull out the paper. He opened it, reading silently. When he looked up into Ellen's eyes, his held confusion.

"It's a letter."

"Well, what's it say?" she asked.

Without answering, he handed it to her.

Friend,

You're here, so I'm gone but the fight continues.
They were tracking me, watching my movements, so I
had to hide what information I had.
I left you clues.
You'll know where.

Eric

Ellen reread the letter.

Standing, she whispered, "They were tracking him?" Her brows pulled in.

Taking the light from her, Thomas leaned in to shine it inside the safe. Then, just to be sure, he felt around the interior, knocking on the walls. Nothing changed. No secret compartment presented itself.

Ellen laid the letter on the kitchen counter and picked up the key. She closed her eyes and concentrated. She'd never done this before with an inanimate object and wasn't sure she could.

Feelings of Thomas shifted through her mind before she peeled them away to the metal beneath. The key cooled until it felt like a chunk of ice against her flesh. Images bubbled up. She saw herself and Eric, once again at the Vatican. Images of her as the Guardian, and now with Father Thomas. In her mind's eye, she turned, and a brilliant light beckoned.

She opened her eyes to peer at the key in her hand.

"What did you see?"

"It's connected to this whole thing. In some way, it might be why I'm here."

FAITH OF THE CURÉ

"What do you mean?"

"I'm not really sure." Laying the key with the letter on the counter, she scanned the letter again.

Ellen opened her mouth to ask a question, but as she inhaled, her breath caught. Taking off her pack, she upended it on the floor. Her jacket, two bottles of water, and the file from Dr. Daniel's office fell out. She dropped the pack, picked up the file, and rose to her feet.

"What?" Father Thomas asked, watching her with renewed interest.

"I—" She opened the file on the counter to rummage through the contents.

"What is it? What are you looking for?"

"There," she said and raised a picture from the many in the file. "I knew he looked familiar." With those words, she stepped around her pile on the ground and hurried to the living room. Father Thomas snatched up the key and letter and followed.

"This guy. This guy," she chanted, walking up to the photos on the shelves. She scanned them and then snatched one up. Turning to the priest, she thrust the picture at him. "That guy! The one on Eric's left."

Father Thomas studied the picture for a moment before shrugging and returning the image to her. At his quizzical look, she handed him the photo from her file.

"There," she said triumphantly, her finger on a figure in the back.

Father Thomas studied the picture she'd given him. It was an image of her in Rome. The image was a little grainy, taken from a covert location. Behind her, partially blurry images walked. When Thomas saw it, he reached for the other photo. Giving it to him, Ellen stepped to scan them over his shoulder.

"See. Do you see it?"

"It's the same man," he whispered.

"Yes! He must have been working with Stephen and Eric back then."

"Okay." He nodded. "I see your point." He handed her back the two photos. "But what does that mean?"

Visibly deflating at his words, Ellen again considered the two images of the man. "I—well I don't know, Thomas. But don't you think it has to mean something?"

"I don't know," he said with a shrug.

When he turned from her to reenter the kitchen, she could only hold the pictures. Crouching to the safe, Father Thomas disappeared behind the counter.

Ellen paced to the front window of the apartment, her thoughts in disarray. She tapped the framed image, sifting through what might or might not be useful. When she again looked down at the photos, she turned over the frame and saw the metal clasps keeping it snug.

Tucking the image from her file under her arm, she undid the clasps from the frame to release the back. Taking it off, she tucked it under her arm with the other photo. Behind the backing was a square cardboard insert to keep the photo protected. Taking it out, she immediately saw writing on the back of the picture.

38.9137° N, 77.0358° W
Front and back, with keen eyes they do gaze,
Composed of body and spirit, duality fills their days.
O'er a building of white,
Brother defenders show their might.

Strong and smart, their beauty does blaze,
Guarding entry to the sun's shining rays.
'Neath Power's nemes, wisdom is found,
Knowledge is based, victory is crowned.

"Nope," Father Thomas said from behind the counter. "Nothing else here."

"What?" Ellen called back, distracted by the words.

Coming up behind her, the priest said, "There's nothing else in the safe. It won't move or anything. I think the key and letter are it." Peering over her shoulder, he asked, "What did you find?"

Gesturing at the words on the picture, she said, "Some writing," and handed it to him.

"What's 38.9137 N, 77.0358 W? Do you know what it means?"

"It looks like GPS coordinates."

"G-P what?"

"Um? Global . . . Positioning . . . System, I think."

"I'm sorry, Ellen, but that tells me nothing more than I knew before."

Ellen turned to look at the priest, thinking he must be joking. When she saw honest confusion in his gaze, she turned fully to face him. "No, I'm sorry, Thomas. Even with having all the changes of your time right in front of me, I continue to forget how much everything is different. GPS. It's coordinates." When the same blank look still filled his face, she tried harder.

"Okay. So, there are lines around the earth. Imaginary lines. Some run up and down . . . or north and south. Some run east and west. These are latitude and longitude lines. Although now I'm not telling you right 'cause I'm a bad teacher. The latitude runs east and west. The longitude runs north and south."

"And these lines are on the earth?"

"Yes. On a map. It's a way to know exactly where something is on the earth."

"So, these numbers will take us to somewhere," the priest stated, nodding as he studied the back of the photograph.

"Yes. In theory."

Handing her back the picture, Father Thomas said, "How do we find where they are?"

Ellen took a big breath, thinking for a moment. "We're gonna need a map. A few maps, really."

"There's nothing around here. Where should we find a map?"

"We're gonna need a library. The bigger the better."

Father Thomas was already shaking his head. "I don't know where a library is."

"I do."

CHAPTER 24

When Ellen and Father Thomas walked out of the building, night was falling.

They had been up for hours and would need to rest soon, but for now they needed to use the relative coolness of the night. She knew the general direction to take to get them to the water, but after that, it would be hit and miss. When she lived in Detroit, in another life, she'd had the opportunity to study architectural designs with artistic appreciation on buildings. One building that stuck with her was a library in Chicago. Her study group had argued for long hours about the good and bad of this building. Its exterior color and large roof owls had always held her attention.

They moved through the city streets, silent as specters. Keeping close to the buildings, they flowed in the shadows cast by the light of the rising moon. Cars littered the roads, left where they stopped when The Rush hit. All had been vandalized in one way or another—windows broken out, upholstery shredded. Most had been tagged by spray paint—various names and images wearing through time.

The later it got, the cooler the night became. Like moving

through a desert, the air of the city quickly cooled, the only warmth radiating from the day-heated concrete.

Often, Ellen and Father Thomas saw other people. Each time, they fell back to hide along buildings or behind some object on the street. At first surprised, she came to realize that in a city the size of Chicago, even with the loss of life that must have occurred with The Rush, people would still exist. Short of a world-ending event, humanity would always find a way.

Now, shifting through the destruction of a long-lost civilization, she became one of the inhabitants of this new world.

The people she saw, seemingly shadows themselves, didn't live life as she once knew. Survival—if this was even survival—was all they were doing.

When the sky began to lighten, Ellen realized they'd walked through the night but still hadn't made it to where they needed to be. They'd need to find cover soon. Somewhere to wait out the daylight hours. Somewhere to get what rest they could. Somewhere secure.

After pulling the priest into an alley, she whispered these needs to him. It was soon after when he tugged on her jacket and pointed down a side street. A store, its front crisscrossed with bars, sat mid-road. She gave a nod and led him past the street to the alley behind. If they could enter from the back, so much the better.

When they located the building of their choice, it was to find the rear door fortified and unbreachable.

"If we can get into the building next door, we should be able to make our way into this one. Maybe from the roof. There's no alleyway between these buildings."

Father Thomas nodded and followed her to the next building. Pulling on the door, they froze when it gave a loud squeal of protest upon opening. Silent minutes passed. When no one came to investigate, Ellen gave a nod, and the two of them moved to the rear of the building. They lifted and pulled, and the door closed with an almost silent groan. They stood again, listening to the unwavering silence.

Making their way through the ground floor, Ellen kept on the lookout for stairs. She figured if they could get to the roof, they could easily get to the other building. No flying through the air this time.

When they found the door marked *Stairs*, they entered, lit the lamp, and began the climb to the roof. Twice they paused, having heard some noise, but neither time did anything threaten them. Ellen figured people may be living in this building—and maybe in the next—but if they didn't try to hurt her and Father Thomas, they, in turn, would let them be.

When the stairs ended and they still hadn't reached the roof, Ellen thought her great plan had just hit a snag. Just then the priest tugged on her sleeve and pointed to the right at another door, and on it was a plaque. Almost illegible with dirt and rust, she rubbed a fist over it. *To Roof*, it read. Ellen sighed, nodded to the priest, and creaked the door open.

The dark stairwell greeted them with silence. With her light in hand, Ellen led them up the last floor to the roof. From there, it was easy to step across to the other roof.

The only things they found in the other building were dust motes and rodent droppings. All was quiet and appeared to be long abandoned.

They located a small room off a large meeting space. It had two exits, one leading back the way they had come, and another to the kitchen and the back of the building. They quickly barricaded the one to the back with easily removed items and shoved a chair under the knob of the one they had come through. If need be, they agreed either could be utilized quickly.

Dropping packs and bedrolls, they curled up, expecting to drop off immediately.

Ellen lay awake, eyes open in the almost perfect darkness, thinking of what tomorrow would bring.

"Do you think we'll get to the library tomorrow?" Father Thomas's voice came to her as if from a disembodied presence.

"I hope so," she whispered. Then thinking to clarify her answer, she added, "I remember being there. What it looked like. What the area looked like." Shifting, she turned more toward him. "It's a large building taking up a city block, so I'm certain if we can get close, we'll be able to find it."

"And you think it's there that we'll find what these numbers mean?"

"Coordinates. I'm sure the numbers are coordinates. And we hope to find where they'll take us."

"Yes, yes of course."

The room was quiet for a while, and then Father Thomas said, "I wonder how far it will be."

Ellen's brows wrinkled. "What kinds of transportation are there? Surely, people can't walk everywhere."

In the dark, she heard him shift, seeming to come to a sitting position. "No, though most often people walk. There are horses, and we might be able to locate a couple, maybe even a wagon . . ."

Ellen kept her thoughts to herself, but she was thinking that if they were subject to traveling by horse, this was going to be a long journey.

"Trains are running."

She sat up, her attention riveted to the sound of the priest's voice. "Trains?"

"Yes. Some of the larger cities are civilized. Commerce happens. Goods and people transported."

"But I didn't think there was any electricity."

The floor squeaked as he shifted, and then a bright flare of light had her squinting and turning her head. When she looked back, Father Thomas was putting a match to the wick of a short, fat taper of a candle that was set in a metal, circular pan.

"If we're not going to sleep, we might as well have some light."

Settling back, he regarded her from across the small room. Sitting, she wrapped her jacket around her legs.

"So, trains," she said.

"Yes. There are steam engine trains. When it became apparent that not only were the machines that make the electricity out of operation, but so were all the components, people needed something. We didn't always have electricity, you know. Why, even now, we're sitting here in light without the use of electricity."

"Yes, of course," she conceded. "Good to know about the trains. And about the cities—at least some of them." She tapped two fingers on her upper lip in thought.

"At least we'll have that option if the coordinates lead us somewhere farther away." With a deep sigh, she again looked at the priest. "Let's hope they don't point us overseas or something."

A faraway, dreamy look came to his face. "I've always wanted to see other lands than those where I was born. I've read books and seen pictures, but it must be wonderful to be there. The smells, sounds, and feelings of other places."

She had to smile. This was a side of the priest that she'd had yet to see. "It is wonderful. I'll miss it."

"Can you tell me about places you've been?"

Ellen lay back, putting her hands under her head to stare at the ceiling of the little room. She relaxed, letting her mind wander. What to tell him? There had been so many places. All exotic in their own way. A small chuckle escaped her when she thought of China.

"This one time," she began, and the priest mirrored her posture to lie back and gaze at the ceiling, "I found myself inside a giant Buddha."

CHAPTER 25

When Ellen woke, it was impossible to tell what time of day or night it was. Their little candle had burned out during the time they had slept, and the room was pitch black.

She stood and fumbled to the door. Listening on this side of it, she hesitantly cracked it open. Dim, late daylight filled the outer room. It was just as silent as it had been when they arrived.

She turned back to the interior room, the priest visible in the half-light. Father Thomas stretched, his mouth gaping in a large yawn.

The duo was packed, out of the building, and heading down the street before the sun had fully set.

It wasn't too much longer before they saw the first sign of movement.

"Ah, hell," Ellen muttered. "Did you see that?"

"I saw motion," Father Thomas whispered from the side of his mouth. "Did you see what it was?"

She shook her head, keeping her eyes peeled for more activity.

Just as Ellen was thinking they might have been mistaken, a

figure stepped from an alleyway about a block ahead of them. It was dressed all in black and had its face painted red and yellow, half one color and half another.

Ellen's heart did a flip and her temperature jumped. "Oh dang. This isn't good."

With her hand on the priest's upper arm, Ellen detoured to another street. They kept their eyes on the figure the whole way around the corner, and it never moved. Though she didn't believe it, she said, "Maybe it'll be easy."

After another block, they made another turn, always keeping the direction they wanted to go in their heads. When they thought it had been far enough, and they had made enough twists and turns, they headed back in the direction of Lake Michigan.

A couple blocks from the water, the first thing Ellen saw was the large red building. It had large arched windows across the front and had retained most of its adornment of large owls on the roof.

Before they stepped out from the concealment of the building to cross to the library, Ellen and Father Thomas peered up and down the street.

"Do you think he might have been alone?" the priest asked.

Ellen shrugged. "I'm not sure. Let's give this a shot."

When they made it across the street and up the stairs without incident, Ellen's mind shifted to getting into the building. At first, she thought the door wouldn't open and they would need to find another entrance. But then, she threw her weight into pulling it open, and it gave an inch or two.

"Thomas, help me with this."

Together, they pulled, and one side of the large double door opened enough for them to slip through. Once in, they grasped the door and together got it closed.

Ellen peered out the thick glass door, but the painted figure didn't appear. Finally, not confident but not willing to wait any longer, she turned from the door with the priest following her.

The interior of the library opened into a large atrium. The ceiling soared high overhead into a dome. By the ambient light of stars, she saw that once, the ceiling was beautiful. The glass, now long broken out, was once supported by crossed veins of metal. The metal, or much of it, was still in place, though after this long, it was rusted and weathered. The floor had geometric tiles laid in a checkerboard pattern. Covered with dirt and whatever had been blown into the building over the decades, it still retained some of its luster. As they walked across the expanse, their footfalls echoed in the large, empty space.

The passage out of the large atrium was enclosed in the building and dark. Father Thomas pulled off his backpack and removed his lamp. With the strike of a match, he illuminated their path.

At the rear of the room, they came upon an escalator. Now, they were simple stairs, so Ellen and Father Thomas started up. The books they needed were upstairs.

As Ellen and Father Thomas climbed the last set of stairs, they caught sight of the ceiling. Long, silver, cylindrical columns hung in a pattern that reminded Ellen of a honeycomb. She continued to climb, her head angling back farther to watch the ceiling the higher they went. Finally, she stopped, the priest stopping with her.

"That is so weird," Ellen muttered.

"What do you think it is?"

"Art," she answered immediately.

"Art?" Father Thomas asked, and when she looked from the metal hung from the ceiling to the priest, his furrowed brow had her smiling.

"Lesson one, Thomas. Never judge art." Clapping him on the shoulder, she moved up the stairs and led them into a room still mostly full of books.

When they found what they were looking for in a room full of atlases, globes, and maps, Ellen scanned the vast array of offerings. She stepped to the books with titles standing vertically and read down them.

She ran a finger down a spine and pulled the book from its cradle between the others. *Understanding GPS: Principles and Application.* She turned back to one of the remaining chairs in the room. The chair fronted a long wooden table, marred by burn marks and gashes. Glancing as she walked, she didn't immediately see Father Thomas and hesitated for a moment before noticing him studying one of the globes.

She knew what GPS was—how GPS worked. But without computers, she needed to figure out how to use it to find a location.

Scanning quickly through the broad instructions, her shoulders slumped with relief. The *N* for north and *W* for west on the coordinates assured they would be looking for a spot within North America. She didn't know what they would have done if the coordinates led them across the ocean.

She turned back to the beginning, now trying to decipher the finer points. Not even realizing she muttered, Ellen said the coordinates out loud.

"Thirty-eight degrees, ninety-one minutes, thirty-seven seconds north, by seventy-seven degrees, three minutes, fifty-eight seconds west."

A little over two hours later, Ellen pushed back from the table to study the books she had spread out before her. Rubbing her eyes, she looked around for the priest. It took her a moment, but she found him at the back of the room. He was asleep with a pile of their belongings lying next to him in a bundle against a wall.

She knew where they were going. At least, she knew within a few miles. She hoped the other writing on the back of the picture would lead them to the right place.

They had a destination, but for now, they could both stand to eat and rest. There wasn't much time left to the night, and she didn't want to be out in the open when the sun rose. Best to stay where they were until a new night was upon them, then they could head out with this new information.

She left the priest where he was for the time being. Walking around the room, she inspected each doorway and what lay beyond. When she found an adequate space, maybe an old storeroom, she carried the chair she'd been using into it and then went back for Father Thomas.

"Thomas," she whispered, giving the priest a shake.

"Wh—" he muttered, sitting up and rubbing his eyes.

"I'm done here."

"What did you find?"

Ellen stood and held out a hand to the priest. With a small shake of her head, she helped him to his feet. "Let's get some rest. We can talk about it when we wake. Then we'll have a fresh start."

Still mostly asleep, Father Thomas nodded his agreement. After they picked up their belongings, the two went into the small room. With the door shut, Ellen shoved the chair under the doorhandle and lay down to get some sleep.

CHAPTER 26

They headed out of the city at nightfall.

Awake and prepared for travel, Ellen explained to Father Thomas that their destination was Washington, DC. She had three different maps of the city packed within her bags. Each map gave them a more detailed view of the city. She felt confident that, with the maps, the GPS coordinates, and the words on the back of the picture, they would be able to locate what they were looking for.

But first, to get out of Chicago.

The library where they'd found the maps sat just a few blocks from the shores of Lake Michigan. They discussed it and agreed that the best route of travel was to skirt the edge of the lake, heading toward the east. This would take them into Indiana and then Ohio. From there it would be a straight shot to DC.

They didn't have much with them and would need to forage along the way. Food and water would be scarce, but they would do what they needed to get by.

When Ellen and Father Thomas stepped from the library, night had again fallen. The moon—slightly less than full—sat on the horizon like a balloon caught on a fence. Its light illuminated the city street, allowing them to see they were alone.

After a moment to gauge the night, the two made their way toward the water. If they were to use Lake Michigan as a ruler on their trek east, they would need to keep it in sight.

Ellen and the priest stopped when they reached what was once the marina. When she had lived in Detroit, she'd been to the lake. Her breath caught. Due to The Rush and the ensuing climate changes, the level of the lake was far below anything Ellen could have imagined.

In the distance, the moon's light reflected off what she could only surmise was water.

"Oh my," she whispered.

"What?"

Ellen glanced at the priest, but the devastation pulled her gaze back to the dry lake bed.

"The lake." After a pause, she added, "I just never imagined."

She studied the land that once was the shore. "Let's continue to the water's edge and then skirt it east. It should make a shorter trip. At least, a bit."

Father Thomas squatted to grip a fist full of ground. Standing, he let the sandy soil slip through his fingers.

"Watch where you step," Ellen admonished before heading out.

* * * * *

The figure with the painted face peeked at the two from behind a capsized boat.

They interested him. He'd never seen two just like them.

Other than his tribe, the people he saw crept through this world. They flitted like rodents, running from one spot of secrecy to another.

These two moved through his city as if they belonged.

Even when they had run from the tribe, they'd escaped. Some of his people had been injured in the pursuit of these strangers. Curiosity pulled at him. He watched them for another moment and then headed back into the city. He knew who might want this information, and how it would benefit his tribe.

CHAPTER 27

Dr. Michael Daniels stood within the controlled chaos of the laboratory.

People in white—doctors, lab technicians, aides—all moved in a choreographed dance. It was with deep satisfaction that he monitored them. They all worked for him. Yes, he worked for another, but they didn't know that. If asked, they would each name him, Dr. Michael Daniels, as the final decision-maker to the prosperity in their lives. If he wanted, he could kick them out into the wasteland.

He was who they needed to keep happy. His desires were most important.

"Um, Doctor. Dr. Daniels."

Michael Daniels ignored the voice coming over his shoulder. Knowing it was petty, and reveling in it, he moved forward, monitoring work as if unaware the lab technician followed him.

Finally, halfway across the room, he turned to his underling. Looking down his nose, he regarded the other man without speaking.

When enough time had passed that even the workers around them had begun to fidget, he allowed his gaze to shift.

"What is it, Kenneth?"

"Sir," the tech said, "the team in room five asked me to come and get you."

"Come and get me?"

"Well, um." He hesitated. "They told me to find you and *ask* if you might be able to lend them your expertise."

Partially appeased, Dr. Daniels regally inclined his head. Kenneth stepped out of the doctor's way and trailed in his wake from the laboratory. At their exit, people sighed, and the jumble of conversation again began.

Down two flights, Dr. Daniels preceded the lab technician into room five. Three people, all in suits resembling those worn by astronauts in days past, turned at their entrance.

One stepped forward and popped a seal around the neck of the suit. It dipped forward and pulled off the helmet. When the figure again stood upright, the visage of a young, Asian woman was revealed.

"Dr. Daniels," she said.

"Liu," he said with a nod in her direction. Dr. Daniels disliked using the title of *doctor* for those he supervised—even though they had earned it. He chose to refer to them by their surnames. Hence, Dr. Melinda Liu simply became Liu.

His degrading attitude aside, they both knew she was the smartest, most qualified scientist in The Guild, including Dr. Daniels.

Ignoring his greeting and the set down she knew it contained, she gestured to the large cage that filled the rear quarter of the room. It was built with plexiglass, metal bars running crisscross through the inside length of it.

"We've managed to achieve what we believe is an abnormal

response to the prescribed stimuli."

Dr. Daniels stepped forward to peer at the interior of the cage. Silent, the three suited scientists and Kenneth watched and waited.

"Hm," he uttered. After another moment, he turned and said, "Show me."

Dr. Liu nodded. "Of course, sir. If you would step into the anteroom and suit up, we can begin."

CHAPTER 28

The moon waned and the night sky filled with stars.

Ellen stopped and looked at the sky. She'd never seen so many stars. The sky looked like a blanket of velvet with a million tiny punctures. It appeared so solid and close, she extended a hand thinking she could touch it. When she couldn't, she closed her hand and chuckled.

"Wow. I've never seen a sky like this."

Father Thomas came to where she stood, leaning back to mimic her stance. "What?"

"The sky didn't look like this in my time. Even out in the country." She dropped her head to look at the priest. "Too much smog, I guess."

"Smog? Oh, yes. I know what that is. We read about it. Pollution, right?"

"Yeah. Cars. Factories. All sorts of industries put pollutants into the air."

Ellen peered into the distance. They had put the lake to their left, keeping it within sight. Now, as her vision readjusted from the starlight, she squinted, straining to confirm what she thought she was seeing.

Pointing with one hand, she grasped Father Thomas's shoulder with the other. "Do you see that?"

Following her arm with his eyes, the priest moved forward a step, his own eyes squinting. "It appears to be some sort of structure."

"Out here?" she asked. "We're in the middle of a dry lake bottom."

Father Thomas did a slow circle, scanning the area.

"It'll be morning in a few hours. Do you want to investigate it? There may be supplies. Perhaps a good place to spend the day?"

Ellen knew they should use the hours left of the night to get closer to their destination. But what if they didn't locate another spot to hide out from the heat of the day?

"Let's check it out." She nodded at the priest.

They were almost upon the ruins when Ellen stopped. She looked up. The wall was curved and immense. In the darkness, it was a solid black against the world. Hesitantly, the priest on her heels, she moved closer. No sounds came to her, no smells, or even impressions. When she got near enough, she reached out her hand.

"Be careful," Father Thomas cautioned.

She hesitated, closing her hand in a fist, and then she flexed her fingers to touch the object. Nothing. Cold, solid. Again, she fisted her hand and rapped on the surface. A dull ring hummed through the structure.

"Metal," she said.

Father Thomas was already moving down the length of the barrier, and she turned to follow him. The size of the object dwarfed them, causing her to feel as if she were a bug soon to be squashed.

When they reached the end and turned the corner, a great

expanse of beams and ribs opened before them.

"Wow," Ellen whispered. Her gaze lifted. "It's the bones of a ship."

Ellen and the priest moved up the edge of the decking, staying out in the sandy bottom of the lake, and keeping the vertical surface to their side. The only movement came from the flutter of old clothes caught on spars and poles reaching from the flooring.

"How long do you think this has been here?" the priest asked.

Ellen shrugged. "Since before The Rush. I think those are smokestacks."

"It feels as though it's going to fall on us."

With a nod, Ellen looked up to the topmost rail of the decking. "I know. But I'm sure it's been here for a very long time and is quite stable."

They paced down the line of the decking, now set vertical upon the sand. Soon, they came to a point where a huge gash ripped the decking and part of the hull of the ship. They stared into the abyss, hearing nothing but the wind, not certain if they should proceed.

Father Thomas shucked off his backpack and dug through for his small lantern. When he pulled out a box of wooden matches, Ellen put a hand on his shoulder.

"Wait," she said.

From where he crouched, he looked up at her.

"Let's take it inside the hull and shield the light. The glow is going to be visible for miles, and we don't want that kind of attention."

Thomas nodded his agreement and gathered his things, then

he moved toward the break in the ship. Ellen followed, and together they stepped blindly into the cavernous hole.

"Thomas," she whispered, lost in the darkness.

"I'm here. Come forward a couple more feet."

Dragging her steps to avoid tripping on something, Ellen did as the priest instructed. When his hand met hers in the dark, she gripped him and moved forward. In the complete gloom, sounds came to her as if from a dream.

Ticking of metal still cooling from the heat of the day.

The scurry of small animals shifting among the unknown, which filled the hull.

The breaths of the priest and her own pounding heart.

Then the scratch of a match, and the bright flare of a flame.

Ellen squinted in the light, bringing a hand up to shade her eyes. Around her, the interior of the ship came into view. Everything was in shadows that moved and shifted with the flame of first the match and then the brighter light of the lantern.

Once lit, Father Thomas closed the frame around the flame and the light strengthened.

Around them, a world out of place was revealed. Turned on its side, the walls were now floors, and the floors walls. The room they were in was still partially full of what appeared to be broken and crushed rock.

Thomas swung his pack to his back and stooped to pick up the lantern. When he lifted it, light flooded the area. Ribs of metal ran up and down the sides, which was now also the ceiling, some with spring-like additions to the ribbing. From about halfway up, a mountain of stones flowed to the exit. It looked as if a large quantity of the rocks had been sucked from the cargo hold of the ship upon impact.

Ellen and Father Thomas scanned the area, but there was nothing to be found here but rock.

When Father Thomas moved to put out the light and exit the hold, Ellen put out her hand to halt him. "Wait," she said and took a step up on the pile. She was still for a moment and then let her head drop back. "Can you hear it?"

Father Thomas looked left and right, lifting the lantern even higher.

Ellen emitted a soft hum, relaxing into her shoulders and breathing deeply. When she squatted to run her hand above the stones, the priest took one step forward.

Gingerly, as though grasping an egg, Ellen plucked a stone from the pile. Standing, she curled her fist around it and brought it to her breast. She took two large steps off the hill of stones and once again stood beside the priest. When she looked up from her hand, Father Thomas would swear that for a moment her gray eyes shone in the light.

"We're done here, Thomas. We can leave."

"What do you have? What does this mean?"

Ellen shook her head, but a smile beamed from her. "I don't know," she admitted, "but it's wonderful."

When Ellen and Father Thomas stepped from the cargo hold, the sun was just breaking over the distant horizon. They would need to change their trajectory to continue moving toward the east.

In the distance, another wreck was just visible.

"Let's get to that one," she indicated with a tip of her chin. "We can rest the daylight hours there and then continue on."

Father Thomas lifted the frame around the flame in the lamp

and blew it out. Giving her a small nod, he patted her on the shoulder and headed into the rising sun. Ellen took a moment to peek at the stone in her hand, and then, her smile firmly in place, she followed the priest.

CHAPTER 29

The shore had been in sight for a few hours before Ellen and Father Thomas were close enough to see what that shore would bring. They walked side by side, speaking only when necessary. They were out of food. Out of water. Their packs were firmly on their backs, and one of the side pockets of Ellen's trousers bulged with the stone she'd gotten from the shipwreck.

As they neared, a small marina became evident, and behind it, large affluent homes and a quaint town.

Jutting out from the dry marina was a lighthouse. It wasn't large, not really all that special, but the sight of it brought a smile to Ellen's face. Even after all its years of disrepair, the red and white shone in the morning light.

Long ago relegated to dry dock, just the lines of the lighthouse suggested high waves splashing against its face, crashing over the concrete walkway that tied it to the shore.

As she and the priest passed by the lighthouse heading toward a sandy beach and the town, Ellen looked back one final time over her shoulder. Surprised, she turned fully to gaze in the direction they had come. On the horizon in the morning radiance was the silhouette of the city of Chicago. With a final nod and a glance at the lighthouse, she turned to follow Father Thomas into town.

When they'd first seen the large homes fronting the lake, by their size alone, Ellen could tell that they had cost the owners a lot to own and provide upkeep. Now, however, the homes were vacant, all in varying states of deterioration.

With the sun rising, they would need to locate a place to wait out the heat of the day, but neither she nor the priest mentioned the beach homes.

When they put the marina and its homes behind them, they turned down the main street. Shops lined it, and they walked down the center of the street, staying back from the buildings on either side. They hadn't gone far when a man stepped from a corner.

He was dressed in a lightweight jacket and wore a hat with a wide circular brim. Resting in his arms, cradled like a baby, was a shotgun. He didn't advance on them but allowed them to come to him.

When they halted about twenty feet in front of him, he tipped back his hat and regarded them. "You folks passin' through?"

Ellen glanced at Thomas and then nodded at the man. "Yes. Just passing through. Thought maybe we could come by some provisions here?"

"Where you headin' to?"

"Just a little farther," she prevaricated. "Few miles closer to the coast."

He nodded his understanding but didn't take his eyes from them. Ellen could feel her nerves begin to tickle. The hum of them was like a stranger blowing on the nape of her neck. With a squint, she glanced up at the buildings surrounding them. She was sure he wasn't alone, and the town dwellers had probably seen them coming from a long way off.

"You're welcome to spend the day here. We don't allow weapons though."

Ellen looked from him to the shotgun in his arms and then back to his face without saying anything.

"We don't have any," Father Thomas volunteered, and after thinking of the knives in their possession, Ellen let the lie go.

The man turned partway from them. "Y'all can come this way." Then he walked off the main street to a secondary lane. Ellen and Father Thomas followed him, staying back, keeping their eyes open for other people.

They followed the man for a few blocks, and Ellen realized they were heading back toward the main part of town when they approached a large two-story brick building. The front facade looked like it was fortified at some point, but she couldn't tell what it originally looked like. When the man entered the building, Ellen stopped. Father Thomas turned to look at her, pausing with his hand on a door.

"What is it?"

She studied the front of the building, looking for telltale signs of something. Anything. But there was nothing.

Shaking her head, she glanced around. "Doesn't this seem pretty dumb to you?"

"Dumb?"

"Yeah. Are we just gonna walk into this building?"

Father Thomas let go of the door, allowing it to slowly close, and stepped back to her. "I know what you mean, but we need food and water. We don't have anything, and we have nowhere else to go."

"Yeah, yeah. I know. Okay." She stepped toward the priest and the door. "Just watch yourself." At his nod of agreement, she insisted, "Food. Water. And we're out of here."

"Of course."

She opened the door and held it for the priest. They walked down a short hall and up a flight of stairs to an open doorway. Stepping through, they saw four men in the room as each turned to regard them. Ellen moved back the way they'd come only to realize two armed men stood behind them.

She stopped, and seeing no avenue of escape, she dropped her hands and muttered, "Well, shit."

CHAPTER 30

D r. Michael Daniels stepped from the door of the cage that occupied most of room five. He stripped off his gloves, turning them inside out, and dropped them in a disposal.

Grudgingly, he complimented Dr. Liu on the advancements she and her team continued to make. "You've done very well," he said from over his shoulder, his face turned from her as she, too, exited the cage.

"Thank you, Doctor."

"It never ceases to amaze me, the abilities of the human mind when put under the right stimuli."

"We have our predecessors to thank for a lot of what we know," Dr. Liu stated, walking up beside him. She also removed her gloves and released the straps of her suit, allowing it to fall to her feet. Underneath, she wore a set of green surgical scrubs.

"The breeding programs," she continued, "have allowed us to harvest the best traits from each generation."

As the door of the cage once again opened to admit the two scientists of Dr. Liu's team, small whimpering sounds could be heard from within. None of those without responded, and as the door sealed shut, the sounds were sealed in.

Out of his suit, Dr. Daniels straightened his jacket and faced the woman. "How much longer do you think this is going to take?"

"I'm sorry, Doctor," she said. "I really have no way of knowing that." She stepped to a desk, lifted a clipboard, and scrawled a word or two on the papers. "All we can do is continue our work. I will say," she said and turned to him, "the results seem to be coming faster than previously seen."

"Well, stay on it," he said. He turned from them and walked out of the room.

CHAPTER 31

Ellen paced the small cell, unable to calm her mind or body. Each time she passed Father Thomas on the cot, he pulled his feet in to keep them from being trod upon.

They'd exhausted themselves by fighting and yelling. Once stripped of their packs and frisked—they found and confiscated their knives and the stone—they were forced into the cell. They'd banged on the bars and yelled some more. When one of the men had returned with water for them, she'd tried to reason with him. He'd completely ignored her, sliding the cups through the bars, and had walked out without saying a word.

Now, she paced, and the priest watched. It was killing her that she'd been so stupid. She'd known—she'd *known*—and still she'd walked right into the trap. She was so angry she wanted to punch something.

When the door opened and a man walked in carrying a wooden chair, she stopped and watched him. He put the chair down with its back to the wall, closed the door, and took a seat to face them. He was tall, of Hispanic descent, with shoulder-length black hair. With a khaki shirt, jeans, and cowboy boots, he looked unassuming.

Ellen stomped to the bars and shoved her hands on her hips. "Why are we being held here?"

The man looked from her fuming face to the priest sitting on the cot. Relaxing back, he crossed his legs, linked his fingers, and smiled. "Where are you from?" His voice was soft and had a southern inflection to it.

"What is going on here?" Ellen's voice cracked as she strove not to yell. "We haven't done anything to warrant being placed in a cage."

"Where are you from?" the man repeated.

"Look," Ellen said, "the man on the street said we could spend the day here and get some provisions. We're just passing through."

The stranger nodded and repeated, "Where are you from?"

"Jesus," she breathed. "It's not a big deal. We're from outside of Chicago. We're heading toward the East Coast. No secret. No conspiracy."

"Where exactly are you heading?" he asked, his eyes direct.

Figuring it didn't matter if he knew their destination, Ellen mumbled, "DC."

"What are your names?"

With a sigh, Ellen sat on the edge of the cot next to the priest. With a tip of her head, she said, "He's Father Thomas Johansen. My name is Ellen. Ellen Thompson."

The man approached the bars of the cell. He tucked his thumbs in the front pockets of his jeans and studied them for a moment in silence. "I'm Richard Sanchez, and I'm in charge of this town. I run the security, the politics, and anything else you might think of. This is a good place with good families. Behave yourselves, get what you need and get some rest, and you'll be on your way. Cross me"—he shook his head to emphasize his words—"and I'll put you down."

When neither of them said anything in response, he took a step closer to the bars.

"Do we understand one another?"

Father Thomas and Ellen nodded, almost in perfect sync. Ellen didn't know if something was happening here that would be a danger to them for the next few hours, but either way, they needed to get out of this cage. They'd mind their own business and be on their way.

Richard Sanchez stared at them for another moment and then pulled out a key ring from his pocket. He inserted a key in the lock and, with a click, opened the door of the cell. He indicated for Ellen and Father Thomas to step out.

When Ellen put out a hand to shake, the man looked from it to her eyes for just a moment and then grasped her hand in a firm grip. The images came hard and fast, and Ellen barely kept her eyes on his. It was because she watched him so closely that she saw the double blink and noticed the slight tightening and then loosening of his grip.

Releasing her hand, he studied her for a moment and then offered his hand to the priest. Without hesitation, Father Thomas gave his hand a firm pump.

When he stepped back from the priest, Ellen said, "When can we get our belongings back?"

"You had knives."

"Yes," she admitted. When he cocked his head and raised an eyebrow, she said, "You can't expect us to admit being armed to a stranger." When he didn't say anything, she added, "A stranger who might outnumber us and throw us in a cell."

At that, the corner of his mouth turned up. Keeping them in front of him, he moved to the door and held it open while they exited the cells. In the big room, amid desks and locked gun cases, two of the men they'd encountered sat. When the three of them entered the room, the two locals jumped to their feet.

Richard Sanchez came around to the front and indicated the men. "This is Steve and Max. Guys, take our guests to the dining hall. Get them something to eat, and have Doc come over and take a look at them."

"Yes, sir," one of the men was quick to say. "This way," he said to Ellen and Father Thomas and led them to the door.

Ellen followed the procession and, at the last moment, turned back to Richard Sanchez.

"Thank you," she said.

He dipped his head in response.

* * * * *

The dining hall was just that. A long industrial room lined with grade-school-style bench tables and a cafeteria-style buffet. Two women stood behind the counter. They visited and surreptitiously watched as the two men led her and Thomas to a table.

"Go on up and get yourselves something to eat," one of the men told them. She thought he was Max, but she wasn't sure. "When you're done, I'll take you where you can get some rest."

Ellen nodded, and with a glance at Thomas, she walked slowly to the head of the counter. As they neared, the women quit visiting and eyed them. Under the scrutiny of the women, she and

Thomas collected trays, utensils, and napkins. Placing the tray on a shelf that ran the length of the kitchen, Ellen looked over the offerings.

There wasn't much.

Ellen remembered eating in cafeterias, both in schools and in the workplace. There had always been an abundance of different foods whether they were baked, grilled, or raw. Now, in this time and place, the offerings were sparse, and she knew she would appreciate them more.

With a smile, she met the eyes of the first woman. When she smiled back at her, Ellen glanced at the second woman. The smiles ended there. This woman, older and harder, wasn't so easily won over. Ellen decided to stick with ease and rounded back on the first woman.

"Hello," she said and nodded in greeting.

"Hello!" the younger woman gushed. "We don't get visitors around here too often."

"Gina," the older woman admonished her.

"Oh, I'm sorry. I always talk too much."

"No," Ellen said with a shake of her head. "I'm glad to meet you. Thank you for allowing us to rest in your town and get something to eat. It's very kind of you."

While Ellen talked, the women filled plates with potatoes, gravy, and small, thin slices of some kind of meat. Ellen wasn't sure what it was and decided not to ask. Taking the plate from the women, she moved down the line and poured herself a glass of water.

When the young woman handed a plate to Father Thomas, she held on to the edge. Unable to take the plate, he raised his brows at her.

"Are you a real priest?"

"Pardon me?" The look of confusion on his face remained, and Ellen stepped back toward them.

"Well . . . I'm sorry. It's just that we don't see many religious sorts around here." She released his plate.

Nodding his head, his expression closed, Father Thomas set his plate on his tray and said, "Yes, my dear. I'm a real priest."

"Um. Father . . ." She cleared her throat. "Can I call you Father?"

"Yes, of course, my child."

"Well, Father. Can we visit after you eat?"

"Gina," the older woman said, "I'm sure our guests would like to get some rest."

The younger woman turned a bright pink and fiddled with the ties of her apron. "Oh, of course. Of course, you would."

Father Thomas studied the girl until she quit her fidgeting. When she looked at him, he told her, "I would be happy to visit with you, Gina." At his words, she beamed a smile at him. "Perhaps, after we're settled. Can you come and find me?"

She nodded so hard that Ellen thought she was going to fall over.

"Good. I'll see you soon." He turned with Ellen, and they made their way to one of the tables at the back of the room.

"It's nice of you to agree to meet with her," Ellen whispered as they made their way to a seat against the wall.

"What do you mean?"

"Just, it's been pretty obvious you're not completely comfortable."

"Comfortable?"

She swung her leg over a bench and set her food on the table before answering him. "Sure. With church stuff."

"Church stuff," he parroted as he sat across from her.

Ellen glanced around. There were two other groups of people in the dining hall. One group was two middle-aged women, sipping what smelled like coffee and reading books.

The other was four individuals playing a hand of cards. They spoke in low tones, and occasionally a laugh would come from the group. Max had gone over to sit and watch the game, and they greeted him warmly. Steve stood with them for a moment, and then without a goodbye, he left the room.

Ellen wondered if he'd gone to get the mysterious Doc and why they thought she and Thomas would need someone to "look them over."

For a moment more, she watched the others in the room, and then the call of the food became too enticing. Letting her curiosity go, she turned her attention to her meal and her companion.

Happy to leave the other topic behind, Father Thomas asked, "Did you get anything from him?"

"Yes." She took another bite and swallowed before continuing. She wasn't sure how to explain the images of a much younger Richard Sanchez defending himself and killing a man. The horror he felt at this unavoidable action and the road he took getting his soul back. All she could really tell the priest was, "He's no danger to us."

CHAPTER 32

Ellen lay on the cot in the small room. She was alone, Thomas having been put in a room of his own. Ushered into the small space, she wasn't surprised when she'd heard the key turn in the lock.

She was sleepy. A full belly and a comfortable bed, and it was all she could do to stay awake. Blinking heavily, she took a deep breath and once again reached under her pillow to run her finger over the tines of a fork she'd lifted from the cafeteria. She didn't like being unarmed, and if pushed, a fork in the eye would stop just about any attacker.

A deep breath, and her mind wandered. Another deep breath, and with a jerk, her body relaxed into the cot, drifting into a dream.

* * * * *

Light streamed into the room from windows high on the two-story walls. For all the illumination, the radiance didn't reach the floor level and light up where the woman stood. She didn't know where she was, and she didn't know where she was going. All she knew, for certain, was that she was where she was supposed to be.

The final clue had led her here, and now, finally, she would do what she was meant to do.

Uncertainty filled her. After her task was completed, what would she do, and where would she go? Who would she become? So many things had happened to her, and now, she no longer belonged. Would she always be alone?

She heard her name, and when she turned, she saw the priest.

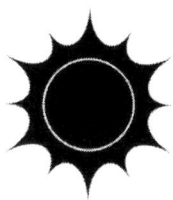

CHAPTER 33

The sound of soft scratching nagged at Thomas's mind and pulled him from the dream.

He lay still for a moment, and then, when the sound came again, he swung to sit on the cot.

When they'd left him in this small cell of a room—a cot, table, and hard-backed chair—he hadn't despaired. He'd slept in worse places. When the lock turned in the door, he'd consoled himself with the thought that it just meant he'd be safe. A moment of worry filled him when he realized there was no toilet, but then he decided if needed, he could yell for someone to let him out.

The sound of scratching had him sitting forward and tuning in to the slight vibration. After a moment, he decided it was coming from the door. He pulled his jacket on as the room had grown chilly. He padded to the entrance and, with a groan, leaned back on the portal.

He didn't say anything, deciding to wait and see what would happen. He was rewarded when a moment later a woman's voice whispered, "Father? Father Thomas? Are you awake?"

It didn't take a stretch of his imagination to recognize the young woman from the dining hall. "Gina," he whispered to her.

Her heavy sigh was audible even through the door. He heard her shift, moving closer to the crack in the structure. "Father."

"Yes, Gina. How can I help you?"

"Father, I don't know how to tell you."

"I'm here for you, Gina. Tell me what you need."

"Something's been happening, Father. Something that keeps me awake at night."

Father Thomas slid closer to the doorjamb. He found he was laying his lips to the opening. "Tell me what's happening. I will help you if I can."

"Father," she whispered.

Then Thomas heard shifting and a sharp noise. There was a bang on the door and the sound of hurried footsteps.

"Gina," he whispered into the doorjamb.

When he heard a door open at the end of the hall, he stood and cocked his head to listen.

Footsteps down the hallway.

Pausing at his door.

The priest kept silent. He watched the floor where a shadow appeared under his door. After a moment, the shadow moved down the hall. Father Thomas stood by his door, silent, for many moments. He waited, thinking Gina might return, but after a while, he returned to his cot.

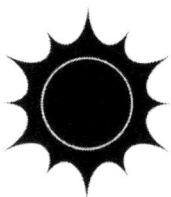

CHAPTER 34

Ellen stood just inside the room as the handle turned. She'd been up for about two hours, her most pressing need to use the toilet. As the door opened, an elderly lady stood in the entry with a large smile on her face.

"Good morning," the woman almost sang.

"Good morning," Ellen replied with a nod.

"Richard asked me to come and get you. Show you the facilities and get you some breakfast. When you're done, he would like to see you and your friend."

Ellen nodded again to show she understood but didn't say anything. Turning, she grabbed her pack from the cot and followed the woman down the hall.

"I'm Maribelle."

"Nice to meet you, Maribelle. I'm Ellen."

"We'll join up with your friend, the priest, at the dining hall." Maribelle walked slow but spoke fast, like a small bird. "Where are you from, Ellen?"

"The Chicago area." Wishing to learn more than she gave away, Ellen asked, "Have you lived here long?"

"Oh yes. I've been here for years. Back before The Rush, you know." She continued to chat as she led Ellen down the stairs. "We used to swim off the dock that leads to the lighthouse when I was a young girl. Some days I can still see it surrounded by water. Then I'll blink and be back to today with everything changed."

Maribelle was the first person Ellen had spoken to who had been alive before The Rush, and she was interested. "Do you remember much of what it was like before?"

"Well," the woman said, then chuckled in a tone that sounded like a much younger woman, "some days are better than others. I'm afraid my memory is fading these days."

"How old were you when it happened?"

"Well now, let me see . . ." Maribelle angled her head slightly up, staring off into the distance. "I believe I was in my early thirties. My Samuel was still alive then. We never did have any children—not for want of trying." She laughed again, causing Ellen to smile.

When they reached an exterior door, Maribelle directed her through it and pointed out a large multi-stall outhouse a distance away under some trees.

"I'll wait here for you, honey. Take your time."

After using the facilities, Maribelle took her back into the building. They wandered down another hallway and soon the woman stopped.

"Here we are," she said, pointing to a door that said *Ladies*. "There's no showers—I'm sorry—and the water doesn't run, but there's a bucket of clean, cool water and I laid out a towel, a sliver of soap, and I found you a toothbrush and some baking soda from the kitchen. I thought you might like to have the use of a mirror. You know, to fix yourself up a mite. If you end up staying awhile, we'll get you set up with time in the shower. Got it all rigged up real fancy. Takes a bit of doing, though. Everybody has to schedule in time."

"Thank you, Maribelle. That's very kind."

"Oh, not at all. Us ladies have to stick together. Provide some creature comforts."

Ellen stepped into the bathroom while Maribelle waited in the hallway. There were three separate stalls with toilets—all empty of water—and a bank of sinks. On the counter between two sinks was the promised water and other items. Ellen didn't touch anything. She double-checked the stalls and tried the tap. No water, not even a sound.

Ellen looked around, scanning for anything that might be out of place. The window was high on the wall, consisting of blocks of thick glass that allowed the light of early evening in but wouldn't allow anyone to see in.

Guessing that everything was as it seemed, she got down to the act of washing and brushing.

After a quick spit bath and a thorough brushing of her teeth, Ellen felt more like herself. She secreted the toothbrush away into her pack thinking, if nothing else, she'd come by this small treasure.

When she stepped outside the bathroom, Maribelle was down the hall visiting with another woman. Seeing Ellen, she finished up her conversation and hurried back.

"All done?" she asked.

"Yes. It was very refreshing."

"Not that you'd remember, being the age that you are, but when I was young, it used to be such a wonderful way to start the day—with a hot shower. Ones we have now, water is warmed, but not like those showers from my youth. Hot water. High pressure.

Heaven." And she smiled with nostalgia.

Ellen thought it would be better that she did not acknowledge a personal experience with the showers in Maribelle's past. That would raise too many questions. When the two women again exited the building, they were on its opposite side. Just across the parking lot was the long building with the dining area.

As soon as they entered, she saw Thomas, and her lips lifted in a smile. She was surprised by the relief and pleasure she experienced at the sight of the priest. They hadn't known each other for long, but he'd become important to her.

Maribelle left her with Father Thomas, and after going through the line to get breakfast—a light meal consisting of eggs, bacon, and toast with jam—they sat to break their fast.

Ellen was barely half done with her meal when Richard Sanchez slid onto the bench next to Thomas and across from her.

"I see you're enjoying the benefits of being near a source of water."

Ellen raised an eyebrow and took another bite of eggs.

"Being able to keep animals. Grow a crop."

Father Thomas nodded and swallowed. "You're very lucky. It's been hard elsewhere to have animals. And raising a garden is often impossible." When the leader of the community gave the priest a look, Father Thomas added, "The heat, you know. It's just too hot for animals and plants."

"Yes, Father," Richard Sanchez agreed. "So, Ellen." He turned back to her. "If you and the good Father here would be interested in staying another day, I could show you around our little town. Maybe entice you to stick around for a while."

Where did that come from? Ellen thought.

"Well, we have somewhere we need to be, but we could hang around for a bit." She looked at Father Thomas for confirmation.

"Yes. I'd like to see some of your operation."

"Well then it's settled." He slapped the priest on the back. Standing, he moved over to speak with two men who Ellen was sure were only there to guard her and Thomas.

CHAPTER 35

Ellen and Father Thomas walked beside Richard Sanchez, and the two men followed in their wake. They'd visited a school room where all the children were taught K through high school, just like in the olden days. Now, as they left the schoolyard, they walked farther into town.

"Father," Richard addressed the priest, "since you showed an interest, I thought you might like to see our growing operation."

"Yes, I would like that very much. People in my congregation—well it's been years now—used to try to keep gardens. So hard, you know, with the heat and the aridness. Very few things would even grow."

Richard Sanchez listened intently to the priest but always seemed to have his attention on Ellen. She noticed this once or twice and thought perhaps she was being a little too paranoid.

"After a time," Thomas continued, "people began to move away. It just wasn't possible to continue living in our area."

"And what area is that again, Father?"

Father Thomas stumbled, thinking perhaps he'd given too much away. He glanced at Ellen, a worried expression on his face.

"I told you," Ellen interjected, "we're from just out of Chicago."

"Yes, you did say that, didn't you," Richard said with a lazy drawl.

"Yes, I did."

Ellen was just taking a breath to get into it with Richard when he turned and pulled open a door. "Here we are," he said with a flourish of his hand.

Father Thomas stayed where he was but bent and peeked in the doorway. "Inside?" he asked.

"Yep. It's the secret to our success."

The priest straightened and entered the facility. Ellen followed him, with Richard taking up the rear, allowing the door to close behind them. Their escort stayed outside.

Just beyond the entry of the building, the entire thing opened to a large space. Within the area, one story down, lines of plants grew in protrusion. There were corn, tomatoes, onions, and other plants that Ellen couldn't identify. A few people wandered the stalks, hoeing and cleaning up the area.

The ceiling, a couple of stories above, was cut with skylights. Filtered sunlight dappled the garden.

"Why," the priest exclaimed, "it's a gymnasium!" He looked at the leader with wide eyes.

Richard nodded and touched the edge of his nose with one finger.

"Ingenious," Father Thomas muttered, already wandering around the rail to stare down at the large indoor garden.

"Come with me, Father," Richard said, taking the priest's arm and directing him to a set of stairs. He glanced back at Ellen to ensure she was following them.

Once down the stairs, Father Thomas wandered away, studying the plants, depth of soil, and watering processes. He stopped each person in turn, asking questions about the facility and its workings.

Ellen stood next to Richard and watched the priest. She was surprised to see him so impassioned by what this community was doing and how they were growing food.

"He's an interesting man," the leader said without taking his eyes from the priest.

"Yes," she answered. "A good man."

"But you haven't known him for long."

She looked at him. "Is that a question?"

"No," he said. "I don't think it is."

"What is it, exactly, that you want?"

With a shrug, he again watched the priest. "You interest me."

Ellen almost thought to tell him to become disinterested, but then she let it go. It would do her no good to stir things up with the leader of this community. They were to keep a low profile, get some provisions, and get to gettin'. They'd already stayed too long.

"We'll need to leave tomorrow night. We have somewhere we need to be."

When Richard didn't answer, she glanced at him. He showed no reaction to what she'd said and continued to stare out into the garden.

Shortly after, Father Thomas came back to them, but all he did was ask if he could stay. He wanted to better inspect the watering system they used. He didn't know if other communities used anything like this but wanted to know how to duplicate it if he had the opportunity. When Richard told him he was welcome to stay as long as he wanted, a large smile split the priest's face.

"You don't mind, do you, Ellen?" He turned a pleading expression on her.

"No, Thomas. Of course not. Enjoy yourself."

Richard turned to her. "There's something else I'd like to show you, Ellen. Discuss with you."

"Sure."

Leading her out the back door of the facility, Richard walked away from the building. She was quick to notice that the two men who'd trailed them here were nowhere around. She followed the leader around a small park and through another building before he stopped in a deserted area and sat on a bench. When she remained standing, he patted the bench beside him. Ellen cleared her throat and grudgingly sat on the bench, keeping as much room as possible between them.

"What can I do for you, Richard?"

"So, we have a problem."

She raised an eyebrow at him. "We?"

"Not *we*," he said and gestured between them, then out to the general area. "But *we*."

"Okay," she said with a nod. "Tell me."

"This hasn't always been the community you see now. This level of tranquility has been hard-won."

"I'm sure." She indicated for him to continue.

"In the last few months, we've had some disappearances."

"Disappearances?"

"Uh, yeah . . . of children."

"Kids?" When he just nodded, she asked, "How many?"

"Three. All between the ages of five and ten."

"Boys? Girls?"

"Two girls. One boy. The boy was the youngest." He leaned forward and put his head in his hands, rubbing his forehead. Waves of tension rolled off him.

"What do you think I can do?"

"Well, that's the thing." He dropped his hands and turned on the bench to face her. "I don't know what you can do, but I'm thinking you can do something."

Now she turned to mimic his stance. "What makes you think that?"

"I'd like it if we could be honest with each other." When she didn't say anything, he continued, "I don't know what you have, but I do know you have something. Something I'm thinking might come in handy."

"Let's say, for argument's sake, that I might have something that *might* help you." When he didn't interrupt, she said, "How would this benefit me?"

Richard was nodding as she spoke. "If you were able to help us, if we were able to stop any more children from disappearing — maybe even get back the ones we lost — I promise I'd get you and the priest outfitted for a journey — better outfitted than you were coming in — and get you on a steam train I happen to know is heading for the DC area."

At that, Ellen sat up straighter and her eyebrows rose. Still not fully trusting the leader, Ellen hedged, "I didn't know anyone had a steam engine running."

"Yep. Been running for years." He leaned back on the bench and stared out over the park. "Surprised you didn't know that."

The possibility of catching a ride on a train to Washington, DC, filled Ellen with well-being. The amount of travel time that a train ride would cut off from their journey was immeasurable. It would more than make up for the time spent helping this community. And maybe, the goodwill would go a long way in seeing them succeed in their hunt.

"Okay, Richard," she said. "Tell me everything."

CHAPTER 36

D r. Michael Daniels stared through the viewing window at the patients beyond. They were close. How much longer could it take?

He had been so excited by Liu's work. He had been so optimistic. He had told Malcolm Whitman about their break-through. His brows furrowed and his head dropped. Maybe he should have kept that information to himself. He turned from the window and paced in the small room. Now Whitman was heading this way to see the progress they had made.

Dr. Daniels stopped again to stare at the children in the room. His brow crinkled again. "No, not children," he said to the empty room. "Specimens."

To continue their work, to show even more progress, they would need more specimens. They could only breed so many of their own, out in the stables. And those subjects were special. Second and third generations.

But for now, they would require blank slates. Fresh from the ranks of individuals that this world continued to produce.

Lost in his world, Dr. Daniels rubbed his eyes with a finger and thumb. When pain flashed through his nose, he gasped and dropped his hand.

"Damn that Ellen Thompson," he whispered.

CHAPTER 37

Ellen and Father Thomas sat on the same bench she and Richard Sanchez had used just an hour before. Ellen filled the priest in on all that the community leader had said.

"So, do you think you can help them?"

Ellen didn't answer right away. She had been giving this a lot of thought and was fairly certain she could locate the person, or persons, who were taking children. Then it would be up to Richard to get any information out of them.

Ellen shook her head and leaned forward with her elbows on her thighs. She dropped her forehead into her hands and gripped her hair. What would this community do with the guilty party once they were found?

She straightened and let go of all the deeper questions. That was for the community to decide.

"Yes, I believe I can locate the guilty party in all of this. I explained, in an abbreviated fashion, what I'm able to do, and Richard and I discussed keeping it low-key at first, seeing if that would be successful. We'll be meeting people this evening." She stood to face the priest. "And I'll be shaking a lot of hands."

Richard came for them a few moments later. He led them

systematically from one area and building to another. She met men and women of all ages and ethnicities.

No one seemed to notice the three of them working their way through the population. When asked why he was introducing the new people, people everyone had thought were moving on, Richard explained she and the priest were considering staying and making their fair city their home. People were excited by the prospect. It seemed it had been a few years since someone new had been added to their ranks.

She felt and saw a host of hopes, dreams, tendencies, and sins. The latter of the small to medium size. It didn't take long before Ellen felt like a spectator—peeking through the curtains into all these lives.

It was about mid-evening when Ellen asked Richard if she could take a break. She hadn't anticipated it, but using her gift was wearing on her. Tired, she arched her back and gave a good, firm rub to her shoulders.

"Yeah. Yeah, of course," Richard replied to her request for a respite. "Let's pop into the dining hall. See if there's some coffee. Maybe some dessert."

"That would be great. Thanks, Richard." Stretching her neck, Ellen rubbed a temple. "It's just more than I ever wanted to know about so many people. Especially, all at once."

"I understand." He gave her back a small rub.

At the touch, Ellen stiffened. Quickly, the leader dropped his hand.

"Sorry."

"No, you're fine. I just wasn't expecting it, you know?"

Leading them into the dining hall, the subject was dropped, and soon their conversation became easy and natural again. They were just finishing a piece of pie when, in a tone just above a whisper, Richard leaned over the table and asked, "So you haven't found anything?"

"No. Just the usual lives of usual humans. At least, ones who have lived through this world."

He frowned and had just opened his mouth to say something when three men came through the door. They were loud in the quiet room—laughing and jostling among themselves. They greeted Richard from across the room, and he raised a hand in welcome.

Richard stood and made his way to the men who were getting cups and pouring coffee. He shook hands all around, inquiring about their night. His ease and familiarity with the men led Ellen to believe they were not only acquaintances, but friends.

Leading the group over, he introduced them to Ellen and Father Thomas and explained the trio had been out on sentry duty—each able-bodied citizen was expected to take their turn at guarding the community.

The group continued their easy camaraderie with Richard much in the way of old friends. Ellen leaned across the table, habit having her reach out a hand to the men upon meeting them. Off balance, she put one hand on Thomas's shoulder.

When the second man, Paul Anders, smiled and gripped her hand, she clenched Thomas's shoulder so hard that he cried out and shifted from her hold.

For a moment, she held both men, neither able to break her grip. Then, with a deep breath like a diver breaking the surface of the water, she released both and sat down hard.

"Ellen?" Father Thomas said, grasping her shoulders, worry in his voice and face. "Are you all right?"

Ellen took another deep breath, her hand to her heart. She placed her other hand on the priest's forearm and nodded. "Yes. Yes, Thomas, I'm fine."

When she glanced up, all the men watched with worried expressions. Except Richard. He stared at Paul Anders, his face tight with tension.

"I'm sorry, gentlemen," she said a bit breathlessly. "I haven't been feeling well tonight. Perhaps I should go and lie down."

The men readily agreed with her. When she went to move, Richard stood on stiff legs.

"Richard," she called to him, but he didn't move, still staring at the one man. "Richard." She raised her voice. This time, he blinked and looked at her. "Could you come with us?" He nodded but still looked dazed.

"Thomas." She pulled on the priest's sleeve. "Grab Richard." The priest moved around the table, and in low tones, he spoke to the community leader. As the three men moved away to a farther table, Richard, Ellen, and Father Thomas walked toward the exit.

Once outside, the three stared at each other.

"Tell me," Richard said. "Tell me what you saw."

Ellen shook her head and took a step back. "It's hard to tell. Hard to describe. Part of it is emotion. Sensory."

"Then tell me what you felt," he insisted.

"It's flashes. The children—Suzy, Anna, and . . . Henry."

"Yes." Richard grasped her arm in a grip that hurt.

"He sold them."

"Sold? What?" Richard stumbled over his words. "Sold them where? To whom?"

"I didn't see that. Just him meeting someone. The transfer of a body. Each time, the child appeared to be sleeping. He was nervous . . . but not about what he'd done. More, he was nervous about who he was meeting."

Richard whipped around and marched to the building, then hit the wall with a closed fist. "Damn it," he muttered. "I've known Paul Anders for *years*."

He swung from the wall and hurried back to Ellen and Thomas. Intent. "Did you see what he got for the children? What did he trade them for? What was his soul worth?"

Ellen shook her head. "I didn't see exactly. Just a plastic bag. It was dark but looked deep green in color." In her mind she saw a plastic trash bag people used for yard clippings. "But small, a few pounds of whatever it is . . . at the most."

Richard turned from them, saying over his shoulder, "Get yourselves back to your rooms. Stay there." And then he was gone.

Ellen and Father Thomas made their way back to the building that housed their rooms, but they didn't go their separate ways. When they ended up outside Ellen's room, she opened the door and they entered without discussing it. Neither wanted to be alone, and Ellen thought they should discuss what had happened and what it would mean for them.

"We need to stay out of any more involvement with this situation," she said to the priest.

"Others might need to know how you knew it was Paul Anders."

Ellen heaved a sigh. "How many of them would even believe what I say? If you take my ability out of it, Paul Anders is a long-term member of this community, and I'm a stranger. They would side with him every time."

"Maybe," Father Thomas said. "Maybe not."

It was a couple of hours later, the sun just beginning to make its presence known in the far eastern sky, when there was a commotion down the hall. The sound of many footsteps and the murmur of voices. Ellen and Father Thomas rose from her cot. Blindly, Ellen grasped the priest's hand.

When the door swung open, Richard stood at the front of a group of men and women. For a moment no one spoke, and then a woman pushed her way forward.

"Can you tell us where our children are? Where is my Susan?"

Ellen was shaking her head, but all she got out was, "I'm sor—" before another woman pushed others aside.

"And my Henry. Where is my Henry?"

Ellen swung to face her, claustrophobia setting in as the crowd pushed its way into her small room. The women became louder, and when one grabbed her arm, she jerked back, falling against the wall.

Father Thomas stepped in front of her, putting his hands up in a placating manner. "Now, people. Please, let's calm down."

Ignoring him, they continued to push in, all talking at once.

Ellen thought she was about to get torn apart when another hand gripped her arm. She yanked and looked up only to be faced with Richard Sanchez. He looked angry and irritated all at once, and she immediately felt safer.

"Follow me, Father," he yelled. Taking a better hold of Ellen, he shoved his way out of the room. People grasped at the three, but as they neared the door, the group moved with them, quieting, then following.

Richard didn't stop when he reached the hall. Keeping his hand on Ellen, he left the building and made his way to the dining room. Once, he glanced back to make sure the priest was still with them. The entire group moved as one through the village and into the larger room. Richard moved to the head of the area, and only then did he release Ellen. She stood between the community leader and priest and faced the now-silent crowd.

"Please find a seat," Richard told the people.

They milled about for a moment, but then everyone sat.

"Most of you have met Ellen and Father Thomas," Richard began.

One of the women from the room stood and yelled, "Where is Henry?" Her outburst got the group riled again, and it took a few minutes for Richard to get control.

Once everyone had quieted, he said, "Mary, just give us a moment, and we'll tell you what we know." She didn't show any agreement with his statement, but she didn't speak again, so he went on. "It's come to our attention, with Ellen's assistance, that someone in our community has been behind the disappearances of your children." At that, a low murmur began.

"Please." He put his hands up. "Please be quiet and let's get through this."

Again hushed, the crowd waited.

"Taking the information she gave us—"

"How did she know?" And again the group started yelling questions.

This time, Richard didn't say a word. He stood with his hands on his hips and stared them down. The noise level dropped immediately.

"As I was saying." He paused to survey the room. When no one interrupted, he said, "As I was saying, we took the information Ellen gave us and did a thorough search of this individual's quarters. We located proof of his complicity in these disappearances."

More murmuring filled the room. Richard let it pass.

"We have him under arrest, and he is being questioned as we speak."

"Richard," a man said, raising his hand.

With a nod in the man's direction, Richard acknowledged him. "Yes, Andrew. You have a question?"

The man, now the center of everyone's attention, swallowed hard, cleared his throat, and asked, "Who is it, and who is doing the questioning?" There were nods and agreement all around in response.

"John Pierson is questioning the individual."

At that, a majority of the group nodded to each other, the atmosphere taking on a decisively positive beat. Everyone knew John's background. He was an older man, in his maturity before The Rush. In his previous life, he'd been a police officer, and he'd retained the training he'd received. He was fair and logical. A calm man who was able to listen to and decipher the facts of a situation.

"He has Max and Nina with him, but he's in charge of the questioning."

"Why aren't you there?" someone in the crowd yelled out, and Richard turned in the direction of the voice.

"Well, 'cause I'm here talking to you good people. We're a community, and as such, each of us needs to know what concerns us all. It's my job to make sure we act as one, and in the most responsible manner possible."

At his words, there was a rush of agreement.

It was quiet for a moment when someone else spoke up.

"So, who is it, Richard? Who's preying on our children?"

Richard deflated. He sat back to lean against the table behind them. He scanned the people. Ellen watched him, not sure what he was looking for. Finally, he said, "It was Paul Anders."

Chaos erupted. People stood, yelling over one another. There were denials, arguments, and a couple of women were weeping. Ellen's attention was drawn to one face in particular. Henry's mother stood alone. She didn't speak, but tears ran down her cheeks.

Richard moved from Ellen's side and walked through the crowd. People moved aside and watched as he passed. When he reached the woman, he took one of her lax hands in his. He rubbed it.

"Mary," he said, his voice loud in the quieting room. She blinked, her gaze regaining focus, and looked at him. "We're going to do everything we can to get the kids back."

Fresh tears ran down her face, but she nodded silently. From behind her, one of the other mothers stepped forward to wrap her arm around Mary's waist. Richard cupped Mary's cheek for a moment, then released her hand to return to Ellen and Father Thomas.

"Let me walk you back to your room," he told Ellen.

"Actually, Richard, I'd like to watch some of the questioning if that would be okay."

He considered her request for a moment, and then with a nod, he said, "Okay. For a bit. You, too, Father?"

"No," Father Thomas said, "I'd like to stay here and see if I can lend some comfort. Pray with some of the families."

"All right," Richard acknowledged. "This way." He raised an arm to direct Ellen.

She looked at the priest. "You're sure you'll be okay?" At his nod, she followed the leader out of the building and into the next.

The atmosphere in the second building was a definite

change. A perceivable chill filled the air. The man, Paul Anders, sat at a small table. On the table were a cup of water and an old ash tray. Paul had a cigarette between two fingers and looked like he'd been put through the wringer. He had a black eye and a split lip. The hand that held his cigarette shook.

"Staying silent isn't benefiting you at all, Paul," an older man with gray hair was saying. He was bent slightly over the table, his back to the door. His stoop was subtle, putting himself in the other man's space.

Paul took a drag on his cigarette, hissing the smoke out. He wet his lips and glanced up at the man leaning over him.

"I told you." His voice shook as much as his hand. "I never did know any names."

"How did they contact you? How did you contact them?"

Paul shook his head, taking a drag from the cigarette again. "I don't have anything I can tell you. They were very careful to make sure I didn't know anything."

"When was the last time you were in contact with them?"

Paul Anders shook his head and kept his eyes on the table.

"May I?" Ellen asked Richard.

At her voice all five in the room looked her way. John Pierson moved away from the table and approached her and Richard.

"What's going on, Richard?" he asked. "We can do without any disruptions."

Richard nodded at John's words but kept his gaze on Ellen. "Do you think you can find anything out?"

For a moment Ellen didn't answer, and the silence dragged on. She stared at Paul, who caught her eye. When she broke his eye contact to look at Richard, her mind was set.

"Yes."

They pulled the table forward and moved the second chair to the same side as Paul Anders. Ellen pulled out the chair and sat down.

"Hello, Paul."

The man glanced up but didn't say anything.

"My name is Ellen. I'm going to ask you some questions, okay?"

Paul sprang to his feet, his chair skittering back to hit the wall. "I don't give a fuck who you are, lady. I don't have anything to tell you." Almost before he'd gained his feet, three pairs of hands were on his shoulders, forcing him back into the chair. His head swiveled as he looked from face to face and then back at Ellen, who sat calmly in front of him. She leaned forward and took one of his hands in hers.

The images came fast, causing her to suck in a breath. With them emotions flooded her brain. Her heart pounded out a beat, and sweat beaded on her forehead. Involuntarily, a moan came from her lips.

From across the room, Richard Sanchez took a step forward.

Behind her lids, Ellen saw images of the children. First, at play. He'd watched them. Selected them. Went into their homes. Breaking the trust of his neighbors and friends before he ever took their children. He drugged the kids and carried them out. Silent, right under their parents' noses.

He took them in the brightness of daylight, when everyone was asleep, to a preselected meeting time and place. He met a hooded man. They met there every six months—whether he had something to sell or not. But he'd always had one. And in exchange for breaking the trust of people who trusted him, he received drugs. Simple and not so simple. What he got, for the children of his friends, was a mixture of cocaine, heroin, and methamphetamines.

Ellen opened her eyes to stare into the eyes of the weakling in front of her. He was whining, pulling on his hand, trying to dislodge her grip. When she tightened it, his gaze shot to hers. Bearing down in her mind, tendrils of vapor like the talons of a hawk dug in and held on.

Paul Anders' eyes bulged in their sockets. He went stiff, and a trickle of blood ran from one nostril. In his mind, the images of the playing children filled her heart with pain. Ellen ripped with her talons, searching for the face of the man in the hood. Closer and closer she got, peeling off layer after layer, until finally she stood in front of him. When he lifted his head and pushed off his hood, she recognized the face of Dr. Michael Daniels.

CHAPTER 38

Dr. Daniels stepped from the exterior door of the satellite station of The Guild. He waited only a moment for the vehicle to pull up. It was loud and smelly, but a luxury in this world. A man jumped from the passenger side to run around the rear of the car. He opened the door, and after a moment, Malcolm Whitman stepped out.

Dr. Daniels extended his hand. Whitman gave it a perfunctory shake and scanned the immediate area.

"Mr. Whitman." Dr. Daniels heard the raspiness in his voice but couldn't help it. Clearing his throat, he spoke again. "Welcome to my lab." Malcolm Whitman had been to this location once before, and Michael Daniels didn't think he'd ever get him back again. It was wonderful and terrifying.

Malcolm Whitman barely acknowledged his words, his attention on the entry of the building. As if remembering, he spun back to the driver.

"Wait here for me." The chauffer nodded his understanding, ducked into the driver's seat, and drove a short distance away. Waving in front of his face and giving a small cough, Malcolm Whitman turned back to Dr. Daniels. "Well, Michael. Show me your project."

Dr. Daniels talked the entire way into the building, through the double doors, through the upper floor, down the stairs, and to subfloor five. Malcolm Whitman didn't offer any contribution to the conversation, but he never stopped looking around and studying the station.

When the two men entered the laboratory, Dr. Liu and her team were hard at work. Grudgingly, Dr. Daniels introduced Malcolm Whitman to Melinda Liu. Malcolm Whitman was instantly enchanted by the Asian doctor. He began peppering her with questions. Questions that Dr. Daniels could have answered if the man had only seen fit to ask them of him.

When Malcolm Whitman placed a hand on the small of Dr. Liu's back and directed her toward the cages, all the while holding an intense conversation, Dr. Daniels fell into a snit. He never had liked Liu, and now she was taking all the credit for work that he, Dr. Michael Daniels, had been responsible for. How dare she be so selfish?

Not willing to be kept completely out of the conversation, Dr. Daniels wandered over to where the two stood discussing what was next in the trials.

"Yes, Malcolm. We're sure about the process to release extrasensory perception and other paranormal powers in the human brain."

Malcolm? Dr. Daniels thought. When did it become Malcolm?

"It won't be too much longer, and we'll be able to run the subjects just like any other machine."

"Fascinating," Malcolm Whitman whispered, his attention wholly on the woman.

"The key, it seems, has been having fresh subjects since they seem to wear out rather quickly. This has been a service"—she turned to Dr. Daniels—"that Michael here is best able to handle."

Michael? Dr. Daniels stared at the woman. He'd never given her leave to use his first name.

"Well, Michael," Whitman said, facing him, "it looks as if they've finally found some use for you." At his words, Malcolm Whitman and Dr. Liu broke into laughter.

Someday, Dr. Daniels fumed. *Someday I'll pay you back for that.*

"Well, this has been most interesting," Whitman said, and again directing the female doctor, he walked away from the cages. "Dr. Liu, won't you join me in the city for a late lunch?"

Dr. Liu beamed a smile at the man. "I would enjoy that very much, Malcolm."

And without a simple goodbye, the two of them sailed out of the lab and down the hall. Dr. Daniels stood where they left him. On some level he perceived the two technicians moving around him and putting away gear, but he was far into his own head.

How dare they? No one treats Michael Benjamin Daniels like this!

Giving a sharp order to the technicians to stay busy and get the laboratory clean, Dr. Daniels left the room, heading for his office.

CHAPTER 39

Ellen stood with Richard Sanchez and Father Thomas over the grave of Paul Anders. When she'd left him the night before, he'd been alive, though maybe worse for wear. She was sure he had a headache from hell, but he'd been alive. He'd been moving around, talking with John Pierson. Richard told her he would be placed in a cell. What would happen to him, she didn't know.

When she'd released Paul Anders in that small room, he'd slumped in his chair. No one had moved, but then he'd stirred, sat up, and reached for another cigarette.

The other people in the room hadn't known what she had done to him, though it was obvious that her touch had affected him.

Then, this evening, the first thing Richard had informed her of was Paul Anders' death. He'd hung himself with the sheets off his bed. Had what she'd done to him led to his decision to end his life? Was his guilt too much to bear?

"What did you learn," Richard had asked before they'd even gotten out of the building.

"I know who he sold them to but not how you can find him."

Richard stopped and turned her to stare into her face, keeping a grip on her arms. "There's got to be a way."

"I believe there is. He met with this man, Dr. Michael Daniels, every six months. That's three months away. I know it means having to wait, but there's no help for that. I know where he met him. You can set up a trap, and once you have him, he can take you to the children . . . if they are still alive."

"Three months?" He dropped her arms and paced away from her, deep in thought. When he wandered back, he said, "I don't know how I can keep people from wanting to try to find him."

"They'll never find him. I came from where he is, and he's very well hidden."

"Still . . ." he said.

"And if they give him a warning that he's being hunted, they'll never find him."

Richard nodded as if seeing her argument had merit.

"The best bet is to be at that meeting. Take him there."

"Okay," he agreed. "You're right. Now I just have to convince the others of that."

Standing over the grave, coming to terms with what she may have done, she knew she'd done all she could. Maybe more than she should have.

It was time to move on.

Richard walked them back to the front of the building that housed the rooms they'd stayed in. Out front on the sidewalk, they'd left their bags along with two large duffels full of food, water, a water purifier, and ancient MREs. On their belts they each sported a large knife.

When Ellen reached her belongings, she unzipped a pocket

and pulled out her baseball cap. She pulled it on, threading her ponytail out the back. Then she turned to look at Richard.

"You're sure you need to go?" he asked, his voice soft.

"Yes. I wasn't lying when I said we have somewhere to be."

A couple of blocks over, a loud whistle pulled their attention. The train would be leaving soon. Without another word, Richard stooped and picked up one of the duffels. Ellen grabbed her bag, and Father Thomas took his.

It only took them a few moments to make the trip to the train tracks. The sight of the large, black steam engine and the cars it pulled filled her with hope and dread. The thought of leaving this man, these people, and this community made her sad, but she knew she was here for a greater good. She had to be.

Richard led them to one of the cars, its sliding door open. He tossed in the duffel and then took the other from the priest to toss it in too. Father Thomas tossed in his smaller pack and Ellen's, then climbed aboard the train car.

When the priest disappeared inside, Richard took Ellen's arm and leaned in. "Come back to us."

Tilting her head back, Ellen looked the leader in the eye. Placing her free hand on his shoulder, she kissed him gently on the cheek.

"I'll try," she said and climbed aboard the train.

CHAPTER 40

The trip to Washington, DC, would take them about twenty-four hours by train. Swaying with its motion, Ellen studied the maps of DC that she'd taken from the library in Chicago. She'd put her thoughts of Richard Sanchez and his town to the back of her mind. She couldn't allow herself to be sidetracked from their primary search.

As luck would have it, the train yard seemed to be close to where the GPS coordinates were taking them. With the overall size of Washington, DC, they might have caught a break. She opened her mouth to tell Father Thomas, but when she looked up from the papers, he was leaning against the corner of the car asleep.

A small smile turned up her lips. He seemed so peaceful.

She studied the maps for a bit more, soon losing the light. She tucked everything away, used her pack as a pillow, and moved closer to the priest so she, too, could find sleep.

The blast of a steam engine jerked Ellen awake. She sat up, feeling the priest stir beside her. It was dark within the train car, the night outside at its deepest.

The whistle blew again, and the train gave a jerk, slowing

almost imperceivably. Due to the time of night, and the slowing of the train, Ellen thought they were close to their destination. She stood, the sway of the train almost driving her to her knees. Stumbling forward, she grasped the wall of the car and heaved the door open an inch. A city ahead was draped in its evening wear. Every so often, a twinkle of light appeared, there and gone with the moving of the train. Like little fairies whisking to and fro in the deep shadows.

Due to the size of the metropolis, Ellen guessed she was correct in her assumption that they'd crossed into the greater DC area. It wouldn't be too much farther before they got to the station.

After one final glance at the city, she made her way back to the priest with wide steps. When she sat heavily beside him, he opened his eyes.

"Are we there?"

"Good evening, Thomas. Yes, I believe we are almost there."

They busied themselves getting their belongings righted. The large duffels were pulled over by the door, along with anything they might need soon. Working with the limited natural light filtering through the cracked door and the slats of the train car, they got it figured out.

"Can you light a lamp for a moment? Give us some light, and we can study the words on the picture before we get there?"

With a nod, the priest had everything out, and a soft light spilled across the car. Ellen unzipped one side of her pack, pulling out the image of Eric and the men. When she turned it over, Father Thomas slid closer and lifted the lantern.

Front and back, with keen eyes they do gaze,
Composed of body and spirit, duality fills their days.
O'er a building of white,
Brother defenders show their might.

Strong and smart, their beauty does blaze,
Guarding entry to the sun's shining rays.
'Neath Power's nemes, wisdom is found,
Knowledge is based, victory is crowned.

"Front and back they gaze," Ellen mused.

"A building of white," Thomas added.

"I guess that gives us something to start with." Tucking the image back in her pack, she watched Father Thomas put out the light and stow it in his belongings.

Now, they sat silently, listening to the clang and hiss of the train, waiting for any change in their motion. It wasn't long before another jerk worked its way down the train, making them lurch forward and then back. A screech of brakes cut the night, and the train came slowly to a stop.

It was a moment before the two of them thought it safe to stand, and within seconds, they had dropped out of the train car. In an area smelling of old oils and surrounded by train cars, they looked blankly at one another.

"What do you think? Which way should we go?" Father Thomas asked.

Ellen looked at the sky, her head back, long ponytail falling past her belt. Soon she spotted the Big Dipper. Running her finger down its handle, she located the North Star.

"There's north. We need to go kinda northwest." She

scanned the immediate area and then looked back to the heavens. "We have some time tonight to get closer to where we want to be. I doubt that we'll find anything before the sun drives us in again, but let's give it a go."

They walked for some time, searching for anything that touched on the clue. There were many white buildings, but none that brought to mind parts of the poem.

When the sun began to rise, and they hadn't located anything remotely like what they were looking for, they agreed to find somewhere to spend the day.

All through the night, they crossed paths with people moving through their lives. Along most of the streets, gas lanterns hung from what once were electric streetlights. She hadn't been to many places, but so far this was the most welcoming. Some buildings seemed to have working stores, bars, and eateries. People coming in and out of homes, and even a woman tending her small pot of flowers. Washington, DC—at least this area of it— seemed to be like a town of people trying to live their lives. They'd seen some people to stay away from, but if they didn't push them, everyone just moved on.

When she and Father Thomas came around a corner, in front of them was an old hotel. What was once an awning that reached out over the sidewalk were now bones casting lines of shade. But the light was welcoming.

"What do you think, Thomas?" Ellen stood with the priest on the sidewalk across from the hotel.

"We do need to stay somewhere."

"I . . . um? How do you pay in this time? I guess I haven't seen anyone using money."

"No," he answered, "it's more a barter system. But thanks to

Richard, we have enough to get us a room for the night." As if thinking about something for the first time, he glanced at her. "You won't mind sharing a room, will you?" Before she could answer, he added, "It's just an extravagant cost . . . two rooms, you know."

"Don't worry about it, Thomas." Ellen patted him on the shoulder. "You'll be perfectly safe with me."

When they crossed the street and started up to the double doors of the hotel, a man with a rifle stepped out. He didn't say anything to stop them but was obviously security. If anything, his presence made Ellen more comfortable.

In the lobby, an elderly man sat behind a long desk. "Hello, folks," he called to them. "Wantin' a room for the day?"

"Um, yes," Ellen said. She had to keep looking around, telling herself she was in another time and place. Except for the man with the gun at the door, this could have been any hotel in her time.

"Just one?" He looked from Ellen to the priest. "Or ya wantin' two rooms?"

"No," Father Thomas assured him. "One room is fine."

"Well, pastor. What ya got to pay with?" After saying this, the man watched expectantly, and Ellen noticed the man with the rifle moved back into the lobby.

Nonplussed, Father Thomas bent over to set his large duffel on the ground in front of the desk. Unzipping the main compartment, he withdrew a box of wooden matches. Standing, he gave the box a shake. The matches inside jangled against one another and the sides of the box. The man behind the counter, and even the man with the rifle, leaned toward the priest. Father Thomas slid open the box, revealing the half-full contents.

The priest tilted his head and lifted an eyebrow. "Good for a couple of days?" he inquired of the proprietor.

The man put out a hand, and the priest closed the box and put it in it. The older man gave the box another shake, smiled, and slid it open to inspect the contents.

Turning, he took an old key from a slot on the wall. Handing the key to Father Thomas, he said, "Up the stairs. Fourth room on your right."

"Thank you," the priest said, taking the key. Bending, he picked up the large bag and slung the handle over his shoulder. He indicated with his chin for Ellen to precede him, and then with a dip of his head for the hotel man, he followed her up the stairs and down the hall.

"You're sure a cool one, aren't you?" she said when they'd reached their room.

"Well," the priest said as he unlocked and opened the door, "I'm just really tired and wanted a safe bed for the day."

Ellen chuckled for a moment. "And you think we can trust them? They might wonder what else is in that bag."

"They might," he agreed, "but they are businessmen. I do, however, recommend we lock the door."

CHAPTER 41

It was fully dark when Ellen cracked open her eyes. She'd had a restful day and couldn't remember anything even waking her. When she stretched out her arms, she remembered the priest and pulled them back quickly. Rolling over, she saw she was in the bed alone.

She sat up, surprised. The room didn't take much more than a cursory glance. There was nowhere to go and nothing to hide behind. Just as she was swinging her legs over the bed to search out the priest, a key turned in the lock and the door swung open.

"Hello, sleepy head." Father Thomas smiled.

"How long have you been up?"

"Not very. I went down and spoke to some people. Asked around about a white building with something on the front and back."

"And?" She sat up, pulling on her trousers. Grabbing her socks and boots from across the room, she again sat on the bed to pull them on.

"Apparently, there's a lot of white buildings. And without knowing what is on the front and the back of the building, no one could give me any idea where to look."

Ellen brushed her fingers through her long brunette hair and pulled it into a quick ponytail. "Well," she said, digging through her pack. "We know we're pretty close. It shouldn't take too long to cover a few miles of streets. We'll have to find something, right?" She stood triumphantly, her new toothbrush in her hand. "I'll be right back. Gonna hit the bathroom and see if I can get a glass of water."

* * * * *

Twelve hours later, Ellen was eating her words.

They had located a ton of white buildings—this was, after all, the capital—but the people Father Thomas had spoken to were right. Without knowing what was on the front and back, anything could be read into the clue.

They were worn out. Night had passed and most of the day, and still they were unable to locate their building. Standing together on a street corner, Ellen put her hands on her hips and pushed her midsection forward to stretch her back. Walking on concrete all night and day wasn't fun on the spine.

Twisting her head, her neck cracked. With a small shudder, she allowed her head to fall backward. When she wearily opened her eyes, she saw it. Above the line of another building, there was one that, from what she saw, appeared to be white. And on the upper corner, a statue.

She squinted, trying to bring the statue into focus. All she could really make out from here were the wings.

"Thomas." She poked at the priest without removing her gaze from the building one block down. When he didn't answer immediately, she poked him again.

"Yes, Ellen. What?" He sounded testy, and she really couldn't fault him. She was tired and hungry too. This day had been trying enough without finding anything.

She looked at him now. He was glancing around as if to find somewhere to sit. He looked as bad as she felt.

"Sorry," she said. "I didn't mean to poke at you."

"No, I'm sorry. I didn't mean to snap. What do you need?"

"Look at this, here." She pointed toward the building. "I can't quite make it out. Wanna wander over and give it a look?"

The priest stood at her shoulder staring at the sculpture. It was the same color as the building, so not easy to see the fine details.

"Yes," he said. "Let's go. Now I'm curious."

They made the trip in moments, occasionally losing sight of the roof. As they came down the block and the building was revealed, Ellen stopped to study it.

Stone steps led to a platform. From there more steps led between two sphinxes and to a large door. Columns ran across the front and sides of the building past the stairs. The top was a step pyramid. On the four corners were statues.

"Thomas," she said, once again poking the priest. He had his head back and was looking at the roof ornaments too. "What do you think of those statues? They look like birds, right? Eagles, maybe, with the large beaks."

The priest nodded without looking away. "Yes. Two-headed eagles."

"Two-headed . . ." Ellen stopped. She turned from the roof to the priest. "Two-headed . . ." She turned to walk away, repeating, "Two-headed . . ." Father Thomas looked from the adornment to follow her with his gaze.

"Front and back . . ." she said.

"Two-headed . . ." he answered.

In a rush, Ellen dropped her pack and unzipped the compartment. She pulled out the picture of Eric and the man. Father Thomas hurried to her, reading over her shoulder.

"Front and back, with keen eyes they do gaze," she read. Looking past the picture, she again studied the eagle. "Front and back. Not on the front and back of a building, but front and back with two heads, right?"

"Yes, yes. What's the next line again?"

"Composed of body and spirit, duality fills their days. Duality. Duality. Two. The two heads," she said.

Father Thomas snatched the picture from her lax grip and read the next line. "O'er a building of white." Looking up, he gestured to the building. "White."

"Brother defenders show their might."

"Yeah, yeah," Ellen said, stepping back to look up at the roof. "White building. Mighty is an eagle. That's them! I'm sure that's them. It has to be."

She turned on the priest and held her hand out. Father Thomas placed the picture in her palm. "What's the next line?"

Ellen took a deep breath, smiled at the priest, and read the next line. "Strong and smart, their beauty does blaze." She looked from the priest to the eagles. "Do you think this is still talking about the eagles?"

"What's next? Maybe it'll clarify it."

"Guarding entry to the sun's shining rays."

Ellen dropped her gaze from the statue on the corner of the building. From here the row of columns that traveled across the front and around the sides blocked her view of the front entry.

She glanced up again. The building had to be three stories tall.

Father Thomas stepped to the side, moving down the length of the building toward the rear.

"There's another eagle here," he yelled. "They appear to be on each corner of the roof."

Ellen gave a nod and raised her hand.

He'd gone that way—she'd go this.

She stepped up a stair closer to the front. A sphinx lay in front of her, near the door. She'd noticed it—it was huge—but until now, she hadn't studied it.

The face was feminine and beautiful. Along with the face of a woman, there was the body of a lion. Wings adorned her headdress, and a figure was carved on her chest.

Another sphinx, sister to this one, lay just past a flight of steps.

Ellen had just moved to take a better look at the second one when the setting sun reflected above the door. There, in a bright pattern, was a representation of the sun and its rays.

"Thomas!" she yelled, not taking her gaze off the sunburst.

From the corner of her eye, she saw the priest hustling to her.

"Look." She pointed to the panel above the door.

"Guarding entry to the sun's shining rays," he said, repeating her thoughts.

"Yes, yes!" She grabbed his hand.

"So, 'Strong and smart, their beauty does blaze' must be referring to the sphinxes."

"'Neath Power's nemes, all wisdom can be found," Ellen recited.

"What do you think it means?" Father Thomas peered over

her shoulder at the back of the picture.

Ellen turned from the giant sphinxes that bookended either side of the entry. She tapped the photo in her hand and walked to the edge of the steps. "It's pretty obvious it is talking about the sphinxes."

"Beauty guarding the rays."

With her back to the sphinx, she silently reread the back of the photo. She pivoted to face the priest, one eyebrow raised.

"Do you know what a nemes is?"

When Father Thomas just shook his head, she said, "So, *Power's* is capitalized and possessive. What if it's a name?"

She jogged back up to the sphinx, and the priest followed.

"What if it's one of their names?" She gestured to the two statues.

"So, what is a neme?" Father Thomas asked.

"Something they have."

Taking the stairs two at a time, Ellen reached the top and approached the first statue from behind. It was large and filled most of the pedestal where it sat, but she was able to slide along it. Inching her feet on the stand and keeping her body pressed to the statue, she moved along it, feeling as she went.

"Careful, Ellen. Be careful," Father Thomas admonished, moving with her but below. He was ready to catch her if she fell, but he feared that would just injure them both.

Feeling over the side and back of the sphinx, Ellen slowly made her way forward. The front paws of the statue jutted out and took up stepping room on the pedestal. She moved down a stair and up again to stand between the legs of the figure. Now, she was face to face with the guardian.

The coincidence that she was once a guardian wasn't lost on

her, and she placed a diminutive hand upon the giant's cheek. For a moment, she stood frozen on this tableau until the priest's voice broke her out of it.

"Ellen? Are you okay?"

She shook her head to clear it and said, "Yes. I'm good."

As she felt along the face and front of the sphinx, she found nothing of interest and began to feel the first threads of discouragement.

What if they didn't find anything?

She finished her circuit of the sphinx and made her way to the second figure.

Utilizing the same process, she felt in every nook and cranny. Running her nails over it, pushing, and pulling. Down the side, around the back, and up the far side, and still nothing. She was fast running out of places to check.

Moving around the front, she again had to go down a step to avoid the lion's leg. When she glanced up to judge where she was, a gap high on the forehead of the sphinx caught her eye. Up a step, she straddled a leg and moved forward. As with the former sphinx, she placed a hand upon the face, but this time, she ran her hand up to the temple and onto the forehead.

With ease, her fingers slipped into a spot under the headdress. When her fingertips touched something, her heart jumped. "I found something!" she shouted over her shoulder to the priest. He shuffled below but didn't speak.

Ellen stretched her fingers, shoving her hand into the crevice, scratching her knuckles on the stone. With just the tips of her digits, she caught ahold of the object and slowly withdrew it from its stone chamber.

It looked like a sheet of paper, but thick. When she opened

it, it crackled with age. When she unfolded the pasteboard, she wasn't sure what to make of it. It was an image—resembling a child's drawing. On it was the outline of a cross. The one central image with a small X in the middle. In the corner rested what looked like a crescent moon.

Ellen turned the paper, then turned it again.

A cross?

"Thomas," she said, turning to where the priest waited.

But she was alone.

"Thomas?" she called.

She glanced around, and only then did she see an object on the concrete at the foot of the statue. She climbed down from the stand where the sphinx rested, moving slower the closer she got to what she'd seen. When she stood directly above it, she glanced around, but she remained alone. When she dropped into a squat, she confirmed what she saw.

A rosary.

Correction—Father Thomas's rosary. She'd seen him worry the beads plenty of times. Had noted the fading on certain beads. The knot between two. Supposedly, broken and mended.

Now, it lay coiled at her feet. And under it, a ripped piece of paper.

Ellen scooped both up and stood.

Come to 201 E Capitol Street for the priest.
Bring us what we want.

"What the hell?" she muttered. Who would have taken Father Thomas? And why? She had no idea what they meant or what they wanted.

She glanced from the ancient paper, to the note, and then the rosary.

The clue would have to wait. She needed to get the priest back.

CHAPTER 42

It had been a long day of searching for the building. A day filled with heat and the intensity of the sun. Sun she wasn't used to. Now, with it setting, she had no time to rest. No time to wait. She had to get to the address.

With all their wandering and searching, she had a pretty good idea of where she needed to go. Over a few blocks, she turned down Pennsylvania Avenue and headed toward Capitol Street. Buildings became less tended, and people more infrequent.

As the sun dropped below the skyline, she had a moment of worry. This wasn't where she needed to be. And she wouldn't be here if not for the need to get Father Thomas back.

Another half mile, and she noticed she was being flanked. They stayed back from her, just dark shadows, but they didn't retreat. When she reached the building, a man sat at the entrance. He stood as she approached. Stopping before him, she glanced around as her shadows took form and closed in.

She held the note out to him and said, "I was invited."

The guard gave a grunt, turned to open the door, and allowed her and her sentries through. Now inside, she heard the hum of voices and followed the sound down a wide hall. The door at the end was shut, and before she could open it, one of her guards pulled it toward them.

With the opening of the portal, the noise level exploded. Ellen recoiled, then hardened herself and stepped in.

CHAPTER 43

Father Thomas saw the door open across and down from him. He sat on a stage overlooking an arena.

His captors stood around him, eating and joking among each other with a jovial air—almost as if they were attending a carnival. The priest could be one of them if one didn't look too closely. Only then would the bands on his wrists and his pallor become obvious. Silently, he prayed. Prayed out of habit and hope. Prayed that all would be well.

When Ellen stepped into the arena and down a long aisle, the noise level—already loud—became deafening. Father Thomas didn't know how the crowd could stand the din. He put a hand up and covered one ear just as the man beside him stood. At his motion, all fell silent.

"Greetings," he bellowed, his voice deep and pleasant. It resonated through the hall.

Ellen's gaze shot up, taking in first the speaker and then the priest. Keeping her eyes on Father Thomas, she gave him a nod when he lifted his arms to show her his restraints.

"Why am I here?" Ellen yelled. Spinning half around, she took in the entire audience. "Why have you taken my friend?"

The man next to Father Thomas stepped forward, closer to the edge of the stage. "Have you brought me what I want?"

Ellen had to shake her head as she stepped forward. "I don't know what you want."

"I think you do," he called. "I think you are the one to bring it home."

Bring it home, she thought. Were they all crazy or was she missing something? "I'll need the priest if I'm to get you what you want."

The man was silent for so long, Ellen thought he would deny her. Then with a quick dip of his head and a flick of his wrist, two men rushed from behind Thomas. Grasping his arms, they pulled him up.

"Wait!" she called, taking another step forward. All motion stopped as they watched her. "You," she dared and pointed at the head man. "You bring him to me." After an exaggerated pause and a sideways glance, she added, "If you dare."

A large smile broke out across the man's face. A smile Ellen returned. Chuckling, he walked back to where the priest stood. He grabbed Father Thomas by the arm and hauled him up.

When a door on the side of the arena opened, Ellen tensed. Father Thomas came out first, at a stumbling run since he'd been pushed from behind. Then the man who seemed to be the leader of this group. Flanking him were four other men. Thomas moved forward, trying to reach her. When he was pulled back, jerked by a rope around his neck, she took a step toward them only to be halted when one of the men put up his hand.

She faced the leader, trying to keep her eye on him, but unable to take her gaze from the priest for long. He had both hands wrapped around the rope that encircled his neck. His breathing was strained, and his face was flushed.

"Why are you bothering us?" she asked, gesturing to the leader. "What makes you think I can help you?"

His voice was gentle when he answered. The deep baritone was soft in the quiet arena. "We've watched you. We knew a sign would come—and then, there you were." He took a step forward, pushing Father Thomas before him.

"I don't know what you want."

"You will. I have been told, you will."

Ellen shook her head. The man came closer, pushing Father Thomas in front of him. From the edges of her eyesight, Ellen saw the protectors drop back. Without giving it too much thought, as the man approached, she reached out and grabbed the leader's arm.

Immediately, the entire arena exploded with sound and motion. People around them screamed and cried—perhaps thinking she was going to hurt the man. The four guards rushed forward, and the leader pulled back from her, but it did him no good. She had a death grip on his arm, and the images erupting in her brain had her clasp all the tighter.

When his protectors began to fight her, pulling on her arm and hitting her in their attempt to get her to release their leader, she barely felt it. One punch to the side of her head had her stumbling back.

Thomas, shocked and only wishing to shield her from harm, threw his body over hers. Protecting her as best he could, his body took the punches.

"No," he muttered between hits. "No, don't hurt her."

The images filled her mind, but Ellen didn't understand them. An object glowed a vibrant gold, shining in the daylight.

People chanted, but she couldn't understand what was being said. The leader stood over it all, the edge of a knife, a slice of his hand dripping red into a bowl. Then a hooded figure. People crying.

When she opened her eyes, she was prone on the ground in the middle of the aisle. Father Thomas had his arms wrapped around her, kneeling by her body, but they were alone. At first, she thought the arena was empty; it was so quiet. When she attempted to sit up, sudden dizziness flooded her. She rolled on her side, her head in her hands. After a moment, the spell passed, and when she looked around, the priest released her. She realized they were in the same situation they'd been in before. Only now, the leader stood close to the back wall, his four guards around him, facing her and Father Thomas.

"Wha—what happened?"

"You grabbed the leader. Freaked them out plenty," Father Thomas was whispering, but it was so quiet, she was sure everyone could hear what he told her. "And you had something like a seizure." He fell back, helping her to her feet. "Are you all right?"

Ellen placed her fingers on her lip, looking at the blood that colored it. Gingerly, she touched her temple with the other hand. She had one hell of a headache. "Yes, yes, I'm okay."

"Did you have a vision?"

She glanced from the leader and his men to the priest. He was staring at her intently. "Yes."

Stepping away from Thomas, Ellen faced the leader and his men. In a voice loud enough for all the people to hear, she said, "What is nehi?"

At the word, the leader gave a jerk, and the guards covertly glanced in his direction.

When she didn't get an answer, she asked again. "What is nehi?"

A buzz started in the arena, the hum of many voices whispering. To Ellen it sounded like a swarm of bees, and the only word she recognized was the one she'd spoken. A moment more, and the leader stepped from within his protective circle. He walked to within a few feet of Ellen.

"Nehi is the name of my third wife," he stated, head held high.

Ellen's gaze held his. "Bring her to me."

For a moment, she thought he would refuse her, but then he gestured to one of his men. The man fled the arena while they waited. When he came back, he had a small woman in tow. Pulling from him, she didn't seem eager to enter the arena.

"Nehi," the leader said and held out a hand to the woman. She ran to him and took his hand. When the leader turned toward Ellen with the woman, Ellen realized she was only a girl.

"Nehi," Ellen said and took a step toward the girl. Nehi leaned into her husband, most of her hidden behind him. Ellen glanced from the leader to the girl and held out her hand.

The girl looked at her husband, and when he gave her a sharp nod, she approached Ellen and placed her hand in hers. Ellen closed her eyes, and after taking a deep breath, she opened them to stare at the girl.

"Where is it, Nehi?"

A loud murmur erupted in the arena but was quickly squelched when the leader sliced his hand down. Now, it was so silent, Ellen could hear the girl's breaths.

"Nehi," she said, getting the girl to look up. "Tell me where it is."

"I meant no harm," she said, her voice soft in the heavy air.

"I know," Ellen said and ran a hand down the girl's hair to cup her cheek. "Where is it?"

The girl looked from her husband to Ellen, visibly shaking. "I meant no harm," she whispered.

"You aren't in trouble," Ellen assured her, turning a stern eye to the leader.

"I only wanted him to see me," Nehi said, glancing between Ellen and the leader.

"It's okay," Ellen told the girl and rubbed her arm. "Tell me where it is."

"Close," the girl said, her gaze flowing to the partial wall behind the leader. The one the stage stood upon.

Spinning, Ellen studied the wall. It was old and weathered with cracks and crevices in it. Turning to the girl, Ellen pulled her forward. At her abrupt movement, Nehi shrank back.

"It's all right," Ellen told her.

With the two of them facing the wall, Ellen leaned over her shoulder to whisper in her ear. "Where is it, Nehi? Where did you put it?"

In the absolute silence, the girl moved forward until she was within a foot of the front wall. With unerring focus, she pushed a plank, and a small opening presented itself. She reached in and withdrew a chalice.

The gasp in the arena was so loud, it felt as if all the air was sucked out of the building. Turning, Nehi held the hierogram to them.

Leaving his circle of protective men, the leader moved past Ellen to approach the girl. When he stood before her, she dared to look up at him. Whatever she saw on his face drew a small quivering smile around the corners of her mouth. He reached out with one hand to take the chalice from the girl, and then he took a half step back. With his other hand, he backhanded her across the face, knocking her to the ground.

"Hey!" Ellen yelled, moving forward. She and Father Thomas were immediately surrounded by guards. As the girl picked herself up from the ground, the leader turned to them. His features were closed off, his mouth tight.

When he again stepped around them, the girl followed. Ellen eyed them as Nehi made her way to the far side of the arena with her husband. Nehi stepped behind him, gripped her fists one within the other, and dropped her head.

"You have recovered that which was lost," he said, moving forward to stand in front of them. "A favor is owed." He spoke to the entire assembly. Looking back at Ellen and the priest, he asked, "What can we do for you?"

Thoughts tumbled through her mind, and rising from them, like out of a lake, came the image of the paper she'd taken from under the headdress of the sphinx.

"Yes." Even to herself she sounded breathless. "I have a favor to ask."

When she stepped forward, she fumbled with her pack, and then with the pocket. Father Thomas moved in, his body tense. "Did you find something? These fools"—his gaze scanned the arena—"grabbed me before you were done."

"Yes, Thomas." She pulled the paper out and turned toward him. Unrolling it, she practically thrust it at him. "It's a cross. A *cross*, Thomas. Maybe you can make something out of it and the symbols."

The priest took it from her. He touched it with his fingertips as though it might strike him. He studied the figure and symbols. Ellen didn't notice the leader move, but from over Thomas's shoulder, he looked on.

"It's a map," he said.

Ellen and Father Thomas spun to stare at him. "A what?" she asked.

"A map." He plucked the paper from Thomas's lax fingers. Turning it to face them, he held it up. "See? It's the National Mall."

Ellen snatched it back from him, turning it one way and then the other.

"Which way is which? How do you know it's a map?"

Father Thomas plucked it from Ellen. "What do the symbols mean?"

The paper disappeared from the priest's grip as the leader snatched it again. He studied it, his brows drawn together. "That I'm not sure about." He cocked his head before shrugging and holding the paper to Ellen. She took it. Pursing her lips, she turned it upside down—or was it right side up? She turned it back over again.

Placing the page flat between her hands, palms in, fingers splayed, she closed her eyes and concentrated.

Nothing.

She again studied the images. A cross, an X, and a moon.

"Is there nothing else you can tell me about this drawing? Nothing more you can give us?" Ellen said, standing before the leader.

"No."

When the leader turned to exit the arena, the girl, Nehi, followed close on his heels. At the door, he turned and gestured for Ellen and Father Thomas to follow him. They caught up just as the group moved through the outer door and into a dark hallway.

They followed the leader and his third wife and had the guards filling up the rear of the group. In the dim hallway, small lanterns were attached to the walls at intervals that allowed safe passage. After a bit, the hall opened to a meeting of the corridors. The leader moved into the corridor to the left, and they all trailed him.

This corridor, wider than the first, had doors opening off it in sporadic locations. It was through one of these that the leader took them.

Ellen stopped just outside the building. Her eyes large, she scoped the yard until she was pushed from behind. Stumbling forward, she caught herself on Father Thomas, but she continued to survey the area, her head back, her face to the sky.

It was as if nothing were between her and the heavens. She knew she would never get used to this view. As she watched, a shooting star crossed above her, and a small smile touched her lips. The morning sun peeked over the horizon, lending a pinkish hue to the edge of the heavens. For a moment, she was one with the firmament. Soaring, nothing around her.

"You have helped us, and now we have helped you," the leader said, drawing all eyes toward him. Pulling hers from the sky above, Ellen blinked and directed her attention to the here and now. "It is time for you to go."

Ellen would have wished for more information from the leader and his band, but with Thomas back and the knowledge that the clue was a map, she was glad to be rid of their company.

"Thank you for your help," she said, just a bit tongue in cheek, and reminded herself that if they hadn't taken Father Thomas and forced her to come to them, they might not know that the cross on the paper was a map. Might not know that they had somewhere to go.

When all the leader did was regally incline his head, she looked around for a way out of the yard. As she glanced his way, one of the guards opened a gate, and they were not so subtly herded to the opening.

Then they were outside the property and the gate closed behind them.

"Well," she said, looking at Thomas.

Nodding, Father Thomas scanned the area as it grew lighter with the coming of another day.

"I think we need to return to the hotel," Ellen said. "We need to get some rest and then something to eat. Then we make a try for what's on the map."

"Yes," Father Thomas said, his voice dragging. "I'm about asleep on my feet."

The day continued to brighten as they made their way back to the hotel. When they entered, no one was at the desk, and that was just fine. They dragged themselves up the stairs and collapsed on the bed. Ellen barely got her shoes off before her mind shut down. What they'd do when they woke, she didn't know. The clues were all there, but the answers were not. She knew the direction they were to go, but not what to do when they got there.

Confusion pushed off sleep for a moment, and then she was sucked under.

CHAPTER 44

When Ellen woke up, the night was fully upon them. Gas flames wisped in lanterns on the street, and people moved up and down the avenue.

She still didn't know what to do with the clues, and since Father Thomas still slept, she slipped out of the room to enjoy the babble of people on the street. Two small wrought iron tables and chairs sat before the hotel, empty now. Claiming one, Ellen sat and studied the clue of the National Mall. She turned the paper around. When Thomas took a seat next to her, she didn't at first look at him.

"You know," she said after a moment. "If this is indeed a map of the National Mall, one item on this map is unquestionable."

The priest took the paper from her and set it on the table in front of him. "The Washington Monument," he said.

"Yes."

"So, we could go there and see what presents itself? I think the image of the moon may reference being there at night."

There was nowhere to go but forward. "Sounds like a plan." And with a nod, she added, "I think that's all we can do."

Father Thomas pushed back from the table, the feet of the chair making a screeching noise on the sidewalk. "Let's go then. I'm ready to figure this out."

Ellen gave him a small smirk. Pushing her chair back, she stood and took the paper back from him. As they walked away from the hotel, she folded the map and put it in the front pocket of her pants.

When the top of the Washington Monument came into view above the buildings, Ellen stopped. Father Thomas turned to her, his brows drawn.

"What is it?" he asked.

"Look at that." She indicated the monument with a jut of her chin. In the night, from this distance, it didn't appear white, but its mass blocked out part of the sky. "I've always wanted to see it."

"And now you shall," the priest said.

"And now I shall," she answered.

The closer they got, the more of the monument came into view until it towered above them. From the sidewalk around the block that the obelisk stood on, multiple walkways led to the center. Even from the edge of the lot, the size of the tower was oppressive.

What was once a grass space surrounding the obelisk, was now dirt and small, scattered rocks.

Taking advantage of the open area, tent cities had sprouted. People sat around open fires, cooking and talking. Children ran around, their voices floating off in the dark. And at the center of it all, jutting into the firmament, was the Washington Monument. Its girth blocked out a large swatch of the sky standing as it had for centuries.

"Have you had any ideas of what we're looking for?" Father Thomas asked.

"No," Ellen answered. "Let's move closer."

No one tried to stop them, and when they stood within arm's length of the obelisk, Ellen placed her palms on the smooth marble surface. She peered up the dark, unlit side.

White marble shone in the starlight. The monument was so massive, she couldn't see the top of the tower. Its murky white surface melded into the night sky so far above.

Ellen ran her fingers along its surface as she continued walking. Smooth and cool, just the touch of it sent a shiver up her spine. As they rounded the corner, a secondary structure stuck out from the side. Slowing, Ellen and Father Thomas made their way to the entry. No doors stopped their exploration, but where they once hung was evident. The interior was dark, and the priest shucked his pack and quickly lit a lantern that he pulled out.

With the light, they saw that the entry structure was full of people. Most sleeping, a few sat in the dark, squinting now at the two who invaded their territory. Ellen stepped in, careful to move between and over the bodies mostly wrapped in blankets. Father Thomas followed her, keeping the lantern high to illuminate their path.

Again, no one spoke, but a couple more watched as she and Thomas crossed their living quarters. When they passed from the structure into the tower, they left the squatters behind. Directly in front of them were the doors of what looked like the elevator. Above the closed double doors, an image of George Washington sat in profile. Around the elevator shaft, the passageway continued.

Ellen scanned the area. Paper, dust, and what appeared to be small chunks of marble littered the ground. On the far side of the entrance, directly across from the first, another set of double doors appeared. This duo was slightly ajar, and one hung askew. Ellen took a moment to peer into the elevator, and when she stepped aside, the priest took her place. The elevator was empty, the control panel on the side dark.

To the side of where they stood, a gate stood partially open. A sign on the front read *Stairwell. Emergency traffic only!*

Ellen gave the gate a push, the scream of unoiled joints harsh in the night air. Freezing, she listened to see if the people outside would come in to investigate. When they remained alone, she stepped through. Here the walls were rough stone. Large blocks of marble stacked up higher than she saw. They were jaggedly cut and were a smoky gray shade. When she laid her hands upon them, a jumble of images—one over another—came to her. Barely discernible, she identified them as workmen laying the blocks, their faces becoming one.

Ellen stepped from the exterior wall to the first flight of steps.

As she and Father Thomas continued to climb the stairs up the monument, Ellen ran her hand over the wall. Every so often, she touched a special block etched with names or figures. Before long, she realized they were representative of different states, countries, or organizations. Each stone block presented her with mental images of where they'd begun their life, the person who'd shaped them, and the placing of them within the monument.

Her eyes open, but her mind turned in, Ellen walked steadily up the stairs. One image blended into the next. All similar in feeling and circumstance. Partway up, the blocks of marble changed in color and texture. These new ones were cut smoother. And they were of a lighter shade. But still the images ran together.

They were more than halfway up when Thomas grabbed her arm. "Ellen," he whispered.

She leaned toward him. "What is it?"

"Do you hear that?" He looked down the stairwell.

Brows crinkled, Ellen peered back down the way they'd come, listening to the dark.

At first, she didn't hear anything and was just about to tell the priest so. But then a deep thump caught her attention. It was a second before she heard another, and she was able to identify it as a footstep.

She scanned the area for somewhere to hide. Somewhere to surprise whoever followed them. When she took Father Thomas by the arm, he gave her a startled look.

"Continue up the stairs," she whispered. "I'll stay here and see who's following us."

"Let me stay . . ." he began, but she shook her head and nudged him up the next set of stairs.

As the priest took the stairs, the light of their lantern went with him. Soon she was in darkness. Complete darkness, she realized. Leaning back to touch the wire meshing of the inside of the stairwell, she slowed her breathing and waited.

Time passed and she began to worry that Thomas would come back down looking for her and scare off their tail. Then she worried that there was no tail. That the sound they'd heard had been a natural noise of the tower. Or perhaps rodents running on the stairs. Then, just as she thought to break confinement, another thump reverberated up the stairs. She froze, concentrating on the darkness below. When a scuff came from right below her, she knew they'd been right. They were being followed.

In the perfect darkness, the flow of air shifted as a body passed by where she stood. Reaching out with both hands, she grabbed what she could—hair in one hand and a cloth, maybe a shirt, in the other—and pulled the person to the floor. She held on tight, sitting on the figure as it bucked and shoved at her, and yelled for the priest.

Heavy footfalls answered her call, and the light came quickly down the stairs behind her.

"Grab ahold. Help me!" she yelled.

Moving quickly, Father Thomas set his lantern down and grabbed the thrashing feet, then sat on them. The body under Ellen quit moving except for large gasps of air that expanded the chest of the body she rode.

When Ellen had her breath back, she rolled the person on their back and sat with her knees on their bent elbows, holding the hands of their stalker with her own down to the cold floor. Images came to her with the skin-to-skin contact, but they were all disjointed and hard to understand. Figures moving rapidly through dark areas, then a boy sitting alone by a small fire.

"Who are you?" she demanded.

When no answer came, she sat partially up, releasing the hands but maintaining her weight on the elbows. In the sparse light of the lantern, the figure was dark within the confines of a cloak and hat. Ellen pulled the hat off and pushed back the collar. She looked into the face of a boy no older than thirteen.

Shocked, she stared at him for a moment and then, swinging her leg off him, she grabbed one arm. She gestured to Thomas to release him before she hauled him to his feet. The boy didn't resist when she pushed him back to the wall.

"Who are you? And why are you following us?"

The boy lifted his head and jutted out his chin.

Defiant, she thought but saw his eyes sparkle with tears in the light of the lantern.

"Thomas," she said, "do we have any of that jerky left?"

The rustle of the priest going through his pack had the boy glancing that way and then back at her. When Father Thomas found it, she took the jerky from his hand. Putting the end in her mouth, she ripped off a chunk and chewed.

The boy watched her actions, and when he licked his lips, she held the piece of jerky out to him. He didn't take it, not at first. He eyed her, his gaze bouncing from the food in her hand to her face, and back again. When Ellen took another bite of the meat, he stood up straight, pulling his body away from the wall. She chewed slowly, watching him the whole time. When she again held the jerky out to him, he snatched it out of her hand and shoved it into his mouth.

Ellen allowed herself a small grin.

"Why are you following us?" she asked the boy. He didn't answer. Just continued to chew the hunk of beef. She wasn't even sure he understood her. "Do you want some more food? We have plenty." When his gaze shifted to her pack, she knew he understood. "You give me what I want, and I'll give you what you want. Okay?"

The boy gave a hard swallow and ran the back of one hand over his mouth.

"Can I have more?" he asked in a soft voice.

Ellen retrieved another hunk of jerky. "Why are you following us?" When he reached for the meat, she pulled it away. "Why. Are you. Following. Us?"

The boy didn't answer for a moment, and then he said, "I'm not following you."

"What's your name?"

Staring at the wall behind her instead of looking at her, he said, "Isa."

Ellen studied Isa for another moment and then handed him the jerky. The boy didn't hesitate this time, snatching up the meat and shoving it in his mouth. Ellen dismissed him to turn back to the stairs. She continued up, Father Thomas following, and the boy following him.

When they rounded a corner of the stairway, the room opened. Old display fixtures lined through the center, and some encircled the edges of the room. They were faded and broken, but Ellen could make out that they explained things about the monument, President Washington, and the city of Washington, DC.

Across the room, she could just make out another stairway visible at the edge of the lamplight.

"Come on," she said. "We're almost at the top."

She didn't expect the boy to follow them, but when she and Thomas started up the final staircase, the boy came with.

The room at the top of the monument wasn't in the extreme dark of the lower portion. Here, four windows, one on each wall, looked out into the night. They were covered with heavy glass at the end of a short port. She moved from one to another until a light in the distance caught her attention.

"Thomas, look at this."

When he came over, she moved out of his way. Peering out the window, the priest didn't say anything for a few moments. Then, with a shrug, he stepped back.

"I'm not sure what that is."

When he moved, the boy slipped in to peek out the window. He had to jump up, holding his chest against the stone windowsill to study the outside. "It's the Herald."

"What?" Ellen swung around at the boy's words.

"The Herald. He sees things, sometimes."

"Sees things? What do you mean, 'sees things'?"

"Things," he said with a shrug. "Come, I'll show you." He gestured for them to follow him and headed down the way they'd come.

Ellen looked at Father Thomas. "What do you think?"

"We might as well give it a try," he said. "We don't have any other ideas, right?"

"You're not wrong," she muttered and headed to the stairs leading down out of the monument.

When they got to the bottom, made their way through the bodies that still slept at the entrance, and exited the building, Isa waited for them on the pavement outside.

"Come," he said. "I'll take you to the Herald." He turned and headed across the dusty lot surrounding the monument.

They hadn't walked far when Ellen looked back. She realized they never would have seen the lights if they hadn't been up in the Washington Monument. In the monument and at night. The map seemed to lead them here.

The fires glowed in a circle around a larger bonfire. A man, slight in frame, paced around the large fire in the middle. He wore old, torn, baggy trousers that were held up with rainbow suspenders. He wore no shirt, and his dark skin glowed in the flames' light. Every few steps, he did a turn or jig, and with the movement, the light shot varying hues up and over him.

When he came around the fire and caught sight of them, he stopped in his tracks.

Isa moved slowly to him and gave a slight bow of his head. "Herald," the boy said, "I bring you two seekers."

The Herald's head wrenched up, his nose in the air as if

scenting them. Then, sidestepping the boy, he danced his way to Ellen and the priest.

Close up, it was obvious he was not only old, but ancient. Thin skin hung from his frame, and muscles, long since given up any thought of bulging, gave a sway to his body as he moved. If not for the faded suspenders, he would have walked right out of his trousers.

As he circled, he sniffed, moving closer and then farther from them. Ellen and Father Thomas kept an eye on him, but neither of them moved.

When he stopped behind Ellen, she partially turned to keep him in her sights. Humming a little tune, the Herald ran his hands up and down the length of her backpack. When he made to unzip it, Ellen dropped it from one shoulder and brought it around to her front. The Herald followed the bag like a hound to a scent.

When he again attempted to open her pack, Ellen had to stop herself from slapping his hands. Just as the zipper on the large compartment began to give, the Herald stopped and switched to the small side section. So quick was he that Ellen didn't see him until it was done. In his hand, he held the small bit of limestone from the shipwreck.

"Hey," Ellen said and held out one hand. Stopping herself, she realized perhaps that was the purpose for the stone all along. If this Herald could give them information, maybe the rock would be payment.

Moving away from her, the old man jigged around one fire and then another. Then he danced up close again, first to Ellen and then to Thomas. For a moment, he stood silently in front of Father Thomas. He ran a finger over the Roman collar the priest wore.

"Speak to me," he ordered with an ancient and raspy voice.

Father Thomas shook his head at the man. "I don't know what you mean."

"Speak to me," he ordered. This time, he took the priest's hand and pulled Father Thomas down with him to sit. "Speak to me."

Confused, Father Thomas looked at Isa.

"You're a priest?" the boy asked. "You wear the collar of a priest."

"Yes." Father Thomas nodded.

"He wants you to pray with him." When the Herald babbled something to the boy in another language, Isa nodded. "He wants to hear a story from a book called the Bible. He says he heard such stories when he was a young man. He wishes to hear them again."

Thomas stared off into the night. He would try. He would give what comfort he could.

Not looking at any of the three who surrounded him, Thomas began to speak. His voice quavered but steadied as he progressed. By the time he'd almost finished one of his favorite stories from the Bible, he paused, grasping for the light he felt sparking in his chest. Tilting his head back, he realized the stars were beautiful in a way they hadn't been in a long time. He placed a hand on his heart and finished his sermon for the old man.

"Which of these three do you think was a neighbor to the man who fell into the hands of robbers? The expert in the law replied, 'The one who had mercy on him.' Jesus told him, 'Go and do likewise.'"

Halting, only then looking down at the old man and boy who sat in front of him, Father Thomas waited. The boy stood and then stooped to help the elder stand. Thomas got to his feet, and Ellen did the same.

Bowing his head, the ancient again spoke in a language Father Thomas didn't understand. "What did he say?"

"'Thank you, Father,' he said. The story reminded him of other times. Times spent with his mother and the love she gave to him."

Father Thomas dipped his head to the ancient. "I am honored to be of comfort."

After a moment, the old man began to circle the priest and Ellen. With his hands splayed, he shifted around them but never touched them. When he hesitated and then seemed drawn to Thomas's side, and then his pocket, the priest stepped back.

"What's in that pocket?" Ellen asked.

Father Thomas's gaze shifted between the old man and Ellen. "The key from my grandfather's apartment safe."

"Show it to him. See if that's what he's after."

Moving slowly, Father Thomas put his hand in his front pocket and gripped the key. He brought it out and showed the Herald what he held. The old man jumped, did a little jig, and waved his hand over Father Thomas's open one.

"Come," the Herald rasped. "Come with me." He gestured for them to follow him. Isa stooped to retrieve a bag that lay outside the circle of fires and then followed the old man. When he and Isa headed back the way they'd come, Ellen shrugged, and she and the priest followed them.

The foursome didn't go far before the Herald turned and headed north, toward the White House.

The beautiful white building, which used to be surrounded by manicured grass lawns, trees, and bushes, now stood stark on dusty dirt lots. The imposing front porch, caged in by large columns, had been reduced to rubble, and part of the roof had collapsed into the building. The white outside, unpainted for years, was gray and peeling.

Ellen stopped, her breath catching. Memories filled her mind, a lifetime of images seen but not appreciated. Her heart wrung for what had been and now might never be again.

Ellen looked back at the Washington Monument. Only from this distance did she see the destruction—the chipped marble and large hunks missing near the top. Had she been aware of the condition of the tower, she might have thought twice about venturing up into it.

When the Herald detoured to take them around the side of the White House and its adjoined buildings, she hurried to catch up.

Along the way, most people dipped their heads and hurried by as they passed, but twice, people greeted the Herald. They visited in low tones for a few moments and then continued, giving her and Father Thomas long, searching looks.

Once, the Herald took them into the dark recesses of an alley. There, he stood, not saying anything. Within a minute Ellen heard the voices coming down the street. Brash. Harsh. Laughing and pushing each other, a group of young men walked boldly down the lane. She shifted and felt a grip on her forearm. It was the Herald. He didn't even look at her but watched out in front of them until the gang passed. He waited another full two minutes before he continued his path.

A few blocks north of the White House, the Herald drew them to a halt. He whispered something to Isa who nodded in understanding.

"The Herald says to be quiet when entering the building. And to stay close."

Ellen looked over the boy's head to the building they were to enter. What used to be a glass front was now broken shards and chipped brick. The sidewalk they passed over had intricate lines of bricks instead of the simple concrete of most.

Ellen stayed close to Thomas and kept her senses on alert as they entered the building.

The crunch of their footsteps on the broken glass stopped them, but when nothing happened, the Herald led them in. They moved around long counters set in the middle of the room, and along one whole wall, a tall counter spanned the length. Every six feet or so, an opening allowed interaction between the people in front and the people behind the wall.

A bank, Ellen thought.

Into darkness, they followed the old man and the boy. Once out of the entry area, the Herald stopped and lit a brand the boy pulled from the bag he carried. When he lifted it, the light spilled into a back room that opened into a vault. Long ago, the door had been ripped off. Bits and pieces of it littered the floor and surrounding area.

Inside the vault were safety deposit boxes. Some of them were open. Some weren't there at all, the gaps in the wall resembling teeth broken out. In the middle of the room, a tall, long table stood. Bolted to the floor, it had withstood time and vandalism with only a couple of deep scratches on the otherwise dusty surface.

The Herald stepped into the small area, followed by the trio behind him.

When he gestured to the boy, Isa shucked the pack from his back and handed it to the old man. In return, the Herald gave the boy the torch to hold.

Digging, the old man pulled out a jangling mess of keys. Large, small, silver, and gold, they shone in the flames. He tossed them from one hand to another and then, with a mighty shake, selected one.

With his free hand, the man walked down the line of boxes, moving his appendage like a divining rod. He closed his eyes, and a low-grade hum came from his chest. When he stopped, opened his eyes, and smiled, Ellen stepped forward to scan the box.

The Herald pushed his key into one of the two keyholes on the box he'd selected. With an impatient gesture, he waved Father Thomas over. Stepping around Isa and Ellen, the priest again pulled the small key from his front pants pocket. The Herald gestured, this time toward the box with a grunt of impatience.

Father Thomas pinched the key between two fingers and gingerly slid it into the second keyhole. He gave a deep swallow, and when the Herald turned his key, the priest grasped his and gave it a turn. A belly laugh erupted from the old man that had Ellen looking over her shoulder to ensure they were still alone. The Herald pulled, and the front panel opened to show the handle of an interior box.

When Father Thomas gave it a yank, Ellen stepped forward. The box slid out of its compartment easily and with only the smallest of sounds. Thomas placed the box on the table and pulled Ellen forward with a hand on her back.

Gingerly, Ellen opened the box, laying the covering back flush. Inside was a satchel. Clean, protected from dust and debris, it was a fine tanned leather. A strap bound the cover to the body of the case. Using only her fingertips, Ellen manipulated the bag out of the box. It compressed to ease over the edges of the box and popped out into her hands.

With a deep sigh, Ellen held the bag like it was fragile.

"Well?" the priest prompted. "Are you going to open it here?"

Glancing at her companions' curious faces, Ellen nodded and placed the bag on the table. She unstrapped the cord and laid the lid back to reveal papers. Fingering through them, they appeared to be pages from a diary. Dates and places marked the time and place of the author. In the front pocket, a single sheet sat alone. She took the sheet out and read it:

> *Friend, my search is at an end, but I know you will carry on.*
>
> *Here is all the information I was able to compile over the years. I know you'll be able to do what I wasn't.*

Ellen pulled papers out of the satchel, scanning them and laying them one after another on the table. When she saw the name Whitman, she stopped to read. The more she read, the wider her eyes got. She stuffed the papers back in the satchel.

"We need to leave," she said, closing the satchel and placing it in her backpack. She settled the pack on her back with a shift of her shoulders and turned toward the exit. "Thank you, Isa," she said as she passed the boy. Turning, almost as an afterthought, she said to the old man, "Thank you, Herald." She bowed to him. The Herald returned her bow.

"Come on, Thomas. We need to get back to Chicago."

"Ellen!" the priest yelled as she went out the door almost at a run. "Ellen, wait!" But she didn't slow, and Father Thomas hurried to catch her.

CHAPTER 45

Little T entered Washington, DC, with three loads of men. They were heavily weaponized and, as a large, armed force, not expecting anyone to give them any trouble.

They'd been given the charge to find the woman and the priest and bring them back to Malcolm Whitman. Little T didn't know why, and he didn't have to. He was a soldier, and soldiers followed orders.

He liked the city of DC. In it, he saw what once was. The monuments. The Capitol Building. Even the White House showed the past and the people they came from in its disrepair. He liked to think, no . . . he knew . . . that even in that time, he would have been an important man.

He had three vehicle loads of men and was meeting with someone who would know if the two he sought had come into this city. And where they currently were.

When they pulled up in front of the building, his men jumped from the vehicles to clear and surround the area. Leisurely, as if he had all the time in the world, Little T stepped from his ride. Straightening to his full height, he towered over all the men in his employ. He waited only a moment when the door of the building opened to reveal a dark maw. If he were a less trusting man—or less vengeful, he thought with a small grin—he might be worried to walk into the dark.

Head held high, Little T walked without hesitation across the sidewalk and into the building.

"T! Good to see you."

Little T glanced around the dim room. From the back, men approached him. He recognized the owner of the voice. His contact. Not someone he would ever refer to as a friend, but someone whom he was glad to have a good working relationship with.

"Parker." Little T acknowledged the other man with a lift of his chin.

"Come on in," Parker said. "Let's have something to eat and drink before we get down to business."

"I'd like to, but I'm on limited time. Do you have the information I need?"

Paulie Parker Meggle, or just Parker to people who knew him, thought about arguing with Little T. Partially, to see if he could get his way with the big man, and partially just to be difficult. Then, seeing the seriousness in his colleague's face, he sighed and filled Little T in on the information he wanted.

"They left the city last night. Sorry, *mon ami*, but you just missed them."

Heat filled Little T's frame, and he wanted to punch something. Maybe Parker's face with the small smile hovering around the corners of his mouth. Well-trained control kept all evidence of his reaction from those around him.

"You knew I wanted them." This was a statement of fact, not a question. Little T's face showed nothing as he waited for the other man's answer.

With a dip of his head, Parker admitted, "Yes. It's true I knew this. However," he said quickly when he saw the flash in the big man's eyes, "they had already jumped a train by the time I knew they were on the move." He accepted a glass of liquid from one of his men and directed the man to serve Little T. Ignoring the man, Little T kept his eyes on Parker, waiting for information he was sure was coming. "By the time we located which train they were on, it was long gone."

"And where was this train heading?" Little T asked, his patience long at an end.

"St. Louis."

Little T's brow furrowed, and he repeated, "St. Louis."

"Yes." Parker nodded. "I have men in St. Louis, and they know you've been on the lookout for these two. It won't be long, and we'll have their exact whereabouts."

As if noticing the man for the first time, Little T took the offered refreshments.

"We'll be in DC overnight. I expect their location from you before morning." Having given his ultimatum, Little T downed the shot of liquor, turned, and left the building, his men scattering before him.

CHAPTER 46

Knowing time was of the essence, Ellen and Father Thomas hopped on the first train heading west. Now, at least, Ellen knew the final move. Knew who and what they were looking for.

A sliver of moon hung in the night sky when she and Father Thomas pulled the door shut on the slowly moving train. They were alone in the car, and as far as they knew, no one had seen them board. Pulling her pack from her back, Ellen slumped down in the corner and breathed a sigh of relief.

"Can you tell me now?" the priest asked. He'd been pestering her the entire time from the bank to the railyard wanting to know what she knew. What had she learned from the papers in the satchel?

"Yes, Thomas," she said with another sigh. "Sit down and I'll show you."

When he sat, she lit a lantern and pulled papers from the satchel. Along with them, she told him of her first memories of being in this time—how she had been unable to move but had heard two men talking. Pointing to the information on the sheet, information Thomas's grandfather had compiled, she drew his attention to the name of the man in charge. The man at the head of the organization known as The Guild. Malcolm Whitman.

"One of the men was named Malcolm Whitman. I heard the second man refer to him by name. How much you wanna bet this Malcolm Whitman is Malcolm Whitman III?"

"You think *my* grandfather worked for *his* grandfather?"

"Yes. Yes, I do. Businesses are often handed down in families. I think the Malcolm Whitman who was in my room is who we're looking for. The person we need to stop if we're going to stop the experimentation on children that's going on."

"Okay," Father Thomas said, nodding slowly. "I follow your train of thought. But how are we going to locate this man? How are we going to find him and stop him?"

"The first thing we need to do is get back to the area of your church. When I woke up, the place was a lab. After I escaped, I walked to your church within a couple of days. And we were able to get to Chicago in three. Somewhere around there is the lab."

Father Thomas used his hand to cover a yawn as she spoke but nodded in agreement. "So, we should be able to find the place where you were kept. This lab, right?"

"I really think we can. In that lab there is a doctor. Michael Daniels. Guy's a dick. I kneed him in the face making my escape, so I'm pretty sure he won't be too happy to see me. He's the one I saw when we were in Richard's town. In that vision. I saw him buying children from Paul Anders. I think he was in charge—at least, he acted like he was in charge. We get to him, and he'll be able to get us to Malcolm Whitman."

When the priest yawned again, Ellen patted him on the leg.

"Get some sleep. There's nothing we can do for now except sit back and enjoy the ride."

Thomas stretched out, using his pack for a pillow, and was soon snoring lightly. Ellen watched him for a bit, remembering waking up in his church. If she'd only known at that time that they would be circling around to the same spot.

Time to give up the search for a bit of downtime. She needed sleep, and as soon as they got where they needed to be, sleep would be a commodity. Ellen stretched out beside the priest and closed down her mind.

The slowing of the train jerked Ellen awake. She sat quickly and glanced beside her to see Father Thomas rubbing his eyes. She stood and stumbled to the door. Throwing her weight into it, she got it cracked open to peer out. She had no idea where they were, but the sun was past midpoint in the sky, heading toward the west. Surprised, she glanced back at the priest. They'd slept through most of the day.

"Thomas, this is your world. Does this town look familiar to you?" The priest walked unsteadily toward her due to the motion of the train. Just as he reached her, she muttered, "Oh, my God."

When he looked out the door, he saw an immense silver arch shining in the late-day sun across a large, dry riverbank. Father Thomas put a hand on her shoulder, swaying with the motion of the train. "It appears we overshot our aim by a bit."

CHAPTER 47

Malcolm Whitman paced within the confines of his suite at the top of the tower. These rooms, this home he'd made for himself, had always felt so spacious. Now, however, he prowled like a caged lion.

That woman. That Ellen Thompson. How could they have lost her so completely? Didn't he have people tracking her? Didn't he have eyes and ears in every city on the East Coast and inland for miles?

He'd read his grandfather's journals.

No, he thought, stopping to stare out the full wall of windows to the night beyond. He'd studied them. Memorized them. He knew every thought and felt every feeling the old man had, had. Through his analysis of them, he'd grown as obsessed over her as his grandfather had been. What insight might she add to his research? Not just her thoughts, her experiences, but her very flesh. She was different. Had always been different. But why?

He paced again down the length of the room.

Turned.

Back to the bank of windows.

Turned.

Now she'd slipped the tails. Disappeared with that priest. But he would have her. She was his prize, and he would have her.

CHAPTER 48

When the train slowed enough for Ellen and Father Thomas to disembark without injury, they jumped down and headed across a burned-out field of dry, broken grass. The sun left small shards of light streaking up from the horizon. Soon, it would be completely dark, and the duo wanted to find safety before they decided their next move. At this point, all Ellen knew was they needed to get to the north side of St. Louis.

Ellen scanned the area. She thought they would ride the train right into Chicago. Then it would take a couple of days to get back to Thomas's church. Now, they were too far west and too far south. It would take them days, if not weeks, to get where they needed to be.

A few blocks into the city, in an underpass, Ellen and Father Thomas saw the flicker of flames. Closer, they saw multiple barrels aflame, and groups of people stood around them warming their hands. As Ellen and the priest got closer, each group turned to eye them.

"Maybe we should go around?" Ellen asked Father Thomas. Just then, one of the women called out, "Father," and hurried to them. She grabbed Thomas by his sleeve and pulled him toward her group. Ellen followed at a slower pace, keeping her gaze on the others.

"Father, we're so glad you've come." The woman still had a grip on his arm. Her smile shined so bright, it made the fire in the drum dim. "Can you tell us the word of God, Father?"

Father Thomas studied the woman for a moment. "What is your name, child?" he asked.

"Elizabeth."

Lifting a hand, Father Thomas placed a palm to the woman's cheek. At his touch, she closed her eyes and bowed her head.

"You are a child of God, Elizabeth." Lifting his gaze from her face, he scanned those around them. Those at this fire and those farther out into the night. Raising his voice, he said to them, "You are all children of God, and as that, you are perfect in his eyes. You are loved by our Heavenly Father, as all fathers love their children."

Father Thomas moved among the downtrodden of this world. As he had moved around other peoples in their travels. His words, his very presence, lifted them. Wherever he spoke, he made a difference.

Hours later, Father Thomas joined her in a spot they'd been given to spend the rest of the evening and the next day. He looked exalted. His eyes shone, but his body was bent in exhaustion.

"They said we could stay as long as we want," the priest said, looking around the small underground room. Outside the walls, in other rooms, others visited, ate, made love, and read to children. They were warm and safe but would not be able to linger long.

"We need to keep moving." When the priest looked up from

his hands, she added, "I'm sorry, Thomas. I know you'd like to stay, but there's somewhere we must be. Something we must do."

The priest nodded in understanding.

"We'll leave at dusk today."

That evening Ellen and Father Thomas made their way across the city. They stayed mostly on the main roads where people traveled. St. Louis was a populated, busy town, almost reminding Ellen of Washington, DC.

People greeted the priest warmly, stopping in their travels to speak with him and often to ask him to pray with them. The priest seemed to be in his element, once again among a flock who needed his words. Each time he spoke, his voice became stronger and surer.

By the middle of the next evening, Ellen and Father Thomas left St. Louis behind. They'd happened on a group with vehicles who got them to the end of the city and directed them toward Chicago.

With one final look back, Father Thomas followed Ellen once again into a wilderness where they didn't know what to expect.

CHAPTER 49

A town came into view at a bend in the road they traveled. Built half in and half out of the old, dried riverbed, it must have been constructed after the Rush.

No lights shone through the dark. The shadowed outline of buildings peeked between a copse of an old, barren stand of forest that surrounded the hamlet. Dawn was showing her bright head over the top of the town, amber light mixed with the dark of the sky—the stars long since faded.

"Morning's coming quickly. Maybe we should find somewhere to spend the day," Father Thomas offered.

"It looks abandoned."

They watched the small town for a moment, and then with a lift of her chin, Ellen led them in.

No sound came from the buildings as the duo moved from the line of trees to well-worn dirt streets. Choosing not to put them in a direct line of sight with anyone who might be in the town, Ellen stayed to the back roads and alleyways. She passed buildings, moving farther back into the town.

When they rounded a corner, and a dark building towered in front of them, she pointed soundlessly to the priest. He nodded.

If danger came, they'd have enough warning that they could make their escape in the hills beyond. Ellen veered toward it, Thomas close on her heels. Finding the front door locked and barred, they moved around the side and into the back area. That door was locked, too, but with a little work, they managed to get a small window open into the lower floor of the building.

Ellen shucked off her pack and handed it to the priest before she dropped to her hands and knees to shimmy through the window feet first. She was most of the way through the window, almost ready to take it on faith and drop, when someone grabbed her around the waist and pulled her in.

She gasped and then expelled the same breath as she hit the concrete floor. Scrambling to her feet, she moved backward in the dark until she hit the wall. There, she pulled the blade resting at her waist. Crouched, hands in front of her, one full of sharp edges, she waited for an attack, but nothing came.

"Ellen," Father Thomas called from outside the window.

"Stay there, Thomas. Someone's down here with me."

"Ellen, I'm coming in."

"No!" she shouted as a grunt and the sound of something hitting the ground outside made her heart leap. "Thomas?" When no answer came, she yelled, "Thomas?"

With her hands out in front of her, swiping left and right with the blade, she shifted across the floor back the way she'd come. The window was on the lee side of the house, and no moonlight helped to illuminate the basement. Once or twice, she bumped into something with her foot as she dragged her feet across the floor. She was almost at the point she deemed to be the far wall when she heard a sound behind her. Spinning, she threw an arm up before something hit her in the head, and she collapsed to the floor.

* * * * *

Ellen woke slowly. Pain radiated from a point just above her right ear around her skull. Sitting, she held her head in her hands, afraid to move too suddenly and feel the stabbing pain.

When she dared, she lifted her head and cracked her eyes. She sat amid loose hay. She touched the point of the pain and looked with wonder at the blood on her fingertips.

She peered out into a semi-dark room through the bars of a cage. Ellen reached out a hand, gripped a bar, and gave it a shake. It didn't move. The cage rested next to a wall, and beyond it there were two empty cages. In the distant corner, a lantern hung from the ceiling. It flickered gently, making shadows on the wall.

Ellen pulled herself to her knees, the top of the cage too low for her to stand, and studied the room beyond her pen.

"Thomas," she whispered.

In the distance, through the walls of the basement, dogs barked. She jumped when a bang sounded.

"No, no!" The voice echoed through the basement, bouncing off the cement walls.

"Thomas!" she screamed.

"Nooooo . . ." When the word transitioned to a scream, Ellen went wild with panic. Banging and pulling on the bars, she screamed the priest's name.

"Thomas! Thomas!" Ellen turned to kick her booted feet against the bars. No one came to her antics, and the screams in the adjoining room went on and on. Finally, unable to stand it any longer, Ellen pushed her hands over her ears to shut out the cries. It didn't work, and the wails worked their way through her fingers until she, too, screamed out in frustration.

Without warning, without a whimper, the screams cut off, and Ellen hesitantly pulled her hands from her ears. "Thomas!" she screamed.

Where were they? She needed to get out of here.

In the other room, she heard a loud clang and then the low murmur of voices. Too low for her to make out the words.

"Thomas!" she yelled again, not caring if they came for her.

Ellen opened her eyes. She was still in the cage. She didn't remember falling asleep. Didn't remember anything after the voices and Thomas's screams. Now sitting, she pushed her snarled, matted hair back over her shoulder, and a few blades of hay fell out. In the half-light she stared, not quite believing what she saw. When she reached out to touch the water in a stainless-steel bowl, her gaze jumped up, skipping around the room, looking for those who watched.

She leaned over the bowl like a dog and sniffed. She was thirsty. Parched. She didn't know how long it had been since she last had a drink, but it felt like days. Her body yearned for the cool liquid.

But, she thought, wouldn't that be the easiest way to drug her?

She wouldn't be so accommodating.

When a door clanged open, Ellen scurried backward until she was pressed up against the bars at the back of her cage. She felt like the animal they'd made her, and she was sure she looked the part.

Another door opened, this one to the room she looked out to. She watched as a man backed through the door, pulling something. When another man followed, Ellen sat higher, stretching her neck to see what they had between them.

A body. *Oh, God! Thomas!*

She'd started forward when she realized the person they carried wasn't the priest. It was smaller. Not a child, but not full-grown. Lank, dark hair obscured the face.

When they continued across the room with the body, ever closer to her, Ellen again hunkered down in the corner of the cage. She saw now that the two men wore masks. Like old-time Halloween masks, they were white plastic with little holes for the nose and mouth. They walked right by her to the cage at the end of the room. Dropping the feet, one of the men opened the cage door to the loud screech of metal on metal.

They tossed the body in the cage, lifting and pushing the legs in after. After shutting the door, one man locked it with a large padlock he took from his pocket. They didn't look her way as they turned and passed back by her. Sliding to the front of her cage, hands gripping the bars, Ellen peered out.

"Hey," she shouted. "Hey, you! Where's Father Thomas? What have you done with him?"

Neither of the men even looked her way but kept moving until they were back through the door. It clanged shut with a finality she found hard to ignore.

When Ellen again woke, the bowl of water was where she'd left it, only now bits of straw floated on the liquid. Next to the bowl was another. This one contained something that resembled a hash. Leaning over it, she sniffed.

Dog food.

How long would it be before she was happy to get even that?

Sliding to the door, Ellen reached out to feel along the

locking mechanism. It was a padlock. Without the key she wouldn't be getting out of here.

When she heard a moan, instinct had her shuffling back before she realized the sound came from the person in the far pen. On her knees, she gripped the bars and tried to see the other prisoner.

"Hello," she whispered, but she didn't get any answer. Not even a moan.

Where are we? Who are these people? And where is Thomas?

The opening of a door had her again moving to the back of her cage. When a group of people stepped into the room in front of her, Ellen quickly studied them. They didn't look like anyone she'd ever seen.

Pale, to the point of having little or no pigment, they were small. They moved toward her, and only when they neared could she see their misshapen limbs. All of them, and it looked like a good dozen people, had bowed legs—bent by their own weight. Their arms, even their fingers, were misshapen. Their hair, all different in colors, hung in tendrils from their scalps.

The closer they got, the farther Ellen pushed herself back. Leaning over, they whispered among themselves and peered at her like an animal they'd caged for their enjoyment.

"Evil," one said, whispering under her breath to the one beside her.

"Sinful," the other whispered back.

The group gripped the bars of her cage from the outside, their fingers like stones in cloth, distorted and malformed.

After another moment, they began to move away, throwing glances at her over their shoulders. When the last one left the room, the door closing after, Ellen dropped her head in her hands. Her sobs, muffled and teary, went on for some time.

Ellen woke when a noose slipped over her head and tightened around her neck. Gasping, she grabbed the pole attached to the noose. At the end of the pole were two of the people from this town. Men. They opened the door to her cage and pulled her out.

Unable to advance on them due to the pole, and unable to get the ever-tightening noose from her throat, she was forced across the room and out the door.

In the exterior room, two more men waited. Grasping the pole, she shoved it back into the two on the end, hoping to break their grip and then get the noose from her neck. They took her thrust and then pushed her back where she went down hard on the floor. The end of the pole on her throat rammed into her. In a gagging, coughing fit, she was easy prey when the two new men rushed her and bound her hands not only behind her back, but also tight to her body.

The four of them walked her outside. It was dusk, but on what day, she didn't know. There had been no way to tell how many days had passed while she was in the cage.

Around a corner of the building, the remainder of the town waited. All gruesomely misshapen. All resembling walking corpses. They were covered from the light of the sun, some with hoods and some holding umbrellas. On some level, she realized they were all adults.

With the fading light behind them, gallows waited past the congregation. His body bound and his neck in a noose, Father Thomas waited on the stand. They'd stripped him of his collar—his badge of who he was—and now his shirt flapped open at the top.

Coughing again, she gasped and yelled, "Thomas!" which caused the population to begin speaking among themselves in their peculiar whisper.

On the gallows, Thomas struggled for a moment only to be clubbed from behind by a man.

At the foot of the steps, Ellen set her foot to the stair and refused to mount the stage. Four men grabbed the pole, yanking her back. One of the men released the pole to swing a weighted bag, connecting with her right temple.

Seeing stars, Ellen dropped to her knees, bent at the waist. For a moment, her head rested on the dust and dead grasses surrounding the gallows, but the men soon had her back on her feet and herded up the stairs to stand beside the priest. Still unable to focus, she felt the warmth of blood run down the side of her face.

"Ellen."

When she heard her name, she turned toward the sound, the image of the priest moving in and out of focus.

"Ellen, be calm."

She blinked hard, giving her head a shake, and concentrated on the man beside her. His face was bruised along the jawline. Where his collar lay open, a wealth of bruising and some dried blood showed.

They yanked at her throat, and the rope went up and over a long pole mounted above the scaffold. It was pulled up and tied off with very little give.

"Thomas," she said, staring at the priest. "Thomas, I'm sorry."

"No, child. No." Taking a step and moving as close to her as he could, he looked back at her. "Ellen, will you pray with me?"

"I'll get us out of this. Don't give up on me, Thomas."

Thomas gave a wry chuckle. Looking from her out to the sea of people, he admitted, "This might be the end, Ellen."

"No. No, I can get us out of this." She looked out too. "I can."

The crowd quieted as one of the men stepped forward. He put his hands up, getting their attention, and they shuffled forward as if to hear him better.

"Good citizens. Once again blasphemers have come into our home."

At his words, some of the people began an awful hissing. Again, he put up his hands and they quieted.

"We will deal with this threat as we have dealt with all others in the past."

Ellen stepped forward, speaking to the crowd and the man. "We're no threat. We were just looking for a place to spend the day."

When she spoke, the man next to her shoved his fist in her stomach. Unable to double over without the rope cutting off her airway, she partially crumpled and dry wretched, coughing and gasping. The man who'd hit her forced an old bandana into her mouth and tied it behind her head with another. Ellen sucked air in and out of her nose, her eyes watering.

"Now then," the man again addressed the crowd. "We'll send these interlopers off—back to the hell from whence they came. Hangman." He turned to the man who'd hit Ellen. "Do your duty."

Tied and gagged, Ellen could only shake her head, a mumble coming from her. The man stepped forward and grasped a lever, and her eyes widened, the mumble becoming a muffled scream.

When an arrow struck the man in the throat, toppling him

backward, the clearing erupted in pandemonium. Ellen's gaze swung around the area, coming to rest on the priest beside her. Wrenching his hands, Father Thomas was attempting to release his ties.

The hangman wavered, swaying with his hands wrapped around the shaft of the arrow. When he again swayed to the front, thinking he'd topple on the lever, Ellen took a step toward him and kicked his sternum solidly with the flat of her foot. The force of her kick had him falling backward, and she almost lost her footing. She rebalanced, barely stopping from strangling herself.

More arrows flew, people dropping in their flight. The leader ran by the gallows yelling to his people, but just as he cleared the stairs, a man in black caught him and, with one swipe, cut the leader's throat.

When the killer turned to look at them and then stepped slowly up the stairs, Ellen began to wrestle with her bindings. The man reached for her, and she pulled back as far as the noose would allow, but he only reached over her head and cut the rope. He moved to Father Thomas and swiftly sliced his noose from around his throat.

Ellen could only stare, catching the priest's eye.

Where moments ago the clearing had been a screaming killing field, now it was silent. Bodies littered the ground. A group of men, all clad in black, approached the gallows. When they pulled back to allow one man to near, she was spellbound by his size. Not just tall, but brawny, he gave her and Father Thomas an enormous, toothy smile.

"Well, hello, Ellen Thompson."

CHAPTER 50

Little T couldn't believe his luck. He'd always been lucky, but he also knew a man made his luck.

Parker's organization had come through. With Ellen and the priest following the dry riverbed, it was easy enough to get out ahead of them. The fact that they seemed to be on their way to Chicago was of little interest. They needed to get to Chicago with him. *He* needed to be the one to give her to Malcolm Whitman.

Little T studied Ellen and the priest for some time. All around them lay the fallen. His men walked through systematically killing the injured. Soon, they would spread out and clear the town. When one of his men walked to him, he gave him his attention without looking away from the scaffolding.

"We've set up in the town hall. It's the big red building on the main street."

"Thank you. See that they're taken there. Give them water. I'll be right there."

The man gave one nod and, yelling at some other of The Main, soon had Ellen and Father Thomas off the gallows. They kept them tied but pulled the bandana out of Ellen's mouth.

Ellen flexed her jaw, swallowing a few times, and tried to talk.

"He—" she began but had to stop to swallow again. "Hey!" she yelled at the big man who was obviously in charge. "Where are we going?"

Moving as if she hadn't spoken, the big man walked away.

When Father Thomas moaned, Ellen jerked at the hands on her. "He needs help. They tortured him." The men with them turned a deaf ear and walked them down one street and then another. When the priest collapsed and had to be assisted back to his feet, Ellen again fought her restraints. "Can't you see he needs help?"

"Just keep walking," one of the men said, giving her a shove in the back.

The farther down the street they got, the more and more they encountered men and women all dressed in black. None stopped. None looked at them. They all seemed to be going somewhere and doing something.

At a large red building, the man following Ellen grabbed her arm and shoved her through the front door. Looking behind, she saw Father Thomas get the same treatment. Partially through the building, they were shoved into a room. This one was empty, with no windows. The door closed behind them and opened a moment later. The man who'd led them here came in with two glasses. He set them on the floor and then pulled a knife from his belt. He wiggled his finger to have her turn around.

Ellen spun but looked over her shoulder at him, not trusting him. Cutting the ropes on her wrists, he left her to shimmy out of the binds still encircling her frame. After cutting Thomas's ropes, he looked at her, pointed down, and ordered, "Stay."

Leaving the room the way he'd entered, he shut the door, and they heard a key turn in the lock.

Ellen took a deep breath, dropped her ropes, and hurried to where Father Thomas stood against the back wall of the room.

"Thomas?" She took his arms, and when he began to collapse to the floor, she helped him to sit. She scanned the room and hurried to where the cups sat. Sniffing one, deciding it was water, she took it to the priest. "Here, Thomas. Drink this. It's water."

Father Thomas's hands shook, but he got a good grip on the cup and downed the water. When Ellen brought the other back and offered it to him, he shook his head.

"You need to drink too."

"You're injured," she argued.

"I'm fine. We're fine. Just drink the water."

Sipping, ready to give it to him if he needed it, she studied the priest. With one hand she moved the edge of his shirt a bit and looked at the bruising.

"Yeah," she said. "You're real fine."

He glanced at her and then closed his eyes. "We're not hanging from the end of a rope."

"Always the optimist," she quipped, earning a small chuckle from him.

When the key again turned in the door, Ellen jumped to her feet. Father Thomas struggled to rise, so she helped him up. The door opened, and the big man from outside pushed himself through it. For a moment, Ellen thought the jam would break with the effort. Behind him, two men waited. When he just stared at them, she said, "So? Who are you?"

He smiled. "I'm Little T, and I have to say, you don't disappoint. All attitude."

"Little T?" She looked him up and down. "Who named you that?"

A snicker escaped the big man, and he shook his head at her. "You'll have food and some more water brought to you. Along with a blanket. We'll be leaving at nightfall."

He turned back to exit the room. Ellen jumped forward, which caused the two guards to intercept her. Little T turned, an incredulous expression on his face.

"Girl, you don't know when to quit."

"What's going to happen to us?" With a gesture to the priest, she said, "He's injured and needs attention. Do you have a medic with your group?"

Little T studied the priest, who leaned against the wall, and then turned his attention back to Ellen. "He'll be fine until we get where we're goin'."

"Which is where?" she rushed to ask.

The big man hesitated. "Chicago."

Stunned, Ellen let him leave the room, his lackeys following. She shook her head and went back to the priest who was lowering himself to the floor.

"Did you hear that? Chicago. What are the odds of them taking us right where we need to be?"

"I told you, Ellen. Everything is going to be just fine."

"Uh-huh . . ."

CHAPTER 51

Little T rarely slept. And more rarely if he was out on the road. When he awoke the next evening, stretched, and looked around, he couldn't help but be surprised. Maybe he'd found rest just knowing that Ellen Thompson and Father Thomas were in his control.

He sat up on the bed he'd commandeered, and with another big stretch, the dream came back to him. He'd been in the tower in Chicago. The one with the large *T* emblazoned on the side. Emblazoned like the building had always been his.

He'd walked through the upper chambers, thinking that he'd been wrong before. That the upper floors were exactly where he was supposed to be. The ability to look out over the land he controlled, to see not only the vastness, but the beauty, was something that he valued.

Little T chuckled at his far-reaching desires. When he threw off the covers and stood, naked as the day he'd been born, a set of raised voices had him slipping into his pants and opening the door. On the other side, two of his trusted lieutenants argued with the guards. As soon as they saw him, all fell silent.

"What's going on here?" For a moment, he thought no one

was going to answer. But then one lieutenant—Martin—stepped forward.

"It's the woman."

Little T sighed internally. He'd known all along that Ellen Thompson would be a bane in his existence.

"Come in." He turned with a gesture for his lieutenant to follow him. While he dressed, he listened to the litany of complaints the man had about their guest.

"And, when we didn't come and get them quick enough this evening, she stood there and banged on the door. And when we got there—"

"Stop," Little T interrupted him. "Are you telling me you can't handle one little girl?"

At his words, Martin flushed. "But T. You don't want her hurt. I'd like to retie her and use a bigger gag."

Again, Little T chuckled and counted himself lucky that he could find the humor in this situation. "Have they been allowed to use a toilet?"

"Yes," came the quick answer.

"Fed and watered?"

"Yes, sir."

"Then lock her and the priest back in the room until we're ready to head out."

The lieutenant's expression closed. "She'll yell and bang and make a general nuisance of herself."

"Well, I guess you'll just have to deal with it."

* * * * *

Seated in his custom seat in the middle of the caravan, Little T watched as Ellen and Father Thomas were brought out and loaded aboard another vehicle. She walked beside Martin, talking and gesturing the whole way. Little T couldn't hear what she said, but the pained look on Martin's face made him chuckle again.

CHAPTER 52

Ellen held the compress to the bruise on the side of Father Thomas's jaw. The woman who'd come to help rechecked a wound on the priest's shoulder. While she gave instructions for Father Thomas's care, Ellen listened to everything she said, nodding and taking it all in. They'd arrive in Chicago the day after this, and finally they'd sent someone to see to Thomas.

She didn't know if the woman was a doctor, but she seemed to know what she was talking about, so Ellen followed her direction and didn't give her any guff.

She'd helped when the woman cleaned the wounds on Father Thomas's torso, and although she wasn't squeamish, she'd blanched when she saw bruising on his jaw from where the people of that town had pulled two of his molars.

Thomas had filled her in on some of what had happened to him in the town. She was certain he'd kept the worst to himself. Pulling teeth and with no anesthetic. All to get him to confess to something he didn't even know. Crazy zealots.

The young healer had given him something to help with the pain—Ellen didn't know what and really didn't care as long as Thomas could rest.

"Are you all right?"

Ellen broke out of her reverie when the woman spoke to her.

"Yes, I'm fine."

"No wounds?"

"No. No, I don't think they'd gotten to me yet when they decided to hang us."

"Ah, yes. The hanging." She pushed Ellen's hair back from her collar. "Let me put some salve on your rope burns."

Ellen thought to tell her no thanks but then decided being contrary was hurting herself, so she sat still, Thomas's head on her lap, while the woman doctored her.

"Have you worked for Little T long?" Ellen asked.

The woman hesitated in her ministrations and then continued. "Yes. I grew up on the streets of Chicago. Little T found me and sent me to train when he found out my interest in medicine. I made him a promise that I would come back to the community and be of service to the people."

"So, you've known him a long time?"

"All of my life, really. Before him, I had no life, no identity. I was barely surviving. Now I am somebody. I have meaning to my life and am respected."

"But he's a gangster. A thug."

The doctor stared at Ellen for a moment. Then she shook her head. "He's a father figure to many. You might not believe it, but Little T cares about his community."

"What about the rest of the world?" When the woman again looked her in the eye, Ellen added, "I just saw him and his men eliminate a whole community of people."

"You mean the people who were going to hang you and this priest?"

Ellen had the decency to flush at the obvious rebuke in her voice. "Okay. I admit they saved our lives, but they still killed willfully."

The doctor shrugged and went back to her patient. "All I know is he's done a lot of good for our community. He keeps us safe."

Ellen let the subject lie.

She and the doctor had been working on Thomas for almost an hour, cleaning additional wounds they found across his ribs and stitching them up, when they heard a commotion outside.

The doctor stepped to the door and cracked it open. People ran down the hall, intent looks on their faces.

"Hey," the woman yelled, stopping a young man. "What's happening?"

"We're under attack," he said. "Stay here and lock the door." Then he turned and ran with everyone else.

The two women sat with the priest who still slept. Cries and screams came from outside the room, and soon Ellen was on her feet, pacing. When another scream floated through the door, Ellen stopped. Looking at the doctor, she said, "I'm going out there."

"You can't," the woman told her.

"I can't just sit here and wait for someone to come and kill us." She stepped to the door and, with her hand on the knob, turned again. "Stay with him. I'll be back."

Stepping outside the room and pulling the door shut behind her, Ellen was immediately enveloped in noise and chaos. Bodies littered the hall, and people ran in both directions. She scanned one way and then the other. She stooped to pick up a large knife from beside a body, then headed toward the screams.

Down the hall and out the main doors, Ellen sidestepped

groups of people engaged with each other. Both men and women fought viciously. Blood flew and body parts fell. A man with crazed eyes ran at her. His scream brought her about, and he impaled himself on the knife she held. He stared at her for a moment, his scream turned to a gurgle in his throat, and then he fell backward off her blade. The sucking noise as his flesh released her steel made her stomach churn.

When she thought she could do so without faltering, she stepped over his corpse and continued across the field in front of the building. Bodies littered the area. As she moved over or around them, something caught her eye. She moved back until she saw it again. The body of a man lay over another—she didn't recognize either of them—and sticking out of the breast pocket of one man's shirt was a white rectangular item. It was the white against the darker colors that she'd seen. When she bent down to take the item, she realized it was Father Thomas's Roman collar.

The sounds of battle came to her, and she put the collar in her front pants pocket.

When they'd been brought here, the field had been quiet—a vast spot full of dry grasses and dirt. Now, the ground ran red with blood. What dirt she saw was torn up by the frenzy of battle.

Across the field, by a small scraggy bush, she saw the unmistakable figure of Little T. He battled four individuals, all better armed than he was. For a moment she debated, but then she hurried to his aid, although she didn't stop to consider exactly why.

When she got close, one of the combatants saw her and stepped from the fight to confront her. He didn't so much as pause before he swung an arm, aiming for her head. He overreached. When she ducked, his swing had him spinning in a circle. With his side facing her, she put her training to use and stomped on the outside of his knee with everything she had. The crack of the joint and his shriek of pain had an unexpected burst of pleasure whipping through her.

Leaving the injured man, certain he wasn't up to following her, Ellen plunged into the fray. Surprising another of the men, she hit his nose with a fist closed around the hilt of her knife. Faster than the first man, he caught her arm and threw her across the ground.

When Ellen came to rest on what was left of the bush, she shook her head to clear it and was halfway on her feet before she could again see clearly.

Ellen glanced at the large knife in her grip. Then she turned her attention back to the combatants just as one of the men got past Little T's defense and clubbed him on the temple with a bat. The big man went down, and for a moment, it didn't look as if he had it in him to regain his feet.

On his hands and knees, he swung out at the men, but the one with the bat got another shot in and caught Little T on his shoulder. Hearing him cry out, Ellen saw three on one and moved to help.

A battle cry left her lips. She rushed the men who had their backs to her. Just as they started to turn, she was there. Sliding between them, she ran the blade of her weapon over the back of one man's ankle. With a scream, he went down, dropping his bat and grabbing his leg. She came up swinging the knife across her body, backhand from right to left slicing the throat of another of the combatants.

Now, Little T was on his feet. The lone attacker tried to flee, but Little T shoved his weapon into the man's chest just as Ellen ran hers into his lower back.

Over the man's shoulder, Ellen and Little T locked gazes. His held pain and anger, hers a level of battle crazy she'd never felt before. When the two of them stepped back, the man collapsed between them. Giving her a second's glance, Little T bent to take up the bat and, with callous precision, put an end to the two remaining men.

Four bodies scattered around them, their blood soaking into the dry, cracked earth.

"I'd say thanks, but I can't let you go," Little T said.

"I know."

"Why did you do that? Why did you help?"

For a moment, Ellen just stared at the carnage. "Have you ever heard, the enemy of my enemy is my friend?"

"No," he said. "Sounds like something smart, though."

"Yeah." She turned from him to mutter, "I see the truth of it now."

CHAPTER 53

Riding in the vehicles on their final leg before reaching Chicago, Little T asked Ellen to sit with him. Father Thomas was again drugged and resting, so she did, not knowing what might come of it.

The vehicle they rode in made its place in the middle of the convoy, safe from any threats. Walking to the vehicle, Ellen couldn't help but notice how Little T's people deferred to him. Not like a dictator, but more like someone they trusted. Someone whose opinion they valued.

She strove not to let it affect her—he was their kidnapper, after all—but the fourth or fifth person who stopped them had her listening without realizing it.

"When we get back to Chicago, the children are expecting you to come and teach a day at school."

"Yes, Jackson," Little T said, trying to move past the other man.

"It's not my fault you showed them that drawing thing you do."

"Yeah."

Ellen fell into step with the big man, and try as hard as she might, she couldn't stop the question. "What drawing thing?"

"Huh?"

"What drawing thing? That guy . . . Jackson. He said you showed them a 'drawing thing.' What did he mean by that?"

"Ah, man." She would have sworn he blushed. "My granny showed me how to draw perspective. Like a train track or road fading into the hills. I showed a couple of the kids, and they told a couple more, and now they all want to learn about it."

A few steps farther and Ellen asked, "How many kids do you have where you live?"

They'd reached his ride and climbed in. "A lot," he grumbled.

Ellen dropped the subject for a few miles, and then when Little T seemed particularly preoccupied with the steepness of the terrain, she asked, "Are any of the children yours?"

He glanced at her, his gaze jumping back to the roadway. "What do you care?"

"I don't really," she answered. "Just trying to get a feel for who you are."

"I'm the man who's going to sell you to my boss. To get you, he'll let me name my price."

Ellen kept her gaze out the front window of the vehicle, not giving him the reaction he seemed to be wanting. "Who is your boss?" She finally looked at him.

"Why you wanna know?"

"It would be good to be prepared. I'm wondering why he wants me. Or is it Father Thomas he wants and I'm just collateral damage?"

"It's you."

"And he is . . . who?" she prompted.

Taking a deep breath, Little T said, "Malcolm Whitman."

"Malcolm . . ." A laugh caught in Ellen's throat, and she coughed. Getting her breath back, she gave in to the laugh and let it roll out of her.

Taking his eyes from the road, Little T yelled over her laughter, "What's so funny?" This only made her laugh louder. He shook his head. "Nuts."

Late in the night, before the sun made its presence known on the horizon, the caravan pulled onto a street just off downtown Chicago.

Interested in where they were and, more importantly, how to get out again, Ellen watched as they passed businesses and landmarks she could remember. She wasn't interested in getting away now that she knew they would be meeting Malcolm Whitman. All the time thinking about how they were going to, first, locate him and then get to him, and here they were going to be delivered right to him.

The vehicles turned in to a large parking lot and formed a *U* twisting back upon themselves. As soon as they stopped, people climbed out and began unloading gear.

Behind her, a door crashed open, causing her to jump. She swung around, knees bending and fists coming up, only to see children and a few adults pouring out of the building. The children ran to greet adults, laughing and wrapping their arms around them.

Ellen stood, stunned by the warm, natural reception. Father Thomas walked up to stand beside her, and they observed the families.

"So normal," she said.

"Yes. I guess we could be captives of worse sorts."

"What about Father Patrick and what happened at the church?"

"I've been talking to people about Little T and the Main," he said without looking away from the reuniting families.

"And?"

"It seems, at around the time of Father Patrick's death, Little T was just coming into power. He was having some pushback from a couple of different factions. Other alphas who thought they should be leading. Couple of different people I spoke with thought the group at the church sounded like one of these."

"So, it wasn't Little T? It wasn't his command that killed Father Patrick and tortured you."

"Seems like it wasn't. Fact is, I was told it was Little T who personally killed the leader of that band. Part of a coming of age or something. How he got rid of his competition."

Ellen leaned back against one of the vehicles, slid her hands in her pockets, and for a moment, she relaxed. Felling the hard edge of the collar against her fingers, she pulled it out and turned to the priest.

"I found something of yours."

Father Thomas stared at the collar for a moment, and then his gaze jumped from Ellen's eyes back to the collar in her hand. For a moment, she thought he might not take it, and then he reached for it. When he took the collar, his hand trembled gently. Cradling it in his palms like a beloved object, he again looked at Ellen, a bright smile crossing his face.

"Thank you, Ellen. I thought it was lost for good." With the expertise of long use, he affixed the collar to his shirt.

Turning to him, Ellen straightened his shirt, brushing dirt

from his shoulders.

"Looks good," she said, smiling at the priest. He returned her smile and turned to look out over the throng of people.

For another moment, Ellen and the priest watched the families gather their belongings and head into the buildings.

"Thomas." She drew his attention. "Little T is selling us to Malcolm Whitman."

"Ha!" He shook his head, and a smile spread across his face. She couldn't help but smile with him.

"You see, Ellen. Some things are just meant to be."

"Thomas, Thomas, Thomas. You may have me believing yet."

Ellen straightened and wiped the smile from her face when she saw Little T and another man approaching them. She'd never seen the man before, so he must have been here while they were on the road.

"Come with us," Little T said without preamble.

"Where are we going?" Ellen asked without moving.

Little T sighed. "Why are you so difficult?"

"I have a right to be difficult. We're your prisoners, right?"

"Well, if you're my prisoners," he said, a hand on his hip, "then you have no rights. So, let's get a move on." He walked away from them.

Ellen stood still for a moment and then Thomas gave her a prod. She stared at him, and when he shrugged, she pursed her lips and followed the three men.

In the building, people moved around, children running between the adults. The smell of something cooking had Ellen's stomach growling. When she realized the smell was becoming stronger, she quit dragging her feet.

They entered a large room full of round tables surrounded by folding chairs. Most of the tables were full of people eating and talking. Laughter made it warm and inviting. When they sat at one of the tables, women with platters came by and scooped some sort of stew into bowls that sat in front of them. Warm bread completed the meal.

Ellen couldn't believe how hungry she was and wondered if her yearning was making the taste of the food that much better.

People began to filter out, and the general noise level in the room dropped.

Her mouth was full when Little T looked across the table and said, "Who is Malcolm Whitman to you?"

CHAPTER 54

Ellen choked on her food, and with a large swallow, she got the mass down. She sat back on her chair, took a deep breath, and said, "What?"

"You heard me. Who is Malcolm Whitman to you?"

"In truth, I've never met the man."

"Why did you laugh when I told you that's who wants you? If you knew anything at all about him, you should be scared witless."

"I was just surprised."

"Uh-huh. So, you've never met him. Know nothing about him. But you were surprised to find out it was him who wants you."

Ellen glanced at Thomas and then back at Little T.

"Well." She hesitated. "We've heard *of* him."

"What have you heard of him?" Little T sat back and crossed his arms over his massive chest, making it known that he wasn't going anywhere until he got the answers he wanted.

"What's he to *you*?" she deflected.

"Oh no. You're going to tell me what I want to know. And you're going to do it right now."

Ellen sat straight up and faced Little T. "I'll tell you, truthfully, I don't know why he wants me. I have no idea what he hopes to get by having me in his possession."

"Well, girl. He wants you something awful."

"Do you know a Dr. Michael Daniels?"

Little T had an image of the man on the elevator. "What do you know about him?"

"So, you've met?" Ellen leaned forward, her attention caught.

"I wouldn't call it that."

"Well, he thinks I have something he can use."

"What?"

"I'm not sure."

Little T turned from her, waving a hand.

"I'm telling you the truth," she practically yelled. When he just looked at her, she added, "I don't know what they think I can do. What I have. I think they think it will aid them in their experiments."

Now, Little T sat forward. "What experiments?"

"So, now it's my turn not to believe you."

"What do you mean?"

"You work for Malcolm Whitman. You're his lackey." Little T's face turned dark. "You do and get for him. And you're going to tell me you don't know what he's doing? What his entire daily motivation is?"

"I have no idea what you're talking about." When he glanced at the man on his left, all he got was a shrug. "Malcolm Whitman's motivation is money. Ruling people and making money."

Ellen partially stood, leaning over the table into Little T's space. "Malcolm Whitman's *last* motivation is money. I have no idea what he hopes to discover, but his family has been searching for at least three generations. They were doing experiments in his grandfather's time, and they still are."

"How would you know what they were doing a hundred years ago?"

Ellen flopped back into her chair and mumbled, "Because I was there."

CHAPTER 55

Little T listened to Ellen Thompson's story with half an ear. He thought she might be crazy. And the thing was, he believed that *she* believed it.

Halfway through her story, he almost stopped her. He'd need to lock her up—keep her away from his families. Maybe what she had was catching. Was she contagious? Then she started to tell them about the experiments on children.

What could Malcolm Whitman hope to discover? If it had been going on for three generations—and now he realized he was giving Ellen Thompson's story some credibility—what could they be looking for?

And she had the priest buffaloed. He was totally on board with her delusions, interjecting things about his grandfather. Stories and pictures. Obsessions.

But if what she was saying was true—the tales she told about the kidnappings and the disappearances—how long would it be before Malcolm Whitman looked for children closer to home? Children from his community.

Could he discredit her story and risk the lives of the children? The trust of his people?

If anything she said was the truth, even if it was only *this* Malcolm Whitman doing these things, he had to act. He had to stop him. Had to end this insanity before it touched his community.

Little T sat up straight and gave Ellen his full attention.

CHAPTER 56

When Little T stared at her, Ellen's discourse fell silent. She'd been talking nonstop for almost an hour trying to get the men at their table to believe her. Father Thomas threw in information and went along with everything she said, but she had the feeling they all thought she was nuts.

When Little T turned her way, his gaze intent, her words stuttered to a stop.

Here it comes, she thought. He'd gag her and have her taken to Malcolm Whitman. They wouldn't care. They'd just be glad to have her special brand of crazy out of their lives.

When Little T opened his mouth, Ellen tensed. "How do we stop him?"

"What?" Her eyes opened wide. She wasn't sure she'd heard him right.

Little T folded his hands on the table between them and leaned forward. "How do we stop him?"

"Y-you believe me?"

"I ain't sayin' I believe everything you've been saying . . . portals and guardians and whatever. But, if Malcolm Whitman is experimenting on children, we have to be part of putting that to a halt."

"Yes." She swallowed hard. "You don't have to believe everything. I can work with that. But I believe, and Father Thomas believes, that I'm here to stop Malcolm Whitman. To finally stop this generational torture of children. It's got to stop, and thank you, T." She laid a hand over his. "We need you. If we're going to end this, we need you."

Little T turned his hand to grip hers.

"Where do we start?"

CHAPTER 57

The plan was easy, Ellen thought. Get to Malcolm Whitman and put a stop to him. Once the head was cut off the snake, they'd take the fight to Dr. Michael Daniels. And how to locate him? That was the easy part. Father Thomas knew exactly where his church was from here. She knew how long and in which direction she'd walked after getting out of the laboratory. Little T had an army at his disposal. They were already out looking, and they'd find him in no time.

Now she paced. Little T had sent a runner to Malcolm Whitman to inform him that she and Father Thomas were in his hands. Little T wanted to make a trade.

The messenger hadn't been gone even a full hour, but Ellen was worried. How long would it take? How would Malcolm Whitman want the transaction to go?

She had her newly acquired blade strapped, hilt down, along her spine under her shirt and jacket. No matter what, no matter what might happen, she wouldn't be going back to the laboratory as a captive.

"Ellen," Thomas called to her from across the room, "come and sit."

Knowing her pacing was making him nervous, she nodded and walked to the edge of the couch he reclined on. As soon as she sat, Little T walked in and she jumped to her feet.

"Well?" she asked.

"Runner's back. He wants you and the priest. Says to bring you right through the front door."

"Arrogant son of a—"

"Ellen. His arrogance will be his downfall," Thomas said.

Nodding in agreement, she turned to Little T. "Well? What are we doing?"

"Let's get you tied up, little girl, and catch us a bad guy."

* * * * *

Ellen sat in the back seat of Little T's vehicle with Father Thomas next to her. Little T and his driver rode in the front seat. Her hands were tied in front, as were the priest's. The ties looked real, but Little T had shown her how the knots could be slipped in the event that she or Father Thomas needed to get free. A vehicle traveled in front of and behind theirs. Little T knew what Malcolm Whitman expected. He needed to project strength just like they thought he would.

It didn't take as long as she thought to get from the family compound to Malcolm Whitman's tower. A city without traffic allowed them to drive straight there.

When their convoy of three pulled up in front of the tower and Ellen climbed out of the vehicle, she looked up at the face of the building. A hundred feet up the side, a large *T* claimed ownership of the facade.

"You put that there?" she asked, gesturing with her chin.

Little T followed her gaze, his smile breaking. "I like it."

"I'm sure."

In the next instance, the front door opened, and with a flurry of activity, a group of men all dressed in black suits swept through Little T's group. Confiscating weapons and pushing Little T's crew around, they did their best to claim dominance over the area. Then, standing on all sides of Ellen's group, they ushered them into the building.

"Your men will have to stay here."

Little T just stared at the self-proclaimed leader of the group.

"Mr. Whitman wants you and the prisoners on the elevator. He's waiting, and he doesn't like to be kept waiting."

Little T grabbed Ellen and Thomas by their bound hands and pulled them toward the open elevator. Ellen and Father Thomas had been instructed to keep silent, but when the elevator door closed and the car jerked into motion, Ellen couldn't help asking, "How is this running?"

"Don't know, don't care," came the terse answer.

Within moments, the car jerked to a stop. As the door slowly slid open, Ellen had her first glimpse of the owner of the voice she'd heard upon waking in this reality.

"Ellen Thompson." He blocked their exit. A guard on each side, Malcolm Whitman excreted arrogance. For the first time all day, the tension released from Ellen's shoulders. In her experience, arrogance was a cover. It shielded cowardness. When pushed, this man would break.

With a waving gesture, Malcolm Whitman said, "Come, T. Come in. Let's have a drink. A celebration." Turning from the elevator, he reentered his suite. The two guards stepped within the elevator as Little T exited. Each taking a prisoner, they yanked them out and shoved them after Whitman and Little T.

On the other side of the door, the suite opened — the entire wall one of glass. Ellen stared for a moment but moved forward when she was pushed again. Her handler spun her around and shoved her down with a hand on her chest, so she flopped down next to Thomas.

"Thanks." She sneered at the man who'd manhandled her.

When he backhanded her across the face, she sat stunned, her head turned.

"Ellen." Father Thomas sat forward, attempting to shield her from further violence.

"Hey, hey," Little T yelled and moved to place himself in front of the prisoners. "They're still my property. Till you pay me for them, they're still mine."

"Yes, of course, T. Of course. My boy just got too exuberant." Tapping his hand down, he approached his men. "Patience, boys. Patience."

Turning back to Little T, he said, "Now. How about that drink."

Ellen rolled her tongue in her mouth, feeling the split on her lip and tasting blood. She stretched her neck one way and then the other. The blade at her back felt red-hot. She touched her lip and wiped the smear of blood on her pants before she sat back against the sofa.

"I'm okay," she whispered to Father Thomas.

From the other room, they could hear the two men talking. Discussing the transaction of their sale. Ellen and Father Thomas sat quietly on the sofa, the two guards standing nearby.

Ellen saw Malcolm Whitman walk to the door of the room and gesture to the guards. One stood over the priest, effectively stopping him from rising, and the other grabbed Ellen by the arm and pulled her up.

"What are you doing?" she growled at him, pushing away, but he wrenched her forward, dragging her from the room. "Thomas!" she yelled as the guard shoved her into another room. Trying to rise, Father Thomas was pushed back onto the sofa by the man standing over him.

At the entrance of the main room, Little T asked, "What are you doing? What's going on?"

"Just a little sport for my boys."

"I thought you said you needed her."

"Her brain will still be intact. They know not to hurt the brain."

Little T looked at Father Thomas struggling to rise from the couch. When the guard punched the priest, knocking him back against the sofa, Little T started forward.

"I wouldn't if I were you." Turning, Little T saw that Malcolm Whitman had pulled a pistol from the interior of his suit coat. And that gun was now pointed at him.

"What are you gonna do with that?"

"I thought you might not be so willing to hold to our bargain, and I see I was right."

When a muffled crash came from the other room and stole everyone's attention, Little T grabbed Malcolm Whitman's arm and wrenched it up. A shot went off into the ceiling, the sound of the weapon only slightly louder than the sound of his breaking bone. The air filled with the smell of spent gunpowder and the scream from Malcolm Whitman as he lay at Little T's feet and held his useless arm.

The guard watching Father Thomas had turned and headed

back to assist his boss. Now, Little T turned the gun on the guard. "Stay right where you are," he warned.

Malcolm Whitman got to his feet and fled the room, still holding his broken arm tight to his body. Little T glanced toward the fleeing man, and the guard moved at him. When a stoneware bowl crashed on the guard's head and he went down, Little T looked for a moment at the man on the floor and then at the priest, a glazed expression on his face.

Little T nodded at Father Thomas and then went after Malcolm Whitman. The priest stared at the man he'd just hit. When another sound came from behind him, he spun and ran to Ellen.

When the man got Ellen to the back room, he pushed her inside and closed the door at his back. Ellen slipped the binds from her wrists, giving a silent thanks to Little T for his foresight. Then she turned, and when she saw the look on the man's face, she spit at him. He grabbed her upper arms and yanked her against him.

"You're a stuck-up little bitch, aren't you?"

Ellen twisted her arms and laid a hand over each of his. When the images came, she smiled. Staring into his eyes, she whispered, "At least I'm not some Momma's little baby wannabe. Right, Stanton?" Pursing her lips and pouting, she whispered, "Didn't your mommy love you?"

The guard's eyes bulged, and he tried to push her away from him, but she hung on.

"Poor Stanton. All the other kids had mommies who loved them, but not Stanton's. Stanton wasn't good enough."

"Shut up!" he yelled and wrenched his hands from hers.

"Stupid Stanton. Is that what they called you? Stupid Stanton, stupid Stanton," she singsonged. When he covered his ears and turned away, she pulled the knife from the sheath at her back.

When the gun went off in the other room, he turned, a maniacal smile on his face.

"It's over now, bitch. Time for you to die." He rushed her, causing her to fall back until she hit the wall. Grabbing her by the throat, he slammed her into the wall, hitting her head. Ellen saw stars and blindly drove the knife into him.

She heard him catch his breath, and again, he slammed her back. Ellen pulled the blade and ran it into him again. This time, his grip on her neck loosened and then dropped away.

When Father Thomas burst into the room, she was standing over her assailant, her knife coated in gore, a pool of blood spreading on the floor.

"Ellen," he said and hurried to her. Taking her hand, he helped her around the body on the floor. When she didn't respond to him, he took the knife from her lax hand and set it down. Holding her hands between his, he rubbed them to warm her.

Finally, she looked at him.

"Thomas?"

"Yes, I'm here."

"I had to, Thomas. I had to."

"I know, my dear. I know."

They stayed this way for some moments before Ellen blinked and looked around the room. "Where's Whitman?"

"Trying to escape."

"Where's T?" she asked, bending to pick up the knife and move toward the door.

"He went after him."

Ellen followed the priest out of the room and across the main lobby of the suite. Little T and Malcolm Whitman stood outside the doors to the elevator. At first, they appeared to be merely talking, but when Ellen and Thomas got closer, they saw Whitman had another pistol—twin to the first. He and Little T were in a standoff, neither able to best the other. Both at risk of being shot.

When the doors whirred behind Malcolm Whitman, a smile spread across his face. The doors opened, and Ellen saw what Whitman didn't. She stepped forward. "Wai—" she began.

Turning the gun toward her as he stepped back, he said, "Just stay right there." He finished his step, but there was no car to enter. Pinwheeling his arms, a scream tore from his throat. Father Thomas jumped forward to grab him, but he was already falling.

All the way down, his scream echoed off the walls of the elevator shaft, and a hollow thump sounded at the end.

Ellen, Thomas, and Little T peered over the edge.

"Ick," Ellen said, causing Father Thomas and Little T to look at her.

The three took the stairs down, and when they got to the bottom, the doors of the elevator were open. Passing the shaft, Ellen kept her gaze averted as they hustled by.

None of Malcolm Whitman's men were around. When Little T's lieutenant told them all the men in black suits had run away, Ellen figured they could tell it was Malcolm Whitman who had fallen.

"There's something else, boss," Little T's lieutenant said.

Little T looked up from studying the pistol in his hand with a raised eyebrow.

"Got news there's a large group coming across the old lake. Movin' into the city."

Nodding, he pocketed the weapon. "We need to check it out."

Ellen put a hand on his arm. "We aren't done with this, T. We need to locate the laboratory."

"I know, girl. But we can't have an outside force moving in. We need to secure the city or there won't be anything to come back to."

"All right, all right. But just remember. We have to find those kids."

"You think I don't know that?"

Ellen just nodded, not happy about the delay.

"You comin'?" he said from the front seat of one of the vehicles.

"Yes. Yes, we'll come," Ellen said as she and Thomas hurried to take a seat before the caravan swept them away to the shore of the dry lake.

CHAPTER 58

By the time they got to the edge of the lake, a crowd had already gathered. It took a bit to get the vehicles through the throng, and even then, they had to get out and walk to the front.

In the distance, moving across the sandy lake bottom, a group of animals and people came their way. When recognition hit, Ellen pushed through people in the crowd. She pulled on Little T's arm, stepping in front of him to get his attention.

"Wait! They're friends."

A few minutes more, and she stepped down the dry embankment. First walking and then breaking into a run, Ellen flew into Richard's arms.

"We've come to help," he said, "and bring home our children."

"We're glad to have you." She looked over the group that gathered around them. "All of you—welcome." She and Richard stood to the side and let the group move past them toward the Chicago coastline.

Father Thomas led Little T to them, speaking to people as he came.

Little T stopped when they reached Ellen, and the two leaders faced off.

"Richard." She ran a hand down his arm. "This is Little T." When she introduced the big man, she held out a hand toward him. "T, this is Richard Sanchez. We stopped in his town on the way to DC."

When Richard held out a hand, Little T gripped it, the skin-to-skin making a crack. "Good to have you here. Can use all the help we can get."

"Good to be here."

The four of them—the two leaders, Father Thomas, and Ellen—made their way to the shore with the last of Richard's group. People were already chatting among small groups.

"So, Ellen," Richard said and turned to her, "where do we go from here?"

"Back to T's headquarters?" She looked around at the groups, leaders, and workers, and back to Little T. He was nodding, and he turned to the people.

"We're waiting to hear from the scouting parties. We *will* locate the laboratory that Malcolm Whitman oversaw. We will take down the man, Dr. Michael Daniels, and we will free the children who have been taken from their homes."

The crowd, both Little T's people and Richard Sanchez's, cheered at his words.

CHAPTER 59

It wasn't until the next morning that the scouting parties located the lab. Under direct orders from Little T, they didn't approach the building. Sending two runners back with the news, the bulk of the party hunkered down to observe the night and get new orders from their leader.

Ellen paced the confines of the community center when the word came in. She'd barely slept the night before, her mind in a turmoil of details. When she'd thought to get something to eat, she'd come across Father Thomas and a gathering of people—some from each group—holding a candlelight vigil in the main room. His low voice filled the area as he intoned the Lord's Prayer.

Ellen stopped and bowed her head, her knowledge in her beliefs unsure but ingrained from childhood. When Father Thomas finished, and the answer of "Amen" went 'round, Ellen raised her gaze to that of the priest. With a nod at her, he returned to comforting those who sought him out.

She was almost to the kitchen when a shout came. She joined in with others as they filed out to see the runners come home.

Little T and Richard Sanchez stepped out, and Ellen realized the two leaders had been in a private meeting. When Little T moved forward, the crowd fell back to allow him passage. He spoke for a moment with one of the men, then looked at Richard Sanchez. With a nod to the other man, his gaze encircled the mass of people.

"Load up!"

Whoops answered his order, people running to get their gear and get to vehicles. Ellen watched the frenzy, suddenly feeling left out and alone. With a deep sigh, she pivoted only to find Richard right behind her.

"Aren't you coming?" he asked.

"Richard, yes. I just wasn't sure which way to go."

Putting out a hand that she took, he said, "Ride with me. You are the catalyst for this, Ellen. You need to be there in the end."

* * * * *

By the time the caravan went a few miles, the noisy exuberance had died. Packed into the vehicles, they sat with stony expressions looking to the coming conflict.

When word came back through the ranks that they would be pulling over and making camp for the day, Ellen felt the discontent move through them. But no one lagged—not T's or Richard's—and soon makeshift tents were up to protect them from the worst of the sun's intensity.

Food was laid out and groups gathered to eat and visit. Around the encircling bulk of vehicles, armed guards watched, ever vigilant for the lone scavenger or a larger force.

When she wandered past a small crowd of the two groups, she paused when someone called her name. Looking, she saw a woman stand and waved her over. With a smile, Ellen changed her trajectory and made her way to the woman.

"Hi," she began. "Patsy, right?"

"Yes!" She said it with such enthusiasm, Ellen had to stop herself from stepping back. "Here, come sit with us." Patsy pulled Ellen by the arm to where a group sat.

"Sit, sit." Patsy practically pulled Ellen down with her. At the contact, a flash of images swam through Ellen's mind. *Easy, breezy,* Ellen thought. Happy and not too bright, Patsy was no threat. "You all know Ellen."

The group nodded to her, a chorus of hi, hello, and welcomes.

The conversation flowed from subject to subject, and at some point, Ellen quit listening—just allowing the hum of it to pass over and through her. It had been so long since she had experienced something so innocent and normal as this group. The laughter warmed her, allowing her to feel, at least for the moment, like she belonged.

As the conversation flowed, Ellen lay back against the warm soil. Even with the canopy overhead, the sun's light shone intensely. She draped her arm over her eyes. The voices lulled her, and soon she drifted to sleep.

* * * * *

She snuggled against his strong body. Comfortable. Warm. She felt safe and maybe even loved.

The image flashed, and she was up and running. The hall was narrow, and the overhead lights flickered with a strobe effect. Movement caused her to bounce back and forth, striking the walls.

"Ellen."

He called her name, but not with love. Not with longing.

"Ellen."

Fear streaked down her spine, sweat beading on her forehead. The lights flickered again, making a hissing sound. When she looked down, her hands were covered in blood.

* * * * *

Ellen woke with a gasp, her arm falling from her face as she partially sat. The group had changed. Some leaving, some coming. Patsy was gone, and for the most part, Ellen was alone. When she sat up, some of the group looked her way, smiling.

Be polite, she thought. *Smile back. Nothing is wrong. With the right effort, they will never know you're not one of them. Not really . . .*

When she stood and turned away, no one stopped her.

Near the vehicles, she saw Little T and Richard Sanchez. They were deep in discussion, so she turned the other way. It was good that the two leaders worked well together.

The sun was almost at the line of the horizon when she found Father Thomas. He, too, was with a group of people, but he saw her before she could turn away.

"Ellen," he called.

Plastering a smile on her face, she moved toward him. When she reached him, he seemed to sense her disquiet. He pulled her into the crowd and threaded her arm through his, effectively locking her to him.

"Richard has given us the plan for tonight. They say the area with the laboratory is just a few miles ahead. Once we are moving, it won't take us long to get there."

"Good," she said, and then admitting she was out of the loop, she added, "So, what is the plan?"

"The runners said there are three doors to the building. The windows are boarded up, so access will be limited. They're considering that you were underground, and they think the children may be being held there. But no matter what, the entire building will be searched. Dr. Daniels needs to be located, as well as any of his team who can be found and identified."

Ellen nodded as Father Thomas spoke. The next evening, they would be at the end of all of this. Win or lose, it would be over and done.

CHAPTER 60

As the sun's dying rays streaked across the darkening sky, the caravan was already on the move. Within two hours, the leaders said. Within two hours, they would be there. They'd be there and they'd finish this.

Entering the complex, the scouts directed them, and the vehicles pulled up in front. There was no reason to be overly stealthy, as they'd be going in hot and noisy. Everyone unloaded, and weapons were pulled and readied. Quivers filled, sheaths tightened, the occasional firearm rechecked. Conversations flew back and forth, and those watching the buildings reported that they didn't see any motion inside.

When the front door was breached, Ellen wasn't anywhere near, but she heard it. Her first thought was to wonder what was happening. What had happened to all the organization? Suddenly, it seemed as if everyone was doing whatever they wanted. She hadn't seen Little T or Richard Sanchez since they'd arrived. Were they aware people were filing into the laboratory? It was chaos.

Ellen had her long knife in the sheath on her back when she headed toward the main building. She had a lantern in her hand but had chosen to keep it unlit, using the light that crept through the boarded-up windows to investigate. She kept looking for Father Thomas—another face she hadn't seen in a while.

People moved past her in all directions, and she couldn't find any order in their movements. When she reached the door, no one monitored it. No one stood guard.

Inside, the windows were covered, and the rooms were dim and moody. In the distance, voices could be heard, but she wasn't sure if they were the ones she was with or the ones they'd come to conquer. She slowed, taking her time to move through the rooms, watchful for any movement. She looked for something familiar. She'd gotten out of this building. Having come out, she should be able to go back in.

There were shouts ahead when two factions engaged. Then all was silent. Ellen moved forward down a long hall until she noticed bodies lying where the hallway opened into a large room.

When something pulled at her, she turned away from the room with the dead and went down another corridor. She moved away from the fighting, away from both her people and those they'd come for.

It wasn't long before she was all alone.

Her footsteps echoed in the hallway. Though nothing familiar jumped out at her, she continued to be tugged forward.

She'd almost reached the far end of the hall when a panel slid open, a hand reached out, and she was jerked inside. She dropped her lantern, and it crashed in the hall as the panel slid shut. She wasn't blinded, though, since the small area—another hallway—was lit by flickering wall sconces. She looked from them to the hand that held her—Dr. Michael Daniels.

"Well, Ellen," he whispered. "How nice of you to join me."

The raspy voice—the one she remembered from her first

wakening—filled her with a kind of dread. A shiver ran up her spine and her hand clenched, wishing for her knife. But she needed him alive. She needed to locate the children.

"Where are they?" she asked.

All he did was raise an eyebrow. "They? Why they're roaming around my building. Prying into my private business."

"Not that *they*. Don't act dumb." She wrenched her arm from his grip. "The children. The children. Take me to them."

"Oh." He paced down the hall a few steps. "My little darlings. Come with me, Ellen." He lifted an arm to indicate down the hall. "Come, and I'll show you."

Ellen's mind spun. She needed to get help. Needed to get Richard, Little T, or Thomas, but the good doctor was here. Here and now. And she had to get to the children.

"Lead on, Doctor." She took a step toward him.

Right away, the hall transitioned to a set of stairs that the doctor took down. At the top, Ellen looked back the way they'd come. An image of the panel opening and a man coming through came to her mind. How glad she'd been when he'd gone the other way. That he hadn't seen her. Now, it seemed, she was back. With one final look, Ellen followed the doctor down.

They passed three small landings with exit doors before reaching the one the doctor wanted. He pulled it open and walked through, not waiting to see if she'd follow, confident she would.

Ellen stepped into a corridor. It looked just as she remembered. Across from her, the janitors' closet door was closed. Down the hall, evenly spaced sconces gave off a yellowish light.

Feeling as if she were in a dream, Ellen wandered past the doctor and down the hall. She heard him fall into step behind her but continued. A bit farther, and the window into the lab came into view. She crossed to it, to stand in front of it, her hands resting on the sill.

"Where are all the people?" she asked.

"What people?"

"When I was here before, this room was full of people. People in white coats." Facing the doctor, she again asked, "Where are all the people?"

"They're long gone, Ellen." He stepped to her to place a gentle hand upon her arm. "Now, it's just you and me."

CHAPTER 61

Father Thomas was frantic. He'd lost Ellen, and he couldn't seem to find anyone who knew where Little T or Richard Sanchez were. He needed to find them. He needed help to locate Ellen.

When he came around another corner, he was practically running. A group of people, busy searching the room, didn't have any information for him. Finally, the last person pointed him in a direction. He said he'd seen Richard Sanchez through that door. His pulse hammering, sweat beading on his brow, Father Thomas made his way to where the man had pointed.

When he saw Richard at the end of another hall, the priest broke into a run.

"Richard!"

At his shout, the leader turned his way. Almost falling into him, Father Thomas came to a halt and Richard caught his arms, stepping back.

"What is it, Thomas?"

"It's Ellen," the priest breathed out between pants. "I can't find her anywhere." He scanned the area, his gaze frantic. "Have you seen her?"

Already shaking his head, Richard told the priest, "No. I lost sight of her right after we breached the front. Maybe she's with Little T."

"Maybe. Maybe," the priest allowed. "Have you seen him? You're the first one I've been able to locate."

"No." The leader put out his hands in a pacifying gesture. "Don't get all keyed up. Let's find T. I bet you he knows just where Ellen is."

By the time they found the big man, the sun was peeking over the horizon, and the exploration of the property was dwindling. No one had found anything. It was as if it had been wiped clean. And no evidence of access to the supposed underground laboratory.

The two leaders stood by a back wall, whispering. They kept looking at the priest who paced the room. When they approached him, he stopped pacing and stood to face them, hands on his hips.

"We've decided to divide people into groups. Systematically search the grounds. She must be here somewhere."

Thomas dropped his head and sighed, "Thank you." Though inside he was thinking, it was about time. "Where do we begin?"

It took longer than the priest would have liked to organize the people into groups and get them moving back through the building. They were tired and hungry, some of them not even knowing who Ellen was.

Thomas went with one of the crews. When they came across the broken lantern in the middle of a hall, most of the people stepped over or around it, but Father Thomas kneeled, illuminating it with his light.

"I think this might be Ellen's."

The leader of this group made his way back to the priest. He kneeled beside him and studied the broken bits. "I don't know, Father. This could have come from anywhere." He gave a shrug, pushed back upright, and followed his crew down the hall.

Father Thomas didn't believe him. He knew she'd dropped it. He felt it in his bones that she was in trouble, and he was tired of dealing with others and their misgivings about it. This lamp was the first evidence he had that something had happened. If she went calmly, why did she drop the light? He was certain she had been taken.

CHAPTER 62

From the laboratory, Ellen followed the doctor down another of many hallways and a back stairwell. She was in a maze, and she knew it. How would she get out of here?

When Dr. Daniels opened a large double door and preceded her in, she stopped at the door. This room she knew. Like the hallways, it was illuminated by wall sconces. In the center, a secondary room was walled with glass. The glass box contained an imitation of a home.

"Do you recognize it?"

Ellen pulled her gaze from the parody and looked at the doctor. When he smiled, something crept into her gut. It churned, and sweat broke out on her upper lip. She stepped closer to lay her hands upon the glass walls. She peered in as a certainty embedded itself in her brain.

Moving along the wall, she approached the entry. At her touch, the door opened, though she'd been certain it would be locked. Standing for a moment in the portal, Ellen stepped in, the doctor close behind her.

In a fugue state, she floated around the room. Touching items, opening drawers, and even sitting on the bed, she couldn't come to terms with what the presence of this room meant.

When the doctor pulled a chair to sit in front of her, she just stared at him. "You know, don't you, Ellen. You know who lived here."

"It can't be," she said and again studied the room.

"It can be. It is. You were my father's prize before you were mine."

He stood and paced the room.

"What made you want to leave after all this time is uncertain." When he stopped in the middle of the room to study her, she cringed. "You always seemed so happy."

"No!" she shouted and, springing from the bed, pushed past him and out of the door. She was halfway across the outer room when he called after her.

"Don't you want to see the children?"

Ellen halted in her flight. Heart pounding, she turned to the doctor.

CHAPTER 63

Father Thomas let the group he'd been with move on without him. He wouldn't go any farther without exploring this area, and he wouldn't waste any more time going back to look for Richard Sanchez or Little T. It had been him and Ellen for most of this, and it would be him and Ellen now. He wouldn't abandon her.

Methodically, from the beginning of the hall to the other end, Father Thomas peered along the lines of the building, studying corners and the junctions of walls. Tapping, he listened intently to the sounds, searching for anything. Anything at all that stood out.

Coming down the wall, nearing the spot where the broken lantern still lay, he had his ear to the wall and tapped his way to the other end. He knocked his knuckle against the plaster, and just as he was going to take another step, he stopped, his gaze losing its focus. Then, his head moving like a marionette, he stared at the wall. With a step back, he again laid his ear to it.

His knuckle hit the wall. The answering sound was hollower than it should be as if there were a large space behind it. He moved along the section of the wall, tapping until the sound changed.

The priest stepped back, looking down the section that he was sure contained a door. Now, how to get it open?

CHAPTER 64

Ellen couldn't believe what he'd just said. "The children?"

"Yes. Do you want to see them?" Each word the doctor said brought him a step closer until he was standing right before her.

Thoughts of the room behind all the glass swirled in her mind. Memories, she realized. Needing to block it out, to save her sanity, she concentrated on what he had said. "Yes. Yes, I want to see the children."

"Good, good. I thought you would." Putting out a hand to indicate their direction, Dr. Daniels opened the outer door and stepped through. This time, he waited for her to follow him and moved farther down the hallway, his gaze remaining on her. "The children have really been a wealth of information."

"What are you doing with them?" she asked, trailing his path.

Smiling, glancing back at her often, Dr. Daniels seemed excited to have someone to discuss his work with. "It was a belief of my father's, that with the right stimuli, children—especially the very young—could manifest special abilities."

"Special abilities? What do you mean by that?"

"I think you know," he said with another smile.

Ellen scooted around him, stopping them in the middle of the hall. "No. No, I don't. Tell me."

"Clairvoyance. Extrasensory perception. Precognition. Telekinesis, just to name a few. We don't really know what the brain might be able to do. There's so much in there humans don't even utilize." With a shrug he stepped around her and continued down the hall.

Ellen's head drooped, and she moved her hands to her hips. *Crazy,* she thought. *The good doctor is certifiable.*

"Are you coming?"

Lifting her head, staring blindly back the way they'd come, Ellen nodded and followed the doctor toward the children.

CHAPTER 65

Father Thomas had almost decided he was mistaken. He'd stepped back from the wall to lean against the one across the hall. He'd been all over the panel—looking, feeling, and still nothing. Now, he dropped his head back to hit the wall he leaned on. With stanch determination, he raised the lantern and glared at the barrier across from him.

When the light reflected on something in the corner, he again thought he was mistaken. Dreaming. Wishing. Then it reflected again, and his heart jumped.

He stepped forward and reached up to the molding that ran along the wall and across part of the ceiling. A decorative portion hung down, just within reach. Nothing happened until he ran a fingernail down the side. With an almost silent *snick*, the panel slid open a crack.

Father Thomas was afraid to breathe. He stuck the tips of three fingers in the gap and pushed the wall open.

Again, he lifted his lantern to illuminate the small room on the other side. It looked like it had some sort of lighting farther in, but before stepping in, he set the lantern down to pat his pockets. When all he could come up with was his Bible, he stared at it for a moment before mouthing a short prayer. He laid the Bible across the runners that allowed the wall to move, picked up his lantern, then stepped into the room behind the wall.

It only took him a second to realize this was a landing. Small lights illuminated a set of stairs. He hesitated at the top, listening. No sounds came to him. Not from without the area or down the stairs. He was completely alone. Father Thomas looked back at his Bible guarding the opening in the wall, allowing his passage back. He was sure Ellen had come this way. Possibly not of her own design. The priest took a big breath and descended the first steps of the stairway.

When he reached the first landing, he opened the door to peer out. No lights lit this floor. Heavy with silence, there was a musty odor accompanied by a slight chill. Again, he was going on faith but decided Ellen hadn't gone this way. Shutting the door, he continued down.

The next landing and door opened to a lit corridor. Father Thomas exited the stairwell, and when the door shut behind him, he jumped. Grasping the knob, he turned it and opened the door. Relief made his head swim. He shut the door and again looked down the corridor.

This hallway had dark paneling with doors at even intervals. When he walked to the first one, he read a gold placard mounted on the door: *Dr. Melinda Liu, MD.*

Father Thomas looked from the first door down the hall. Offices. These were the doctors' offices. Ellen *was* here the day she escaped. She'd told him about it. Dr. Michael Daniels had an office here. His office was where she found the folder on herself.

He didn't think Ellen was here. She'd been to Dr. Daniels' office. Why would she return there? Would one of the other offices hold any interest for her? He didn't think so. Father Thomas returned to the door to the stairwell. He had a moment of panic when he gripped the doorknob, picturing in his mind that it was locked. That he was locked in—underground in a large crypt. But then the knob turned, and the door opened.

Father Thomas inhaled deeply and blew out a steady breath. Stepping into the stairwell, he kept moving down.

CHAPTER 66

Ellen continued to follow the doctor. Not knowing how she was going to get to the surface, she decided to put that in the file of "don't think about it." *Stay in the present. Worry about the future when it comes.* The fact that this mantra could see her into even deeper trouble wasn't something she took time to consider.

When Dr. Daniels halted in front of another double door, Ellen almost ran into him. She drew back as he threw the doors open, exclaiming at the top of his lungs, "Kids, I'm home!"

The doctor entered the room, but Ellen stopped before the doors.

What was she doing here, following a crazy man through this maze of rooms? From the other side, muted by the door, Ellen heard the doctor's voice. Did someone answer him? Were the children really in there?

"Only one way to find out," she muttered and pushed her way in.

The lighting in the main room was dim, but she saw multiple glass cages like the large one in the first room. In each cage, some just sitting up in bed, and some seeming to be performing some activity, was a child. She guessed that they ranged in age from three to thirteen. The youngest, sitting in bed, was all large round eyes and eerie silence. The eldest stood against the glass wall talking with the doctor. When she neared, they all looked toward her.

"Who is this, Doctor?" asked the girl in the glass box.

"Ellen." He turned at her approach. "This is Sarah." With a sweeping gesture, he included the rest of the room. "And the children."

"My God, Dr. Daniels. What have you done?" Ellen whispered.

"I told you she would never understand."

Ellen jumped when a voice came from the dark behind the cages, and out walked the nurse, Marissa. The quality of her voice drove nails through Ellen's ears.

Gaze jumping from the nurse to the children, to the doctor, Ellen whispered, "I thought you said we were alone."

"Now, Ellen." He dipped his head, that smile coming to his lips. "You can't expect me to tell you the truth."

"Why is she even here?" Marissa advanced on her, pointing a finger like a dagger.

As Ellen stepped back, the doctor moved in between the women. Turning to the nurse, he asked, "Is everything prepared?"

For a moment she continued to glare at Ellen. Then, seeming to give a full-body shake, she said, "Yes, Doctor. I've gathered all the documentation."

"What documentation?" Ellen insisted. "What are you doing now?"

"Ellen"—Dr. Daniels turned toward her—"I would love to have you with us, but now I see that just can't be. With our laboratory compromised, Marissa and I will be moving on."

"Where, Dr. Daniels? Where will you be moving to?"

With a small "Tsk, tsk," he shook one finger at her. Behind him, Marissa moved back into the darkness.

"At least tell me what will become of the children."

"We'll be disposing of our subjects." He didn't notice when Ellen blanched at his words. "We'll begin again in another location."

A rattle of metal caused her to turn her gaze to where Marissa had gone. The nurse reappeared, a metal tray in her hands. On the tray were syringes.

"Shall I continue, Doctor?" the nurse asked.

"Yes, yes, Marissa. Carry on. When you're finished, we'll be on our way."

Giving a curt nod, Marissa headed toward the nearest cage.

"Wait!" Ellen yelled at her. She slid by the doctor but was jerked to a halt when Dr. Daniels snagged her arm. With a grip like a clamp, he wouldn't let go, even as she pulled at him.

The sound of a door opening had her turn frantic eyes to where the nurse entered a room. Ellen watched as a child of six ran to the back corner of the small cage. Seeming to understand what was happening, the other children, except the baby who was crying in terror, began yelling instructions to the first child.

Done with any sort of compromise or discussion, Ellen turned on the doctor. She grabbed him by the collar with one hand and, with the other, punched him straight in the nose. His exclamation of pain had Marissa halting in her path to the child. Blood dripped on his shirt, and he released Ellen. Seeing Ellen coming for her, Marissa hurried. She set the tray on the bed and took one syringe. Popping the cap, she hurried after her cowering prey.

Ellen flew through the doorway, grabbing a handful of syringes as she passed the bed. Just as Marissa kneeled to grab the child, Ellen jabbed three of the needles in her shoulder and depressed the plungers.

With a yowl like a cat, Marissa came to her feet and turned on Ellen. She took a swipe at her with the syringe. Ellen leaned back, avoiding the killing blow. Grabbing Marissa by the wrist that held the needle, Ellen punched her much as she had the doctor. Marissa went down, pulling Ellen with her. Ellen caught herself on one hand, released the nurse with the other, and half jumped over the prone woman.

When she found her balance, she turned to confront Marissa. There was no need, however. The nurse was seizing. White foam pooled in her partially open mouth, blood running from her ears.

Ellen turned to the child, thrust out an open hand, and said, "Come with me."

CHAPTER 67

Father Thomas followed the sounds: shouting and crashes. If Ellen wasn't here, he'd be very surprised.

When he pushed open the double doors, the first thing he saw was a man in a white lab coat, blood streaming down his front, getting to his feet and moving toward the door. When he saw movement, he looked just as Ellen fell over a woman. A moment later, she emerged from what appeared to be a glass box with a child holding her hand. Father Thomas turned his attention back to the doctor.

"You're not going anywhere." He gave the man a shove back. "Ellen!" Father Thomas yelled across the room.

"Thomas!" was her answering shout. "Don't let Dr. Daniels leave."

"Didn't think so," Father Thomas said. He gripped the doctor by a lapel and spun him back into the room. He pushed the doctor into a chair and bound him to the arms with a cloth from the exam table. Then he turned toward Ellen.

"The children, Thomas. We found the children."

* * * * *

It didn't take Richard Sanchez and Little T long to come across the Bible in the juncture of the wall. Stooping, Richard picked it up and then handed it to Little T.

"Guess the priest was right."

"Paulie," Little T called one of his lieutenants. "Get the dogs."

Richard was nodding. "Smart. Very smart."

When the hounds were brought up, their handlers let them sniff the Bible and then took them within the wall.

On the way down, the dogs became confused and backtracked on the floor where the offices were. After that, they were on a straight shot to the priest.

When Father Thomas heard the barking in the distance, his first thought was that the doctor must have had animals kept for other experiments. But as the sounds got nearer, he stepped to the door, cracked it open, and watched.

First came a small group of dogs, pulling men with their leashes. Right behind them were the two leaders. Father Thomas heaved a heavy sigh as he stepped from behind the door.

"Little T!" he called with a hand raised in the air.

The dogs circled him, sniffing up his legs.

"Priest." Little T threw all decorum to the wind and picked him up in a large bear hug. "Where is Ellen?"

When he could breathe again, Father Thomas said, "In the room. And she has a surprise for you. The lot of you."

The search party pushed into the room, pulling the priest in their wake. There in the center stood Ellen, a child in her arms, and surrounded by others.

Two of the first searchers, a man and a woman, called a child to them. Laughing and crying, they hugged the child and each other. Then another came forward, then another. By the time they were finished, all but three of the children were claimed.

"What about these?" Little T asked. "Aren't they yours?"

"No," Richard Sanchez answered. "How will we find where they belong?"

"Here," Ellen said, starting back across the room. "There's some documentation. Maybe it tells us something about the children."

When she saw Dr. Daniels still bound to the chair, she stopped. "What will we do with him?"

Little T walked to the doctor, looking down his nose at him. "This is the man doing all the experimenting?"

"Yes," Ellen told him.

"I say, we kill him. Right here. Right now. Be done with it."

"Oh, T," Ellen said with a sigh. "We can't do that."

"Why?"

"We just can't. He was wrong, and we don't want to be wrong too."

"Take him with us," Richard said. "We'll figure it out later." Then he turned to the people crowding around them. "Let's get these children somewhere safe. They all look like they could use a good meal."

No one argued with him, not even Little T. Ellen ensured Dr. Daniels' hands were bound, and when he tried to talk to people, explaining his side of things, she had him gagged.

"I may have stopped them from killing you, but we don't need to listen to you." She stopped Richard Sanchez to point out boxes behind the glass cages. "Information on the remaining kids might be in those boxes. It's documentation Dr. Daniels was taking with him."

Nodding his understanding, Richard gave orders to have the boxes brought above ground to their camp.

By the time the group returned to the safety of the camp, the sun was setting. Most of them had been going for over twenty-four hours and tempers were getting short. Along with the children, the search party needed a good meal and a warm bed.

The unclaimed children were taken in by families and cared for. Ellen instructed that the boxes be brought to where she and Father Thomas's belongings were laid out. Soon enough, the camp had settled down. Except for the guards who monitored the boundaries of the camp, everyone slept. Everyone except Ellen. She began with the nearest one and worked her way methodically through the boxes. It didn't take her long to see some of the documentation related directly to the experiments. What was done, to whom, for how long, and what the outcome was. These she set aside. She couldn't allow this information to go any further. It began three generations ago. It had to end with her.

Within the boxes, she located information on the children. Some she identified easily as the ones belonging to Richard Sanchez's group. She thought she'd found information on the three unidentified children. She'd show it to the others this evening. Perhaps, they could locate their families. She also found information on the ones who were selling the children to the doctor. Ones like Paul Anders in Richard's town. They'd have to roust them out. And in the bottom of the box, something about stables. It would take both communities to clean this festering wound from their world.

By the time the sun had gone down, and the campfires lit, she was thoroughly exhausted but had read what there was to read. Her only surprise was that there was no information on her.

Dr. Daniels indicated she'd been with them for some time. She'd thought she might get more insight into her past, but it seemed not to be. She had no memories of any time spent with Dr. Daniels or his father, and she didn't know if she ever would.

Standing, she bent to pick up a box stuffed with the papers she planned to burn. It contained detailed information on the experiments on the children. She glanced at Thomas and was surprised to see his eyes open.

"Good evening, Thomas."

"Good evening. Have you slept at all?"

She shook her head. "I'll sleep when I'm done." Hefting the box, she walked out to the large bonfire in the middle of the camp.

People gathered around the fire. She set down the box near the flames. From the corner of her eye, she saw Father Thomas, Richard Sanchez, and Little T approaching her. Worried they'd try to stop her, knowing no one could have this information, Ellen took a handful of the box's contents and tossed them in the flames.

As she reached for another handful, Richard grabbed her arm. "Ellen, what are you doing?"

"I'm burning this trash."

"But it might be useful."

She was already shaking her head. "No, Richard. This would never be helpful to anyone."

"But there might be something, some little thing, that the right people—good people—could turn into something beneficial to all people."

She stared at him, a small smile on her face, and then slowly shook her head. "That's what people always think. Take something bad, and I'm sure we can make something good from it, but you know what, Richard? Someone always uses it for bad."

She wrenched her arm from his grip and bent to grab the whole box. Lifting it, she dumped it in the fire.

"No!"

Ellen spun at the shout, barely getting out of Michael Daniels' way. His hands still tied behind his back, he ran straight into the flames, kicking the contents that burned.

"My work," he intoned in a high keen. "My work!"

"Dr. Daniels!" Ellen called, trying to grab him from the fire, but she couldn't get close enough without getting burned.

Catching the new fuel, the fire climbed the doctor's pant legs while he furiously stomped to save the papers.

"Please, Dr. Daniels!" Ellen called to him. Shielding her face with her hands, she stepped back even farther from the heat of the flames.

With the doctor's first screams, Richard pulled Ellen away from the fire. Some of the people in the clearing screamed, and some cried as the doctor crumpled into the fire, but most stood stoic and watched, remembering the children and their captor.

The next morning, the bonfire burned out, and Ellen asked that Dr. Daniels and Marissa be buried. Some complained, wanting to leave them where they lay, but she was insistent. If they wouldn't help her, she'd do it herself. She knew they needed to be better than those they had stopped.

When Father Thomas picked up a shovel and helped her dig, others joined in.

When the burial was complete, Ellen stood by the grave. People moved away, packing up to leave this place.

"Thomas, could you say something?"

Nodding, Father Thomas stepped up beside her. He took her hand and spoke. "Moses said to him, 'As soon as I go out of the city, I will spread out my hands to the Lord; the thunder will cease, and there will be hail no longer, that you may know that the earth is the Lord's.'"

CHAPTER 68

They reached Little T's community by the end of that day. They'd traveled through part of the daylight, pushing to get home.

People broke into groups, some planning on heading across the dry lake to Richard Sanchez's home. Some of Little T's people would be going with, and some of Richard's would be coming back. The leaders were already planning trade. They also spoke of groups that would go out into the land, locate the stables, find the places where children came from, and stop the sellers. There were three children whose families needed to be found.

Father Thomas was a central part of this planning. It seemed he'd found his flock after all.

Ellen walked away from Richard to climb a small knoll. They had said their goodbyes, and now she watched the activity below her. She knew her time here was ending. She could feel the doorway getting closer. Soon, it would be here for her. Where would she go? Would she be returned to the plane of the Guardians?

Thomas approached her from out of the dawn, morning just a promise that would soon be fulfilled. When she heard thunder rolling across the mountains in the distance, a smile crossed her lips. Right on its tail, a breeze blew through the camp. Heads rose, and questioning looks passed between people. Rain. They were smelling rain in the distance.

Nature was coming back. Life would prevail.

"Ellen," the priest said as he neared her. "What now for you? Will you stay here with us?"

"I don't think so, Thomas."

The priest looked around at the frenzy of activity. "You should. There's plenty that needs doing."

"I'll be going. I can feel it coming for me." Father Thomas looked at her, concern in his eyes. She gave him a reassuring smile and rubbed his arm. "You know, I wondered my entire time with you. Why am I here? What could have been so important as to pull me back?"

He nodded at her. "We've done important things. Stopped bad men. Freed children."

"Yes," she agreed. "All important. But these things could have been done without me. Richard and his people could have and would have found their children. They would have met Little T and his people. Stopped Dr. Daniels and Malcolm Whitman."

Now he turned fully toward her. "You don't think that's why you were brought here?"

"No," she said, "but now I know why. I know what was important enough. Important enough to save the world." As he stepped closer, she felt the doorway calling. As the sun peeked over the hills in front, the portal began to open behind.

"What, Ellen? What is that important?"

"I came because of you, Thomas."

His brow furrowed, a question in his eyes. "Me?"

"And faith," she said, a small smile curving the corners of her lips. She placed a palm upon his cheek. "The faith of one good man."

Both lights—the sun and the gateway—broke at the same time, blinding the people in the clearing. Blinking, their eyesight cleared, and she was gone.

EPILOGUE

Steely gray eyes opened behind the barrier of a helmet. *I'm back.* The familiarity of the confines of the suit of armor felt like a well-known friend.

When the flash of a blade entered her sights, she countered. Throwing up an arm covered by a heavy leather cuff, she stopped its arc. She wielded a wicked blade, sharp on both sides, a small guard protecting her gloved hand. She reflexively swung the weapon in her other hand—a worn club, stained but strong. At the end of a length of timber, a round stone was strapped to its end.

The ball of the club connected with her opponent, cracking not only the helmet, but the skull beneath. She scanned the area, quickly taking in the fallen bodies and fighting groups. The sounds of metal on metal and the cries of men filled the day.

Okay. So, this isn't the realm of the Guardians.

The whistle of a projectile had her ducking and twisting. With surprise she noticed a man between her feet. Alive, she thought, but unmoving. A moment of surprise had her hesitating, almost too long.

Another whistle brought an arrow with it that she managed to deflect with the shaft of her club. Twisting, she threw the dagger, impaling the man with the bow.

A moment later, she heard the unmistakable thunder of horses' hooves.

* * * * *

THE END

OTHER TITLES BY
VICKI B. WILLIAMSON

* * * * *

ELLEN THOMPSON THRILLERS

Finding Poppies
Key of the Prophecy

THE PEDAGOGUE CHRONICLES

Maya's Song
Sylvan's Guise
Tessa's Flight

To learn more, please visit:

Vickibwilliamson.com
Facebook.com/FindingPoppies

65005013R00189